REDEMPTION

BOOK FIVE IN THE DOMINION SERIES

S. E. LUND

ACADIAN PUBLISHING LIMITED

COPYRIGHT

FOREWORD

"The day misspent, the love misplaced, has inside it the seed of redemption. Nothing is exempt from resurrection."

— Kay Ryan

"Love is stronger than death."

– Robert Fulghum

CHAPTER 1

WINTER IS EXCEPTIONALLY cold this year.

Without access to news, it's impossible to know whether this is widespread or just a freak turn of weather in the eastern seaboard. It feels colder. The skies are grey, have been overcast for weeks on end and we have to resort to wood fires to keep warm. Luckily, the mansion is old and there seems to be a fireplace in every room so there's always a crackling fire to sit beside, warm your toes.

When I realized I wouldn't be leaving Soren's compound, returning to either the cottage by the ocean or my apartment in Boston, I decided I have to either find a new home for my cats, which was unlikely, or bring them out to the compound. There's been so much hardship since the plague struck that I feel a bit guilty going to so much trouble to bring the cats to Soren's, but I can't stand the thought of them starving to death in the city.

I arranged to have the cats brought to me. When they arrived at Soren's compound, they hid under the beds for days, crawling up into the box springs to hide. After a week, during which time they only came out to eat and use the litter box, they finally crept out and cautiously explored the suite of rooms I have been assigned. During the second week, they begin to sleep with me on the bed. I find it a comfort to have them here, although I don't remember them. From my journal, I know they were company for me during the long days I spent studying before I received the files from my mother's archives.

All month, I've had trouble sleeping. It isn't just the cold. What keeps me awake at night is what I know is coming and what I dread. Soren expects me to help him gain his own kind of Dominion over humans – a tyranny of his priests instead of one of vampires. I can't do it and live with myself, so the only option I can see is to find a way to escape.

In the evening, after Julien and I spent the entire day plotting our escape, Soren calls me to his quarters. Of course, I know Soren might be able to read my mind and discover everything Julien and I discussed. Michel thinks it's only possible after Soren and I share blood, but I'm not so sure. If that's the case, by now, the effects would have worn off. Soren didn't intrude into my thoughts while Julien described the security arrangements in place at the compound, so I have hope.

Maybe Michel's right. *Maybe* it's only when we share blood that Soren can tap directly into my mind.

I hope that's the case for if not, it'll be next to impossible for us to fight him.

I don't want to help him resurrect his monstrous 'brethren', as he calls them – the rest of the Twelve. I have no idea what they are, but they're monsters. The way Kael killed dozens of humans with no thought told me that pretty clearly.

I'll do whatever I can to avoid that future. If Soren resurrects all eleven of the remaining twelve, how many mortals will they kill? Hundreds?

How many more will die because of my assistance? Thousands?

I can't comply with that. There's no way I want that on my conscience for the rest of my life. So when a guard comes to my room, I expect the worst.

He jerks his head to the side. "My Lord Soren requires your presence immediately."

I frown and turn to Julien, who's sitting beside me on the couch, a sketch of the compound's perimeter and outbuildings on the back of a cloth napkin from our meal.

He shrugs. "His *Lord* requires it," Julien says with a touch of sarcasm in his tone. "Better go see what *he* wants."

I sigh and stand up from the couch, smoothing my sweater, which keeps me warm against the chill of the compound.

"Hopefully, I won't be long." I bend down and kiss Julien. Maybe this is just an administrative issue, but I doubt it.

Has Soren been listening in and is he now going to punish me for plotting against him? There's only one way to know. I have to go to his quarters and find out. Not that I have much of a choice, with an armed guard waiting to escort me.

I follow the guard out of my room to Soren's quarters, down the dim hallway lined with dark paneling and portraits of noble lords from past centuries. The guard opens the door and admits me to the interior of Soren's suite. Candlelight bathes the walls of the anteroom with a warm white-yellow glow. In the corner, a large grandfather clock ticks, the pendulum swinging back and forth in a slow rhythm. It's old and has a spring loaded clockwork inside, the rich wood pierced by dozens of tiny wormholes, attesting to its age.

In this new post-apocalyptic world, in the zones affected by the plague, the old is new again. Only the oldest machines and devices with no plastic or materials made from fossil fuels remain in working order.

I enter the interior rooms and make my way deeper inside, only to come upon Soren reclining bare-chested on a settee, with a sleeping Gabrielle lying on top of him, her face nestled into the crook of his neck, her blonde hair cascading down her back. She's wearing a gown that bares most of her skin, with diaphanous draping that leaves little to the imagination. Soren's eyes are closed, and he's humming something soft, one hand stroking her hair.

It's such an intimate moment. Soren is so gentle with her. I feel like I'm intruding on these two lovers lying in each other's arms, getting solace or comfort from the other's touch. I take a step back, trying to hide on the other side of the doorway.

I wait, wondering if he even knows I'm there.

If he does, he says nothing. Instead, he hums, the tune soft and lilting – almost like a lullaby. He summoned me, so he knows I'm coming. Then it occurs to me this little scene feels like it's been set up so I'll see him like this – showing Gabrielle affection. Finally, when I grow impatient and upset that he's trying so blatantly to manipulate me, I step back into the room and clear my throat.

He cracks open one eye and sees me. While I watch, he stirs and strokes Gabrielle's cheek.

"Wake up, little one," he whispers.

Gabrielle blinks rapidly as if she's been asleep. She stretches like a cat waking up from a nap, her back arching. She yawns and looks up at Soren. When their eyes meet, a very intimate smile passes between them. The smile of lovers exchanging a knowing glance.

She leans up and kisses Soren, her kiss deep and lingering, one hand sliding down the bare skin of his chest to his waist and then up to caress his pectorals.

He pulls away and smiles at her. "Later," he says softly and glances my way. His ice-blue eyes are piercing in their intensity. "We have company."

She turns as well and when she sees me, she smiles coyly as if she's a child caught doing something naughty. She pulls herself up and off of Soren's body and straightens her gown, which has pulled down considerably to expose her voluptuous bosom, the skin on her breasts creamy white and smooth. I catch a glimpse of faded bite marks on the inside curve of one perfect breast.

"Excuse me," she says with a giggle as she passes me, her sweet perfume following in her wake. I watch her leave and then turn back to Soren, who's sitting up, running a hand through his long fair hair.

"You wanted to speak with me?" I say, arching one brow.

"Yes." He stands, stretching his arms out and up over his head. When he does, a huge pair of alabaster wings spread out behind him.

He's showing off, trying to impress me, seemingly enjoying the fact that I caught him in an intimate moment with Gabrielle and am now watching him parade his nearly naked body in front of me with those gorgeous wings…

"What do you want?" I ask, impatient to know why I'm there. He pours a glass of blood and holds it out to me. I shake my head, not wanting to be too friendly with him.

"Suit yourself," he says and drinks down the glass of blood, licking his lips in an exaggerated manner like he's deliberately trying to provoke me.

"We have to talk," he says, his voice firm. "Sit."

I clasp my hands behind my back. "I prefer to stand."

He makes a face of impatience and sits on the couch, watching me, his arm thrown over the back, his wings folding up into nothing. "Michel told me you were stubborn."

I say nothing in reply, trying to keep my cool, determined not to respond to his jibes.

I hear him sigh. "Very well, be like that." He stands and comes over to me, looking down at me from under a frown. "I want to call a truce with you," he says simply.

"A truce?" A shock races through me. What does he mean?

"Yes," he says, his hands on his hips. "If you help me resurrect the rest of the Twelve, I promise they won't kill a single mortal."

I glance at his face to see if he's being honest or is playing me. "What?"

"That's right," he says and starts to pace the room, walking around me in a circle, watching me as he walks. "I *could* kill you with a thought for plotting against me. I could let you run away and try to fight, for my amusement, of course," he says with a grin, "but it would delay me resurrecting the rest of my brethren. I could create another iteration of your genes and let them grow to maturity, doing it right this time, but the simplest thing would be if we were to cooperate. I'll make sure the rest of my brethren have adequate preserved blood to revive them, so there'll be no need for anyone to die. How's that sound?"

"So they don't have to kill in order to be revived?"

Soren shakes his head. "Not at all. They need blood. Kael is a bit more bloodthirsty than all the others, and likes to 'cull the herd,' as he calls it. I don't believe any of the others will complain if the terms of their resurrection are that they drink harvested blood."

I frown. "Why do you need them? Can't you rule on your own?"

He sighs. "I need company."

"What about Gabrielle?" I ask, thinking he looks quite happy with her.

"Gabrielle's fun, but she's not one of us, and she's *not* Marguerite, despite looking identical to her in every way. Marguerite was her own person – a Viking princess. Gabrielle is just a girl raised in modern culture. With all your modern human technology, genes only get you so far. Experience is the real determinant of a person's character. Besides, only another like me can understand what this existence means. The Twelve are my brethren. They're the only ones of my kind." He stops in front of me, his expression serious.

"Another like you?" I ask, still uncertain about Soren's origins. "What *are* you?"

He smiles, his eyes narrowed. "Why should I tell you – an unbeliever?"

I cross my arms. "Tell me what you are. If you want me to cooperate, I need to know why you want the rest of the Twelve back. I don't believe that you're lonely."

He makes an exaggerated pout. "Oh, Eve, so mean to me… You don't believe that I'm lonely? That I can feel sad that my brethren are in stasis? That Kael and I are the only members of our kind alive?"

I shrug. "Sorry," I say, trying not to sound too saucy. "I guess I don't trust you. I don't know what your game plan really is, or what your endgame is. I'm afraid you'll use me and then betray me."

"Fair enough," he says and sits back down on the couch. He pats the seat. "Please sit down beside me. You make me nervous when you stand up like that, as if this is some kind of interrogation instead of a meeting of minds."

"Meeting of minds," I say with a scoff. I relent and sit beside him, very aware of his bare torso, his perfectly sculpted abdomen, chest and arms, the skin alabaster white like his platinum hair. "You aren't cold?" I ask, gesturing to his chest.

"Why does it make you uncomfortable to see my bare skin? Are you that attracted to me?"

I glance up and down his body in disbelief. I am not attracted to him. Although his physique is perfect, like a statue come to life, I despise him.

"You think I'm beautiful," he says simply.

I can't deny he's attractive. Beautiful is the right word to use. To my ascended vampire eyes, his skin seems to glow as if he's lit from within and every feature is perfect.

"Most humans wear clothing."

"I'm not human," he says with a grin.

"So you claim," I say, refusing to admit anything. I glance away and study the room, noting the opulence, the grandness of the furniture.

"Oh, ye of little faith," he says with a laugh. "Doubting Thomas to the end."

Then I remember reading my journal entries about the letters to Julien from Brother Novae about being a Doubting Thomas and I wonder if Soren has been playing Julien all along. Is it just a coincidence that two people involved in Julien's life use that saying? It doesn't seem likely...

"*Tell* me what you are," I say again, more firmly. "If you want me to cooperate, you have to start telling me the truth. I'm sick to death of operating blindly. Michel thinks I should obey him based on trust but he's done nothing but lie to me from the start. Why should I obey you, help you, when you won't tell me the truth either?"

"Oh, Eve," he says with an exasperated sigh. "So dramatic... This is war, and in war, there's such a thing as chain of command and need to know. I'd have thought Julien would have explained this to you by now."

"He has but I need to know this," I say, adamant. "The soldier has to believe he's fighting for a just cause."

Soren shakes his head. "Wrong. Usually, the soldier is in the army because he's hungry, plain and simple. In the end, he fights to keep his fellow soldiers alive, and nothing more. The politicians and generals have just causes to believe in. The soldier only cares about staying alive and protecting his brothers in arms. You should care about that as well."

"I do," I say. "I care about all my fellow mortals, or at least, I still care about mortals," I say, correcting myself. I keep forgetting that I'm not mortal any longer. I still *feel* mortal. My immortality means nothing to me at this point. It's not real to me yet.

"It'll become real to you the first time you watch a mortal be born, live out their life and die of old age," Soren says, and then I realize that he *can* read my mind. I feel a sense of hopelessness descend over me like a cloak at the fact that nothing I think is private. As long as Soren can read my mind, there's no way Julien and I can escape, no matter what we do.

"That's right," Soren says, his voice soft. "There's no way. Give it up, Eve. Cooperate. You'll get your heart's desires. Every one."

I frown and grind my teeth, hating that he has access to my every thought.

"Is there no way I can block you?"

He laughs at that. "As if I'd tell you if there were. Eve, sometimes you're so naïve. It's sweet, really. So stubborn. So naïve. So strategic. If only you were as easy to control as sweet Gabrielle..."

"I'm not," I say, thankful that I'm not like her. But I bet Marguerite wasn't easy to control.

"She wasn't," Soren says and I almost growl in anger that he's reading my every thought. He leans closer to me. "She was very much like you, in many ways. Perhaps that's why Michel is so smitten. He can barely resist you. He couldn't resist her either."

"He *killed* Marguerite," I say.

"He did," Soren says, the corners of his mouth turned down. "I'll never forgive him for that. If I have to keep him alive for eternity so I can torment him, I will."

He turns to me and I see the determination in his eyes. He really means it.

"Why was she so important?" I ask, surprised that he feels so much about Marguerite even now, eight hundred years later.

"I *loved* her," he says as if he's insulted.

"But she was a mortal," I say, unable to understand. "Before you turned her. And you're a –" I say and hesitate, not really knowing what he was. He's more than a vampire. Something else entirely, but I can't accept what Michel claims.

Angel...

"Immortal," I add, unwilling to call him an angel.

"Yes," he says, almost rolling his eyes at me. "What's that got to do with it? Do you really think I don't feel the same emotions? Do you feel more intense emotions as a vampire?"

"Well," I say, considering. "Of course. Yes. Much more intensely."

"Exactly," he says and leans back, like he's satisfied. "I feel everything a mortal does, but much *much* more intensely. I *love*, Eve," he says and turns to me, his gaze holding mine, his eyes intense. "I love *deeply*. More deeply than you ever could. When I found out she was dead..." He says nothing for a moment but his skin flushes pink and his eyebrows knit together. I can hear his breathing become more rapid. Then he seems to get ahold of himself and closes his eyes for a moment. "I hate more as well, and I need revenge even more intensely."

"Against Michel," I say, nodding in understanding. "You're doing everything to hurt him. Creating me. Putting us together. Making Julien want me as well."

Soren cracks a smile. "I dangled you in front of Michel like a ripe piece of fruit. He couldn't resist. You can't believe how pleased I was that he succumbed to your charms..." He smiles to himself for a moment. "And of course, what Michel has, Julien wants. Noble Julien, loving his brother's lover. How tortured he is about it!"

"Why do you get pleasure out of their pain?"

He turns to me and frowns. "They killed Marguerite. Since they're immortals, I want them to feel pain for eternity."

"*Julien* didn't want to kill her," I say, wanting to defend him at least.

"When he saw she was going to die, he killed her quickly so she wouldn't suffer."

"Julien should have saved her, but he was too much under Michel's authority."

"Michel killed her because he could see no escape from her constant sexual demands. He was a priest, for goodness sake. She forced him to have sex."

"Hardly forced," Soren says dismissively. "At least, not after the first while. He took part willingly."

"He tried to survive," I say, defending him even now.

"Julien *should* have saved her," Soren says once more and his voice breaks. Even now, I see his eyes well up with emotion and it shocks me. He turns his head away, but I've already seen his tears. He really does still feel pain about her death.

We sit in silence for a moment as he recovers his composure.

"So, Eve," he says finally, taking in a deep breath. "Collaborate with me. Help me resurrect the rest of the Twelve, and I promise no death. Just bloodletting."

"How can I trust you?" I say, for that really is the question. "What is your end game? Tell me that and maybe I can trust you."

Soren turns to me, his gaze fixed on me. "I'll stop the plague, I'll eradicate vampirism, and I'll restore the Church as it should be. You'll have both Michel and Julien and humanity back from the brink of slavery."

I frown. "I don't want them both."

"Oh, stop it, Eve. You love them both. This tantrum about Michel is getting old. Give in. Be with him. You know you want to…"

"He chose the Church over me."

"He'd be with you this moment if you offered yourself."

"No, he wouldn't," I say in disbelief.

"Go to him and see. Kiss him and he'd be yours."

I shake my head and push that thought out of my head. "What did you mean, the Church as it should be?"

He smiles. "With me at its head."

"You?" I'm not shocked of course, because I knew he wanted to be worshiped. "Do you want to be the Pope or the God?"

"Michel will be my pope."

I make a face of disgust. "You're not God."

"Not *the* god as in God Almighty. But a god nonetheless." He stands and starts to walk around once more. "What is a god, after all, but a supremely powerful being, able to manipulate matter at will? Resurrect the dead, kill with a thought or bolt of lightning. I'll do all those things to prove my powers."

"So more like a god in the Roman pantheon, or the Norse pantheon," I say, holding back a snort of derision. Of course, I don't believe in either God Almighty or the gods. Soren's powers aren't supernatural. They're just based on some ability we don't yet understand or have described scientifically. There *has* to be a scientific explanation for what he does.

I refuse to believe otherwise. I refuse to *believe*. I need evidence and a theory to explain what I've seen with my own eyes.

"You never believed in God?" Soren asks. "Not once? Most people find solace in their belief."

I shake my head. "No," I say, a shiver down my spine remembering all the reasons I don't believe. *Can't* believe. "How could I when I was raped as a child, saw my mother murdered before my eyes? What kind of god lets a small child be abused? If a god is all-powerful and didn't intervene, it's heartless and doesn't deserve to be worshiped. If God's not all powerful, it's not a god and doesn't deserve to be worshiped. Either way, I can't believe."

Soren stops in front of me where I'm standing by the couch. He tips my chin up and looks at me. "Poor Eve," he says and shakes his head. "God doesn't intervene to save little girls from pedophiles because He gave you free will. He lets you choose. That's the price for your freedom."

I frown. "Then why should I worship Him?"

"Because He is the all-father. No other reason is necessary." He strokes my cheek and I pull away. "So hurt when you were a child. If you want, I can take it all away. Every bad memory, every lingering bit of pain."

I step away from him. "It's my history," I say, shaking my head. "I want to know why I'm getting revenge."

"Revenge for what? Your mother's death?" he says, his expression deadly serious. "Let me tell you something that'll blow your little mind." He leans closer to me, his hand cupping my cheek. "She *wanted* to become a vampire."

I shake my head and try to pull away, but he holds me tightly.

"No," I say, and wrestle free of him. "I saw Michel's memories. You ordered her killed because she wouldn't cooperate with you. You forced Michel to kill her. He turned her so she wouldn't die."

"What *did* Michel show you?" he says and then clasps my shoulders in his hands, his face mere inches from mine. "It wasn't the truth, whatever it was." His eyes are intense.

Then, I feel him in my mind, probing my memory. Unbidden, the scene Michel showed me of my mother's death flickers in my mind's eye like film projected on a movie screen. Michel and Soren entering the lab, finding my mother, arguing with her about the cure, and Soren leaving in anger. He orders Michel to kill my mother. Michel turns my mother instead of killing her in order to save her life.

Soren stands back and shakes his head. "That's not what happened. I gave her a choice. She *had* a choice. She wanted to find the cure. She didn't want to die before being able to find it. She *chose* to become a vampire so she'd be immortal and then she could cure everyone once she'd unlocked the secrets to the virus. She was afraid she'd die before she could find it and wanted to be protected. Vampires are notoriously hard to kill..."

I frown. "That's not what Michel showed me. I saw—"

"You *saw* what Michel wanted you to see. Your mother was cooperating. She *wanted* to become a vampire so she wouldn't be vulnerable. She asked if I would approve Michel turning her. Let *me* show you..."

I pull away, because if Michel can alter his memories to show me what he wants me to see, so can Soren.

"No," I say and hold my hand up. "I can't trust either of you. I don't want *you* showing me something you've reconstructed either. I want the truth."

I turn away, determined to leave him and not listen to another one of his lies.

"Ask your mother. Not that she'll tell you the truth either. And if you don't cooperate with me, there's more I can do to convince you."

"I *will* ask my mother," I say, then slam the door behind me. I'm surprised that he let me go. Soren isn't big on giving up control over any situation. But he let me go.

On my way down the hallway, I see Michel coming towards me.

"Eve, you look ill," he says, stopping me, one hand on my shoulder.

"Don't touch me." I pull away and keep going, my fists clenched, jaw grinding.

"Eve..."

I turn back and point my finger at him. "I don't want any more of your lies."

Then I take the stairs to the upper level. I need Julien.

The only one of them who hasn't deliberately lied to me all long.

CHAPTER 2

JULIEN HOLDS me in his arms and rocks me as I cry.

"Shh," he says and strokes my hair. "Tell me what happened."

I shake my head, unable to speak for a moment, my anger and sadness is so great, my throat choked with emotion. I let him hold me, let his strong arms enfold me.

He leads me to the couch and we sit together, his arms still around me, my cheek resting on his shoulder.

"I take it that Soren said some things that upset you."

I nod, and wipe my eyes, still not ready to talk. I try to sort through my emotions and thoughts, but it's still too soon.

Why did they lie to me? My own mother? I can understand Michel lying to me. He has an agenda and it matters more to him than his love for me or my love for him. But my mother?

I would have thought she'd at least tell me the truth. I thought she never lied to me and yet here I am, learning that she lied as well.

She *wanted* to become a vampire…

She *chose* to be turned…

Soren went there for an update and she *asked* him to let Michel turn her.

I close my eyes and sit in Julien's silent embrace. I remember something Michel said – that if Julien knew anything about my mother, he'd die. Now that Soren's planted this seed of doubt – hell, it's a full tree at this point, I don't know what to believe anymore.

I decide to take a risk and speak to Julien about my mother. I need someone to talk to about all this. I take in a deep breath and wipe my eyes.

"Did you know that my mother asked to be turned and is alive?"

Julien tenses, and pulls away. "What?"

I nod. "Yes," I say, still not sure I believe it. "Soren told me that she had been cooperating with him and wanted to be turned so she'd be immortal. Michel turned her at her own request."

"That doesn't sound right," Julien says, frowning. "Your mother is a vampire? She's alive? She was cooperating with Soren?"

"Well, technically, undead, but yes."

Julien shakes his head. "I have no personal knowledge of this, so if it's true, it's all news to me. And hard to believe."

I don't understand why my mother kept this from me. Why did Michel?

I don't know what to think anymore.

So I don't think. I want to clear my mind of all the lies so I climb up onto Julien's lap and kiss him, our mouths joining, tongues entwining. He groans when I rub myself against him and I feel his walls come down. His desire for me is immediate and strong. He wants me, and I need him.

"It's been a while," he says. "Since we tasted each other. I want you."

He picks me up and carries me to the bed, laying me on my back. He leans over me, his hands on either side of my shoulders. He does nothing for a moment other than stare into my eyes. Then, he leans down and kisses me, our mouths joining. We connect and his need for me builds and feeds my own. When our bodies are naked and sliding together, I forget all about my mother, Michel and all their lies, for a time at least. All I think of is Julien, his body strong and firm, the sound of his breath, the sensation of our bodies joined together taking me into the sweet oblivion of release.

~

AFTERWARD, we lie naked, me on top of Julien, my cheek resting on his chest. He strokes my hair.

"They want to turn you against Soren for some reason. I mean, I hate his guts, but I want to know the truth."

"I know," I say and raise my head so I can look in his eyes. "Why can't they tell me the truth? Why is it so important I hate Soren and think he's the one who killed her? Are they afraid I'd side with him against Blackstone?" I lay my head back down, closing my eyes. "I have to ask my mother about it. I have to ask Michel."

"I agree. You can't accept Soren's claims without proof."

I sigh heavily, confused and fed up with this nightmare I've been living for the past year. "How can I know who's telling me the truth? Both Michel and my mother have lied to me or kept the truth from me before. How can I know when they're lying and when they're telling me the truth?"

Julien runs his hands through his hair. "Maybe you have to trust your instincts, and forget trying to know what's true. Listen to what each of them have to say and then make up your own mind who you believe."

I know he's right. All of us have powers to manipulate each other. I have to just think it through and base my decision on the evidence.

"I can't cooperate with Soren without proof. How can he give me proof when I know he can manipulate my mind and show me things that haven't happened, like Michel did? I'll go to Michel and confront him. My mother as well, if I can find her. They have reasons they don't want me to cooperate with Soren or they wouldn't have lied to me. I think I trust them more than him."

"Don't get your hopes up that it'll be easy to figure out. Like I say, trust your gut. That's what you have to learn when you're a cop. Which suspect is the most hinky? Which one seems the creepiest to you when you talk to them?"

"You were a cop?"

He shakes his head. "I was in the military police for a while.

Worked with cops before. I've heard them talk about their gut feeling. They seem to trust it more than evidence sometimes."

"But that means that their personal biases can affect their judgment. They should rely on evidence not intuition."

"My little scientist," Julien says and smiles. He kisses my forehead tenderly. "Are you going to cooperate with Soren?" he says, his voice soft.

"I don't know," I say. "I haven't decided."

"Because, if you don't cooperate with him, he'll punish you. He might kill you and wait for *another* you to be born and grow up."

"I know all that, Julien," I say frowning.

"There are a lot of bad things he could do to you."

I turn to him. "Do you think I should cooperate with him?"

"Yes," he says. "It's the only way to stop the plague before it destroys the world completely. The only way to eradicate vampirism."

I stand up and leave Julien, thinking about what he said. I go to the bathroom to wash up. Then, I'm going to Michel and I'll demand that he tell me the truth. I'll see how I feel after he responds. Maybe I'll have to trust my gut, like Julien suggested. Given how easily everyone is able to manipulate each other, that may be all we have to go on.

But I hate it. I want certainty. I want science and evidence, but it's all suspect now that people can manipulate my mind.

Will I ever be able to trust anyone or anything?

While I clean up, Julien stands in the doorway. I pour fresh water into the basin on the counter and splash some of it over my face with my hands, then wash my body off.

"Good idea," he says, his arms crossed while he leans on the door jamb to watch me. "Don't go to Michel smelling of me or he'll be livid."

"He made his choice," I say and grin at Julien, and try to make light of it, but inside, I still feel a tug at my heart that he gave me up so easily. Soren seemed to think that Michel would go back to me in a moment, if I offered. I won't because I decided we were through before he chose the priesthood, but still… I wonder.

"He chose the priesthood over me. I doubt he really cares."

"Oh, he cares. Believe me, he cares," Julien says with a nod. "He just cares more about his damn religion than his own heart."

"I know," I say and brush my hair, smoothing out the tangles I got from rolling around with Julien on the bed. "But that's Michel, isn't it?"

"He's nuts," Julien says and smiles that crooked grin. "His loss is my gain." Then he comes to me and pulls me into his arms. "Don't let him discourage you. Don't let him upset you. Most of all," he says and kisses my neck, "don't let the bastard touch you. You're mine, Eve. He made his choice. I made mine. I chose you."

"I chose you as well," I say, and kiss him tenderly. I stroke his hair, which is starting to fall a bit onto his forehead. If his hair were longer, he'd look almost identical to Michel. Except – except there's this different look in Julien's eyes.

I can't explain it, but I see it when our eyes meet. I feel like his equal when I look in his eyes, despite the difference in our ages. He still has hope. He still wants to fight. He still wants to have fun.

I think Michel has lost that. He seems as if every moment with me is some kind of diversion from what really matters. As if I was stealing him away from his true mission.

Not Julien.

He's all mine.

~

I TAKE the hallway to Michel's quarters and knock on the door.

"Michel?" I say softly. "It's me."

He opens the door and stares at me as if I'm an annoyance. "What?"

"Can I come in?" I ask, trying to squeeze into the room. "I need to talk to you."

He holds firm, keeping me from entering. "What about?"

"When you let me in, I'll tell you."

He glances over his shoulder into the room and then turns back. "I'm busy. Come back later."

"Now," I say and crane my neck to see inside. "Who's with you?" I ask, and then I see her. She comes into view, dressed in her diaphanous gown. *Gabrielle.*

Soren's replacement for Marguerite.

I can't hide my shock, my jaw dropping open.

"Are you *with* her?" I blurt out, then kick myself that it was my first response.

He frowns and shakes his head. "No, of course not," he says angrily. "I'm telling her about the real Marguerite. I took a vow, Eve. I'm celibate until I die."

"Tell her to leave," I say and watch her, a strong twinge of jealousy in me despite his claim that he's celibate. I don't want to even think of Michel with another woman. If I can't have him, I don't want anyone else to.

"Eve, don't be rude. Come back in an hour."

"Tell her to leave, *now*," I say, for although I'm jealous, I need to talk to him about Soren and what he claimed. I need to see Michel confirm or deny it.

"Just a minute," Michel says with a sigh and closes the door. I wait outside, my heart pounding in my chest. I'm afraid of what he'll say when I confront him.

I don't want him to confirm what Soren said about my mother. If he does, everything falls apart.

The door opens again in a couple of minutes and a smiling Gabrielle leaves, giving me a coy expression when she does.

"Thank you, Father," she says softly and turns to Michel. "I'll come back tomorrow."

Michel opens the door, waving me inside. "Come in, Eve."

I enter his rooms. There's a piano in one corner by a huge floor to ceiling window that looks out over the courtyard. A library lines the wall with thousands of books. And in the other corner is a four-poster canopy bed with thick deep green velvet draping and white sheets and pillows. On a desk by another window is a pad of paper and a quill pen.

A painting of some stage of the cross is on the wall beside it, a fatigued Jesus carrying a heavy wooden cross on his back through the streets, his forehead bloody, a crown of thorns on his head. Around him, citizens jeer and throw rotten food and stones.

It's a really heart-rending scene. One I don't doubt actually happened, for I believe in the historical Jesus. Just not the transcendent one who was resurrected or was God made flesh or any of the other religious crap. Does Michel get some kind of solace looking at that horrific scene?

He closes the door and points to the small seating area with a couch and two comfortable armchairs. I sit on one of the chairs and face him where he sits on the couch across from me.

"Tell me the truth," I say and lean forward, my eyes meeting his. "Did my mother ask Soren to allow her to become a vampire?"

Michel says nothing for a moment, but I see something in his eyes that tells me all I need to know.

"I thought so," I say and glance away, unable to look at him a moment longer, my anger is so strong. I try to calm down, breathing in deeply in an effort to slow my heart rate, which is elevated. A flush spreads on my face and my cheeks heat.

"I wanted to tell you—" he says, but I cut him off, my hand up to stop him.

"Don't say a word."

"Eve, I—"

"*Don't*," I say, my voice shaking from emotion. "No more lies. No more anything. Consider yourself dead to me. She's dead to me as well. Not only did she abandon me willingly, she lied to me about how she became a vampire. You lied to me as well."

I stand to leave, for I don't need to hear anything else. What could he say that would make this all right? He lied to me. He lied and lied and lied. She lied.

I'm finished with him. Finished with them both.

I stride to the door, my eyes filling, vision blurred. I don't want to listen to him try to rationalize why he and my mother lied to me all this time.

"One day, Eve, you'll understand."

I turn to him, sick and tired of hearing him say that same old refrain.

"Well, that day isn't today because I don't understand."

"I didn't want it this way," he says and comes to the door when I reach it, holding it closed, preventing me from leaving. "I wanted another way, but your mother chose for us all."

I turn to him, barely able to see him through my tears. "Yeah, well, you went along with her."

"Not willingly, but she forced my hand."

"How? What does she want?"

He shakes his head, still unwilling to tell me the whole truth. "I told you before that I can't tell you."

"And she won't either, so I guess I'm back where I started. I'm done with the both of you."

I put my hand on the doorknob to open the door but he stops me and leans closer, so that his face is mere inches from mine. I can't help but look in his eyes, and despite everything, I want him to tell me the truth, I want to be able to understand so that I can cooperate willingly with him. Even now, I can't help but want us to be the way we were.

"Tell me, Michel," I plead, my voice soft, breaking from emotion. "Please…"

He shakes his head sadly, and I see real pain in his eyes. "I can't." He holds up his hands as if in surrender. "All I can say is that you shouldn't cooperate with Soren. Please trust me. I know you have no faith, but trust me, and trust the love we feel, what we felt for each other. That will never die on my part. I would never do anything to hurt you."

"I can't trust," I say, my lip actually quivering from emotions welling up inside of me. "I have no faith."

He lets me leave this time, and I push the door open and rush down the hallway, a hand over my mouth to stop myself from sobbing out loud, but that's how I feel.

My mother *did* ask to be turned. She *chose* to become a vampire and then chose to let me think she'd been murdered. Michel lied about her ever since I met him.

He won't explain himself and expects me to simply accept what he says as fact.

He wants me to be like him – accepting things on faith, but I have none and never did.

I stand outside my room in the dim hallway and try to get control over my emotions, breathing in deeply to try to calm myself, but it's impossible. I lean against the door and slide down so that I sit on the floor and I sob silently into my hands.

Julien opens the door. "Eve?" he says when he sees me sitting there, weeping and of course, he comes right to me and picks me up, his strong arms slipping around me, pulling me into his embrace. "Oh, Eve, I'm so sorry," he says and holds me tighter.

I don't say anything. I can't speak.

He pulls me into the room and closes the door, then takes me to the couch where I sit on his lap and cry on his shoulder. I let it all out, sobbing about Michel and my mother and all the lies and deceit.

Julien says nothing. Instead, he listens and strokes my back, wiping tears off my cheeks, and kissing me when I'm no longer wracked with sobs.

CHAPTER 3

LATER, when I've calmed down enough, we talk in quiet voices about what Michel said, and didn't say, and what it all means.

"Can you blame her for wanting to be immortal?" Julien says softly, and I know he's trying to be reasonable in contrast to my emotionality.

I shake my head. "It's not that," I say and consider my mother. "She was always so strongly committed to eradicating vampires. Her choosing to become one was so unlike my vision of her that it's hard to accept. It's that she chose to leave me," I say and wipe my eyes. "I always thought she was murdered. At least I could believe that she was taken from me by an evil vampire."

All my life, I thought it was a monster who killed her and I turned all my hatred towards him, finding him, getting revenge. Then I learn it was actually Michel who killed her and not Soren, but I thought he was forced. Then I discover that she was alive. That Michel had turned her in order to save her. Now, I discover she *wanted* to be a vampire.

I turn to look in Julien's eyes and see such sympathy in them. "She was never taken from me," I say and tears start again. "She left me. She *abandoned* me."

Julien pulls me back into his arms and the tears run down my face once more. This time, I get myself under control much more quickly.

"Soren said that after I spoke with Michel, I should come back and talk to him. Maybe I should go and ask him more."

"You have to cooperate with him, Eve," Julien says and I'm surprised that he might even consider cooperating with Soren to raise the rest of the Twelve. "But I told you before you can't trust anyone," he says and his voice is emotional. "Not even me."

"Not even you?" I say with surprise. "Why?"

He shakes his head. "I'm compellable. I can be compelled."

He's right, of course. He *is* compellable. For all I know, everything he says has been fed to him by someone else trying to control me.

It could be Michel or Blackstone himself.

Maybe even Soren.

I have no idea and now, I feel utterly lost.

I place my hands on his shoulders and look deeply into his eyes. "Julien," I say firmly, trying to use my powers to compel him. "Tell me who compelled you to lie to me."

He smiles softly. "It's no use, Eve. You're new and not nearly powerful enough to overwrite the compulsion of an older, stronger vampire." He shrugs.

"Damn," I say and slump. "I hate this."

"I know. So do I. And while I really don't like the idea of you cooperating with Soren, I think it's the only way."

"You think I like it?" I say in disbelief.

"Eve," he says, his voice dark. "I hate those monsters. He said if you cooperated, there'd be no killing. He'll stop the plague. He'll defeat Blackstone. I don't like the fact that he wants to be worshiped like a god, but you can't stop people from believing. As long as he allows people personal freedom, I can't help but see him as the lesser of two evils."

He nuzzles my neck. "All I know is that I want you to be safe. I wish the world could go away and the two of us could go to some cottage on the coast and live in peace but we have to do this."

"Maybe someday," I say softly and snuggle in his arms. For a moment, I let his warmth penetrate me. Our emotions for each other fill me with peace. I need it. His love is like a drug and I need it to keep me going.

"I love you," I say to him, stroking the scar that runs down the side of his face.

"And I you," he says. He kisses me and I feel the surge of desire he feels for me, but as much as I want to make love to him, I have to finish what I started with Soren.

"I have to go and speak to Soren."

"Can't you delay for a while?" he murmurs into my neck. "Say, ten minutes?"

"Ten? Is that all you need?" I say with a grin.

"Less, if you're ready." He smiles, one side of his mouth quirked.

"When I come back," I say and kiss him quickly. "We'll take an hour."

He sighs heavily. "Okay, if you insist. I hope you're still in the mood..."

I stand up and straighten my clothes. "I'll probably need it even more after speaking with Soren."

He stands up. "I'll be here."

I TAKE the hallway back to Soren's suite of rooms and the guard doesn't hesitate to admit me. It's like he's been expecting me. When I enter, Soren's alone and sitting at his desk, sorting through papers. He doesn't even glance up when I stand before the desk.

"So, was I right?" he says, still studying the paper before him. I step closer and see it's a map of the world with familiar red swatches marking where the plague has spread.

"Yes," I say, my voice soft.

He glances up, his brow furrowed. "Sorry about that," he says, smoothing the edges of the map, which have curled up. "It had to be hard to hear. Did he explain?"

"He said she wanted to be immortal so she could continue to work on the cure for vampirism without worry about being killed."

He shrugs. "Makes complete sense. Still, it had to hurt that she more or less abandoned you. Why do you suppose she did that?"

"To protect me from you, for some reason."

He frowns and sits back, eyeing me over his hands, which are folded in front of him. "Me? What did they say about me having anything do with you?"

"Michel said that in one possible future, I'm your lover. You took me at twelve and made me your concubine. They wanted to protect me from that."

"How racy of me," he says as if this is a joke. "Of course, back in the day, girls were married at twelve, after their first period."

"We're a little more civilized today," I say with derision.

"Back then, fifty percent of women died in childbirth," he says, matter of fact. "Fifty percent of infants died in their first five years of life. Reproduction had to start early to maintain the population, let alone increase it. It was survival, Eve. Not dirty old men."

"Can't it be both?" I say. He says nothing in reply. "Well, whatever the case," I say, having to admit he might be right about it. "I'm glad we have a different system today. I certainly wasn't ready for marriage and childrearing at twelve. No girl is."

He sighs and picks up another map. "I'm not going to argue history with you, or human nature." He glances up at me expectantly. "That's a fool's errand. What's your decision?"

I say nothing for a moment, considering.

Soren stands up, coming around his desk to stand before me. "If you need convincing, take my hand."

He holds out his hand and I stare at it, not wanting to touch him. He grabs my hand anyway and when he does, he shows me some vision and it's very dark. The images overtake reality and it's as if I'm in a different time and place. The sky is grey; heavy black clouds blot out the sun. The land is ruined, the dirt pitted by huge holes, men's bodies lying on the edges. I realize they're the craters caused by massive bomb blasts.

He's showing me a possible future and it's very grim.

Then I see a small group of soldiers standing on the edge of the battlefield. We move closer and I see it's Blackstone and several of his men. They're surveying the carnage and seem pleased by it. I take it the smiles on their faces indicate Blackstone won that battle. If he won, I know that humans have lost.

It sends a shiver down my spine. I can smell the wet earth, and it's soaked in blood, the coppery tang strong on my tongue and in my nose. I gag and then the memory fades and I'm back in Soren's room, my hand in his, his eyes focused on me.

"I suppose you showed me that to scare me into complying."

"I showed it to you because you want – you *need* – evidence. The only evidence I have is the evidence based on my ability to see the future."

"How do I know you're not creating that vision out of thin air? How do I know it's really of the future and not just one thread? Even Michel can't see the final future. We all have parts to play and so the future isn't fixed."

"Michel can't see the final future, or the three choices we have. I can. You have to trust me."

Frustration fills me for it always comes down to that – trust or faith.

"If you can see the final possible futures, everything is pretty much preordained. Every step. There can be no diversion. You already know what will happen. Isn't that rather boring for you?"

"I try to keep myself amused," he says with a grin. "There are three paths at this point, leading to three different futures. The choices we make lead us down one of those three. I'm trying to ensure we go down the best option."

"Best for who? You?"

"What's best for me is also best for you, Eve. And humanity. You have to trust me."

"I don't believe it," I say derisively. "You've given me no reason to trust you."

"Fair enough," he says. "Help me to resurrect one of my brethren and if I betray you, you'll know the truth. But honestly, Eve," he says and his gaze moves over my face. "At some point, you have to go on your gut feeling, as Julien said. Which future do you despise the least? One with me on the throne of the Roman Church in Italy, and humans free of the vampire threat, or one with Blackstone at the helm, with humans enslaved to them and acting as blood bags?"

"What's the third option?"

He just smiles. "The one that will break your heart. The one Michel wants to avoid at all costs. But he's devout enough to go that way, if necessary."

"I wish you'd stop talking in such generalities. Tell me what I need to know so I can make the right decision."

"Can't," he says and shrugs. "That's part of what makes this all so damn difficult. You're the wildcard. You're the keystone. The fulcrum on which all pivots. You can't know. Sorry."

I stand and run everything through my mind once more. As much as I hate to do it, I think Soren is the only way we can hope to stop the carnage. "I need time to decide," I say and start towards the door. "I can't decide on the spot, so you have to give me time."

"How much time?" he says, his voice impatient and his tone blunt. "We don't have time. Every moment the plague spreads farther and there's only so much leeway on this road we've chosen. That's on your head, Eve. Not mine."

"I need time."

"If you need to see more," he says and extends his hand once more. I keep my hand to myself.

"So afraid of what you'll see?"

I shake my head. "I want to avoid going on another vision quest that may or may not be a complete fabrication," I say with a sour tone. "Besides, even Michel argues that all you can show me is one thread. That might not come to pass, depending on what everyone does. Each decision we make affects the possible futures, so it could all change and Blackstone could fail."

"Of course," Soren says and sits back down behind his desk, interested in his maps once more. "I showed you the one possible future in which you die before you can help me resurrect the rest of my brethren. In that future, I'm unable to stop the plague and destroy vampires. In that future, I have no power at all. A useless shell, condemned to live for all eternity but without any power." He looks up from his papers. "I need power to stop him. That's where you come in. Only you can unite us as we once were united before we took physical form. That's our source of power. For some reason unknown to me, you're the only one who can do this. I *need* you, Eve. I'll comply with your wishes if it ensures I get power and can resurrect the rest of the Twelve." He shuffles the maps, and I feel as if I've been dismissed. I turn to go but he calls out after me. "Go do your thinking and deciding. See Michel again. See whether what I've said is true. Both of them are yours for the taking, Eve, and both are mine to take away. Keep that in mind." He glances up, his expression intense. "It's your choice."

"How do I know you're not showing me something from the future I want to come to pass?"

"You can't."

I leave him behind, and try to push his words out of my mind. When I walk down the hallway, I decide to speak to Michel and tell him what Soren has told me, so I can see his reaction. Maybe he'll finally tell me the truth.

I take the stairs to his suite of rooms and knock on the door.

"Who is it?" he says quietly.

"It's me," I say, leaning against the door. "We need to talk."

He hesitates, and then I hear the key turn in the lock and the heavy wooden door swings open.

He stands in the doorway, his vestments off, a white shirt open at the neck and untucked over dark trousers. In his hand is a quill and his fingers are black from ink. He looks like he could be a rock star or male model instead of a studious priest out to save the world.

"Come in," he says, and I can see reluctance on his face, in his eyes, which are dark under a frown.

I enter the room and glance around, half expecting to see Gabrielle, but he's alone. On the desk is a long piece of paper and I see he's been writing. I turn to him and he stands before me, waiting for me to speak.

Instead, I go to him and place my hand behind his head, pulling him down to me for a kiss. I can tell he's shocked by my actions, but he gets over it very quickly, dropping the quill to the floor, his hand sliding behind my head, tangling in my hair, the other hand at the small of my back, pulling me against him. He kisses me back, his tongue finding mine in a very non-priestly way.

Despite everything, a surge of desire for Michel fills me and I can't help but respond. I pull him over to the bed and he follows willingly, and when I lie down across the bed, he lies on top of me and continues to kiss me. One hand moves down my body and he actually groans when he slips his hand under my t-shirt to feel my bare skin. My body responds, my heart swells. How easily I could let him do what he wants... When his hand slips between my spread thighs and fingers find my folds, I groan, my lust surging. I want him inside of me, now.

It's when I hear him unzipping his jeans, and the clank of his belt buckle that I come back to reality and realize what's happening.

I remember why I'm there and pull back.

Michel gasps when I push him away roughly to break our kiss. "Eve..."

I roll out from under his body and stand beside the bed, my body betraying me, my flesh throbbing. I'm angry and cross my arms, watching as he struggles to stand, his erection obvious. At least now I know that Soren told the truth about Michel.

"Yep," I say and can't help but hate myself. "Soren said you'd be mine if I made a move."

"What do you mean?"

"He said that if I kissed you, you wouldn't be able to resist, despite your dedication to the priesthood."

Michel frowns, his expression dark. "I'm weak."

"That's it?" I say, angry now. "Just *you're weak*? Not that you love me and want me?"

"That's a given," he says defensively. "I want you and love you, but

I'm a priest and you are *not* meant for me, as much as I might want you."

I go back to him and hold his face in my hands. "Michel, if you'd only tell me everything, I could know what to do. As it is, I have only partial information. You lie to me, my mother lies to me, Julien is compelled and can't even talk to me about certain things, and Soren manipulates me like a puppet. Tell me everything so I can know what to do..."

"I can't," he says and there's a hitch in his voice. "One day, you'll understand everything. That's all I can say."

"What should I do?"

He shakes his head. "What you must."

I stand before him, filled with frustration, tears welling in my eyes. *Damn him!*

"I loved you," I say, my vision blurry. "You were the first man I ever loved besides my father. I was in love with you."

"You were," he says and smiles, but now his eyes are filled with tears, too. "I was. I am. I always will be."

"But not enough to tell me."

"*Because* I love you, I can't."

"That doesn't make sense," I say and stalk to the door, my heart breaking once more. "Everything you say is shrouded in secrecy, half-truths, half-lies, obfuscation. How can I make a decision?"

"Trust your heart."

"It's broken," I say and open the door. I leave, closing it behind me, wishing once again that I had some other fate than the one I face.

I go to my suite of rooms and find Julien standing at the window, watching the sky. I slip my arms around him and squeeze, needing to feel his solidity. Needing to have him wipe away memories of Michel's touch.

"How'd it go?"

"What do you think? He can't tell me the truth. He can't tell me everything or it would kill me – the usual story." I sigh and enjoy the strong muscles of Julien's abdomen beneath my hands.

"Are you going to help Soren?" he asks lightly.

"I don't know. How can I know?"

"He won't give you long to decide."

"What's he going to do – kill me if I take too long?" I close my eyes. "Part of me wants to run away and see what he does. On his own, or with Kael, he really is vulnerable or else he wouldn't want to resurrect the rest. He fears Blackstone. Maybe I need to talk to Blackstone some more."

Julien takes my hands away from around his waist. "That's a bad idea, Eve."

"Why?" I ask and look in his eyes when he turns around to face me. "The more of Soren's brethren we resurrect, the more powerful he becomes. What if I help him resurrect them all and then he's unstoppable?"

"He said he'd stop the plague and eradicate vampirism. I believe him."

I make a face. "How come you've changed your mind?"

"He's our only chance." Julien shrugs. "If you can't see that…"

"If I can't see that, what?"

"I can't be with you."

"What?" I say and shake my head, totally confused. "You can't be with me if I don't help Soren? When we came here, you were all about me not trusting him!"

"I've changed my mind," he says. "You need to support Soren. Blackstone can't be trusted. If you don't see that, I can't be with you." He shrugs as if it's out of his control.

And it's then I wonder if this isn't Soren's doing. I go to Julien and put my arms around his neck, standing on my tiptoes to kiss him. He resists, turning his head to the side to avoid my lips.

"Kiss me," I say, pressing my breasts against him, grinding my hips against his.

"No, Eve," he says and gingerly pulls my hands from around his neck. "I can't be with you if you don't agree to help Soren."

I exhale heavily. "Soren's compelled you to reject me if I don't agree to help him."

"I'm sorry, but I just can't do it." He backs away from me, and says nothing to acknowledge what I said. I don't let him get away, my hand around his waist. He struggles and makes a face of pain as if my touch actually burns him.

"Eve, stop."

"I'll help Soren," I say, and immediately he relaxes and doesn't pull away.

"Good. Go to him and help him."

"I want you now," I say and press against him.

"Go to him and help him." He pulls away, smiling.

I stop and make fists, wanting to punch something. Anything. I go to the couch and take one of the throw pillows and do just that – hitting it, battering it with my fists. It feels so good and I feel so stupid for doing it, but I am so frustrated that Soren is able to manipulate me like this, using my love for the brothers and especially for Julien to tempt me.

"Just go to him, Eve," Julien says and takes the pillow from my hands. "Go and all this will be over."

I close my eyes and breathe in deeply while Julien places the pillow back on the couch.

I expect that until I actually help resurrect more of the Twelve, Soren will keep Julien from me. The interesting and ironic twist is that I could have Michel right now. Soren's doing, no doubt. He knows Michel can't resist me and is making me either be celibate or go with Michel until the rest of the Twelve are resurrected.

He's evil.

Not evil, Eve. I understand human nature. I understand you.

"Fuck off," I say out loud.

Julien looks hurt, as if that was meant for him.

"Eve," he says, his brow creased.

"That wasn't meant for you."

I can see his brow relax.

What a nightmare…

CHAPTER 4

I TAKE the hallway to Soren's suite of rooms, past the central staircase that leads down to the main floor, and a long row of paintings of noble men born centuries ago. When I arrive at Soren's door, a guard opens it for me and lets me enter.

Soren glances up from the couch where he sits, drinking a glass of blood.

"Come and join me," he says, motioning to the other space on the couch. I pick the chair across from him instead. He motions to his servant, who pours a cup of blood for me. I take it without struggle, deciding that I need it now to calm myself.

"So, I take it you've spoken with Michel and Julien about my request."

"I have," I say and drink down the blood, enjoying its coppery taste. A sense of well-being fills me as it slides down my throat to my stomach. I lean back and close my eyes, enjoying the associated warmth. I open my eyes and examine the glass.

"I'm going to cooperate fully," I say softly. "No more fighting."

He glances at me as if he doesn't believe me. "Good," he says finally. "At some point, Eve, you just have to submit, as hard as that is for you to accept. We all have to submit to someone," he says. "Even me."

"I suppose you'll tell me you must submit to God," I say, trying not to be too irreverent.

"Exactly," he says.

"You're telling me this is God's plan?"

He shakes his head. "No, actually," he says and finishes his glass of blood. "God leaves all the details up to us. It's a big test, to see if we're worthy."

I say nothing. I don't even crack a smile or frown. I know it's not worth the effort to argue with him, or Michel.

"Who's first on the agenda?" I ask, taking another sip of blood. "Which of your brethren will you resurrect?"

"Procel," he says, matter of fact. "He and I were closest after Kael. You'll like him, Eve. He was always a music lover and can play a mean harpsichord."

I say nothing, not planning on liking any of the Twelve.

"Really, Eve, give them a chance. They're not all vicious like Kael. I resurrected him first because he's the most blood thirsty and won't balk at the ugly deeds that have to be done to make this all work out."

"What ugly deeds?" I ask, frowning.

"Dark deeds," he says. "Ones that must be done, whether we like them or not."

I get a bad feeling about this. "Kael is your hitman? The bad cop to your good cop?"

Soren smiles. "Something like that." Soren stands and walks over to his sideboard where a carafe of blood sits on a silver tray. He pours more for himself, waving the servant away. "Leave us," he says softly. The servant bows and leaves the room, backing out, closing the door behind him.

Soren returns with the carafe and pours me more blood.

I let him, not wanting to fight any more. Maybe if I cooperate, I'll finally understand.

"Yes," he says, reading my mind of course. "You *will* finally understand, Eve. Cooperate."

I sigh heavily and drink down the rest of the blood, needing its endorphins to take away the anxiety I feel. It works, and in a few moments, I'm mellow.

"When and where?"

"The cathedral. No death, Eve. I promise that. All the blood will be supplied beforehand. No victims. Just you, me and a few dozen adoring worshippers to give us the juice we need to do miracles."

I nod and close my eyes. Part of me wants to still fight, but the other part recognizes that it's impossible. Soren knows everything. He controls Julien. Michel won't tell me the truth. My mother is dead to me until she can explain why she gave me up for all those years. Blackstone is a megalomaniac who wants to enslave humanity.

"I give in," I say and a powerful sense of peace overtakes me.

I promise myself I will stop over-thinking every decision. I'll follow my gut.

Right now, my gut tells me that I can't fight Soren at this time, and so I have to see this thing out and learn what it is he plans to do.

Will he really stop the plague? Will he really eradicate vampirism?

"Yes, and yes," he says. "It's what will make me more powerful than ever. You can count on it. That's my motivation. I must be more powerful than ever if I hope to succeed."

"Succeed at what?" I ask, but I'm feeling so calm and dreamy, I don't really even care. I'm asking to be polite. To make conversation.

"Now that would be telling."

I smile. "And you're not."

"No, Eve," he says and I hear humor in his voice. "I'm not. Remember. Need to know."

I open one eye and I see his smile. It's not smug. It's amused.

"I'm so tired of all this," I say with a yawn. I sit up and put my empty glass on the coffee table. When Soren moves to refill it, I put my hand over the glass and shake my head. "I've had enough."

"As you wish," he says and pours himself more.

I stand up and stretch, enjoying the good feelings from the blood. "I know what you've done" I say.

"What?"

"You've compelled Julien to not sleep with me until I've helped you resurrect the rest of the Twelve."

He smiles to himself and takes a sip. "How smart of me," he says drolly.

"You want me with Michel," I say, my hands on my hips. "Why?"

He glances up at me. "Why do you think?"

"To punish them both."

He smiles again. "I wanted two of you, one for each of them, but that didn't work out."

"What happened?"

Soren sighs. "There were three embryos, and two died, leaving only you," he says and waves his hand towards me with a flourish. "One very special child who would unite us all once more."

"They thought they would each get one of me?"

"Yes," he says with a chuckle. "Identical twins for identical twins. They didn't really like sharing Marguerite, although it gave her immense pleasure. They wanted one for each of them. A fighter who could help Julien with his quest and a crusader who could help Michel save souls."

"What happened when they learned that there was only one of me?"

Soren smiles and stands up as well, straightening his clothes, running his hands down his suit jacket. "They drew straws. Julien won."

"Really?"

"I wanted them to share you, but they were against that," Soren says with a dramatic sigh. "They decided to be grown men about it and leave it up to chance. Straws it was. Michel lost. He was supposed to let you go, but he couldn't help himself. He became involved in your life while Julien was out fighting dragons, and he became attached to the idea of having you for himself. He fought so hard, Eve, to deny himself, but in the end, he was weak."

"You enjoy it."

"I do. I love it. I think it's a fair payback for what he did to my Marguerite."

"Why didn't you bring her back to life the way you did the man in the Amman bombing?"

"Timing is everything when it comes to resurrection, Eve. She was burnt to a crisp. All I could do was gather up her ashes and the few bone fragments that remained. Luckily, the hip bone is so dense that it's hard to burn except in a furnace. That was how I resurrected Marguerite as Gabrielle. She's sweet, but she's not my beautiful Viking princess."

"And so you're going to torture Michel and Julien for eternity?"

"Maybe," Soren says and tilts his head to the side. "I'm not going to let them forget what they did. I *could* have created someone else, and not involved them at all, someone with all your attributes, with your talents, and given you to the guild to train, but it was sweet payback to see them both fall in love with you. Oh, Eve," he says and rubs his hands together in glee. "To see them jockey for position in your heart and in your bed. It was so satisfying. Julien was *so* pleased that I took Michel from you for that brief time. He tried to fight his desire for you, but inside he knew he'd fail. He held out for so long and then you went to him and offered yourself just like I told him you would. He was sooo happy."

I frown. From my journal, I learned that Soren made Michel stay in Pittsburgh in payment for resurrecting Julien after he was staked. I eventually slept with Julien and fell in love with him. Then, Michel returned and he and I were once more reunited.

I loved Michel first. I thought I'd never see him again, because it sounded like Soren would keep him away for a lifetime. Julien looked so much like Michel...

Soren was playing us all even back then.

"Michel and Julien knew they'd eventually have to share you. They didn't like it, but that's the way fate works. Best laid plans, and all."

I shake my head. I want to go back to my rooms and lie down, throw a cover over my head against the light and escape reality.

"You can't escape reality, Eve," Soren says, reading my mind again. "You have to accept it, and go with the flow." He makes a wave motion with his hand and laughs at my frown.

"Go to Michel. Give the poor man a crumb, for God's sake."

I turn on my heel to leave the room, my mellow mood quickly dissipating into a sense of gloominess.

"I'm through with Michel," I say, as much to myself as to Soren.

"So you keep saying, but I think the lady doth protest too much…"

I make a face but don't give him the pleasure of seeing my disapproval. I go to the door and before I can get my hand on the doorknob, he clears his throat.

"Eve, you can't escape this fate. Accept it, and be satisfied that in the end, it will be you who is responsible for saving humankind from Dominion. You'll be the one who helps eradicate vampirism. That's quite a legacy. Sleeping with Michel and Julien at the same time is a small price to pay."

I turn to face him. "I won't do it," I say. "No matter what."

He shrugs as if he doesn't really believe me. "Suit yourself. You won't get Julien back until you give in."

"Give in to what?" I say, standing in the open doorway. I know I should just go and not engage Soren any longer, but I can't help myself.

"To your own desires," he says.

"I chose *Julien,*" I say, determined to fight him. He thinks he knows my heart, but he's wrong. "Michel lost me when he lied to me time and time again. I can't forgive him for lying continuously. A woman can only take so many lies and then you reach the breaking point. It doesn't matter why Michel lied. What matters is that he chose lies over the truth."

"Yes, but that's such an easy choice to make, Eve. Julien's been there for you from the start, waiting in the wings, biding his time… He's done everything you've asked of him, except tell you what you really needed to know. Because he can't tell you that."

"Not his fault," I say defiantly. "You and Michel manipulate him, compel him, make him do things he wouldn't do of his own choice."

"That's completely true, but here's something that'll freak your little mind out. What *would* be his own choice? Would he even *be* with you, if it weren't for me?" He glances up from his glass of blood, the slightest smile on his lips.

What does he mean… Is he trying to suggest…?

"Don't play mind games with me," I say, unwilling to let him think I'm upset at what he's said. "Julien loves me. I can tell. You're interfering with him, preventing him from being with me until I help you raise all the Twelve."

"If that gets you through the night," Soren says, waving his hand at me dismissively. "You'll never know, will you?"

I *despise* him. He doesn't deserve to be a god…

"Oh, Eve," he says from across the room when I turn to leave. "Who does? In the end, all that matters is that a god has the power necessary or not. I will have the power. You'll help me if you want your Julien back. If you want to stop the plague. If you want to eradicate vampirism."

I don't look back, for I don't want to see his self-satisfied grin. Instead, I leave the room, closing the door behind me.

INSTEAD OF RETURNING to my rooms, I walk around the perimeter of the compound, needing the fresh air to calm me down. Soren can make me so angry that I lose my senses. It does me no good to argue with him. He enjoys it. What I should do is comply and maybe I'll learn more about his plans if he gets no resistance from me.

After a complete circuit, which takes about five minutes, I sit on the low stone retaining wall outside the rear door and watch the clouds scudding past. I want the plague to stop and the sooner the better. I want to eradicate vampirism and it looks as if Soren has cracked the code on that, but whatever he does makes the vampire die. Only Soren can resurrect them. Will he pick and choose who he resurrects? There are hundreds of thousands of vampires… Unless he has some kind of mass release process that will spread the antidote around the world, targeting bloodlines like he tried earlier, it'll take a very long time to get rid of vampirism.

Whatever the case, I have to expect that it will benefit him, give him more power, so he can rule as a god the way he wants.

When I return to my rooms, Soren is just leaving. A guard accompanies him and he catches sight of me as I round the corner.

"Eve," he says, smiling. "I was just looking for you. I want to do some resurrecting tonight. Procel awaits. Prepare yourself. Meet me in the entry at eight."

I nod, but I'm not pleased. Inside my rooms, Julien is waiting for me, sitting on the couch, his arms spread over the back. He looks happy to see me and pats the couch.

"Come and sit with me," he says. "You look like you need a back rub."

I approach him, and despite needing his touch, the suggestion that Julien is acting completely under compulsion and may not even want me, nags the edge of my mind.

"I'm fine," I say, not wanting to be duped. "What did you and Soren speak about?"

"Sit," Julien says once more.

I do, sitting about a foot away from him. He moves closer and pulls me into his arms. "That's better," he says, and brushes hair back from my cheek. He leans in and kisses me then buries his face in the crook of my neck, his breath tickling me and at the same time, sending a thrill of desire through my body.

I can't help but think of what Soren said to me and now Julien's touch is no longer welcome. It's suspect. I lie beneath him while he searches my body with his hands and mouth, kissing my face, my chin, my jaw, then down to his bite mark, while his hand slides down my body to cup a breast, tweak my nipple and then slip between my thighs, to cup my mound. My thighs do not part like they usually would and my eyes are open.

I can't help it. I can't stop this thought from driving me crazy.

Did you do this, you bastard?

But of course, he won't tell me. This is Soren's way of showing me that he's in control. Of *everything*.

I sigh and tears fill my eyes. Julien's touch is cold to me now and he must sense it for he rises up and stares in my eyes for a moment.

"Eve..." he whispers, his breath a bit ragged from desire.

"I can't," I manage, squeezing my eyes shut so that I don't have to look in his face and see his expression for I no longer believe it.

"What's the matter? Why can't you?"

When I don't respond, and instead, roll out from under his warmth, my arms wrapped around my body, he takes hold of me and forces me to face him.

"Tell me what's the matter? I need to know!"

I wipe my eyes and look in his. He's frowning, his brow furrowed, his blue eyes, usually so good-natured and loving, are dark.

"Soren made me doubt you," I say and sniff like a child. "He suggested that you may not even really love me and that you've been compelled to believe you do. Now, I don't know what to believe."

He shakes his head, and takes in a deep breath. "I love you, Eve. I do with all my heart. How can you doubt me?"

"Because I know he's compelled you before. How can I know what's the result of compulsion and what's the result of your true feelings?"

He sits in silence for a moment, and I know he has to admit that what I say is true. "I don't know what to say," he says finally, his voice low and sounding defeated. "I only know what I feel, here," he says and puts his fist against his chest. "I love you, Eve. At this moment, that's all I know. Who knows whether it's because of Soren or because of me? I can't know. Neither can you."

"Unless Soren completely erases all his compulsion. Then I'd know."

He shakes his head. "How could you trust him? He might say he's eradicated all his compulsion, but can you believe him? In the end, you have to go with what's here, now."

He pulls me onto his lap, and brushes tears from my cheeks. "I'm here, now. I want you. I love you. Enjoy what we have while we can. Who knows what might happen tomorrow?"

My gaze moves over his face, at the strong jaw covered in a thin dusting of stubble, the soft full mouth, the dark arched brows, the blue blue eyes that seem to pierce right into my heart.

"Even if he made you love me?"

"You'll never know for sure," he says. "So don't even think about it again. That's all you can do."

I sigh and melt into his body, needing to feel his strength around me. I love Julien. That much I know is true. I love him deeply and totally. If Soren has forced him to think he loves me, it was no doubt to make Michel jealous.

I hate that I'm a pawn like this, in Soren and Blackstone's game of power, but there's nothing I can do to know for certain that Julien loves me on his own volition or under Soren's.

"You're right," I say finally. "I can't ever know. No matter what he says now, I'll never know the truth. If he says he compelled you, it might be to hurt me. If he says he doesn't, it might be to appease me."

He runs his fingers down my cheek. "That's right. Just love me, Eve. I'll love you back. That's all we ever really have."

And so I do. I wrap my arms around his neck and kiss him, deeply. I relish in the feel of his warmth against me, the sound of his breathing, heavy now with desire, and the feel of his tongue against mine, hungry for me.

I let him lay me down across the couch and his weight on top of me is so reassuring, and his erection hard against my belly tells me that whether Soren made him love me or whether he loves me on his own, he desires me. He needs me right now.

I need him.

For the next hour, we delight each other with our bodies, our moans and sighs joining together as our senses do until there is only one body and one mind.

I don't care whether Julien is truly mine or if he's Soren's creature.

It doesn't matter anymore. I need Julien and love him. As long as he wants to be with me, as long as he seems to want me, I won't hold back.

If that's what Soren wants, so be it.

It's what I want and need as well.

CHAPTER 5

We lie together, our bodies damp with exertion, our limbs entwined. My head is on his shoulder, my thigh thrown possessively over his, my hand on his abdomen, running over his muscles. He's a perfect specimen of a man, so strong and well-developed. He's beautiful in his vampire paleness.

"I have to help Soren tonight, to resurrect Procel," I say, not looking forward to what lies ahead. "I needed some good brain endorphins to help me get through the evening."

We lie together for the afternoon, and speak in soft voices about what will happen and what lies in store for us. Finally, when I see the time, I get up and go to the washroom, have a quick wash and stare at myself in the mirror. I look tired and need some blood to get me through the evening. I'll be sharing blood with Soren and Kael as part of the ceremony and their blood is so powerful, I won't need anything for a while. But right now, I need some to feel better about tonight.

I go into the other room and see Julien lying on the couch, his arm behind his head, his muscles so nicely on display. He really is such a beautiful man...

I bend down to kiss him and then go to the sideboard for a glass of blood. It's preserved so it has that bitter taste, but it goes down fast and the warmth distracts me from the deeds I have to do tonight. I stand in front of my wardrobe and select the white gown that Soren made me wear the last time. He wants the crowd to see me as some kind of high priestess and so I have to look the part.

I pull it on and then return to the bathroom to do my hair, piling it on top of my head the way Michel suggested the last time I did this.

It's when I'm finishing my hair that I hear a commotion and peek out the bathroom door.

Soren bursts into the room followed by guards dressed in full regalia.

"Where's Michel?" he says, alarm in his voice. "Is he with you?"

I frown and enter the living room. Julien has pulled on his jeans and stands bare chested before Soren, his feet bare, his hands on his hips.

"I haven't seen him since earlier," Julien says. He glances at me. I shake my head.

"I haven't seen him either."

I feel Soren probing my mind.

I haven't seen him. Honest.

Soren comes right over to me, his face red, his brow furrowed. He grabs me around the neck and lifts me up as if I weigh nothing.

"Tell me where he is!" he shouts, and I swear I see murder in his eyes. His hand grips my throat, squeezing so hard it hurts and I can't breathe.

"Stop," I manage to grunt despite his grip on my throat.

"Tell me where he is!"

I feel him probing my mind again, furious that I won't tell him where Michel is.

"If you've developed a way to block me, I'll kill you," he says, his voice low and menacing. I feel him search my memories of the last hours and he sees everything that's happened. He sees me go to Michel, he sees me return to Julien and us making love.

He shakes me, and by now, I'm starting to black out, my vision narrowing, sparkles in the periphery of my vision. I'm sure he's going to kill me.

"I'll kill you," he says, spittle coming out of his mouth he's so enraged. "I'll start over again. I don't care. If you've found a way to block me, you're of no use and I'll kill you with a thought."

I know he could do it, and I grip his hands, trying to pry them loose before I black out completely.

Julien comes over and tries to pull Soren's hands away from my neck, but he can't. Soren is too strong. I feel as if my windpipe will break, and tears are running down my cheeks as I gasp and can't get any air inside my lungs.

Before I black out, he lets go and I slide to the floor. My throat is crushed, and I struggle to breathe, but soon, my vampire healing abilities start to work, and under my fingers, I feel my throat start to open, the bruising start to heal.

In a moment, as Julien kneels over me, pouring blood into my open mouth to help the process along, I start to recover.

I take in long gasping breaths, my vision returning to normal. The pain starts to recede and I look over Julien's shoulder at Soren, who stands watching, his hands on his hips, his expression dark.

Of course I can't block Soren. I have no idea where Michel has gone. The last I saw of him was when I went into his room and kissed him.

It's then that I realize that Soren can't read Michel's mind. If he could, he would have known where Michel is.

Soren can't read Michel's mind!

That realization fills me with a mixture of glee and dread. So, all along, Soren couldn't read Michel's mind... They must have been right about Soren – he can't read Michel's mind – or maybe my mother's. Or my brother's.

But he *can* read my mind and I wonder if it was sharing blood with him? But Michel shared blood with him as well...

My mind whirls with this new information and I feel darkness from Soren, as if his anger could reach right out and strangle me from across the room.

I meet his gaze and his face is paler than vampire-pale, his jaw set. His fists are clenched.

Yes, so now you know. It won't change things, Eve. I can still read your mind and through you, I'll know their every move.

I stand up and my knees are a bit weak so I hold out the glass of blood Julien handed me and he fills it once more. I drink that down, needing the blood to continue the healing process. Julien leads me over to the couch and I sit on it, head down and let the blood warm me and its healing properties mend the damage Soren did to me.

When I'm feeling almost back to my old self, when the pain is gone and I can breathe normally again, a wave of emotion fills me. Of course, it's then that I realize why my mother left me. If she stayed with me, Soren would know everything she did. Soren couldn't read her mind, but he could read mine.

My mother left me because Soren can read me but not them.

She didn't *choose* to leave me because she didn't care, or because she cared more about her quest to find a cure for vampirism.

She left me because if she stayed, Soren would know everything about her and her quest – through me.

I still feel loss at not being with her for the past decade, but now I start to understand why she let me go. She felt she had to so that Soren didn't know she was alive.

He must have made me in such a way that he could read my mind and that is why I have been so strategic to everyone.

I am the conduit. I am the one through which he sees the three of them.

It doesn't matter, Eve. Everything is still the same. You have to help me in order to stop the plague. In order to eradicate vampirism. This changes nothing.

Of course, it changes everything to me. This is why Michel won't tell me anything. This is why my mother and brother have been kept apart from me. Glee fills me, because now I feel as if I can trust them all. I can let things happen without needing to ask for the truth.

Everything has been done to keep Soren from knowing whatever it is they don't want him to know.

Don't feel too smug. You still need me to get what you want.

"We need each other," I say out loud, not wanting him to think that we are going to be talking intimately in my mind. "As long as you do what you promise, I'll do what I promise. That's about as much as we can agree to."

I'll let Michel and my mother and Dylan do what they have to and trust that they know what they're doing. Finally…

It feels like a huge burden lifted off my shoulders. I smile and stand beside Julien. I still don't know if he loves me for real or if it's just compulsion, but at least I don't have all the other things to worry about.

"What are you going to do without Michel?" I ask, turning to Soren, barely able to hide my delight at his plight. "You need a priest to do the ceremony."

Soren smiles. "Julien will suffice."

I shake my head and stand closer to Julien. "He's not a priest. He gave that up centuries ago, in case you forgot."

I feel smug that Soren is now in a bind. He needs someone like Michel to do the rite.

"Julien was an ordained priest. In case you forgot, Eve, once a priest always a priest, in the eyes of God."

I frown and turn to Julien. He shakes his head. "I'm not a priest, Soren. I've broken every vow a thousand times. I don't really feel it any longer – a calling. I stopped feeling it when the Pope went against my father. That was eight hundred years ago and nothing has changed."

Soren walks over to Julien and grips Julien's face between his hands. Before I can respond, Soren meets Julien's gaze and although Julien struggles to pull away, he can't.

"Julien, you feel love for the Church once more. Your utmost desire is to become a priest once more. You can't wait to put on your vestments and say mass with me tonight. Do you understand?"

Julien is helpless to refuse.

I stand helpless while Soren compels him to love the priesthood once more. I can almost see it in his body as he acquiesces to Soren's orders, his body slumping a bit, his face relaxing. There's this look in his eyes as if he's had an epiphany.

I clench my fists but there's nothing I can do. Soren is the most powerful of all the Ancients and he can compel any ordinary mortal or vampire. Julien is like putty in his hands.

Soren releases Julien and I can hear Julien's intake of breath, as if he's been inspired.

"When do we start?" he asks, impatient to go and do this resurrection.

Soren smiles and glances over at me. "Like putty, Eve."

Soren turns back to Julien and looks him up and down. "You need vestments. White, of course. And a nice thick cross made of wood, I think. That will be a nice touch."

Soren snaps his fingers and one of the guards leaves the room. I assume he's going to get some vestments for Julien, who stands quietly, watching Soren like he's waiting for his next orders.

I grit my teeth, hating this but there's no sense in fighting now. I have to do my part, help Soren resurrect Procel. Then, I'll at least know whether he was telling me the truth about no killing.

My heart rate is still a little elevated by the news that Soren can't read Michel and my mother and Dylan after all. They were right about themselves, but wrong about me.

This changes everything.

Not everything, Eve. You still have to help me if you want the plague to stop. You still have to raise them all before I'll use my powers to end vampirism.

You still have to comply.

"I'll comply," I say out loud.

"Good," he replies.

The guard returns with a set of vestments on a hangar laid carefully over his arm. Julien seems eager to get them on and takes the clothes from the guard. His expression is reverent and I wonder what he would be like as a priest. What happened to him, way back when, to turn him against the Church? Was it really the Cathar battle that made the difference and separated the two brothers?

It must have been heartrending for Julien to have made his break from Michel, after going to seminary together and after protecting each other all those years.

Of course, I think about Michel and wonder where he's gone…

And why he's gone. I hope it wasn't anything I did. Perhaps he was planning on leaving – he did say he wouldn't comply with Soren. I thought he was just being dramatic.

I imagine he's gone to meet with my mother and Dylan so they can plan something. I can't imagine that either Michel or my mother will let Soren gain power. There must be something in the works.

But Dylan… he wants his sister back. Soren has him by the heart and so I doubt he'll truly be helping in any plot against him. At least, not until he has Sarah back alive.

Julien finishes dressing while Soren and I watch, and then he stands before a mirror and runs his hands over his hair, which has grown a bit longer since the first time I met him in the coffee shop. He looks more like Michel now.

With the vestments on, he looks even more like his brother.

"Let's go," Soren says, his voice impatient. He rubs his hands together and glances over at me. "You can come with me," he says. "Julien will go in a separate vehicle with Procel's containment. I want you by my side, Eve. The masses will be happy to see you and me together."

I nod without replying. I hate the idea of this performance, but my end game is to stop the plague and end vampirism. That's the greater good and so I have to cooperate with Soren, I have to trust Michel and my mother to find a way to stop him from being some kind of angelic tyrant.

I'm crushed, Eve, that you think I'd be a tyrant and not a benevolent dictator…

I glance at him and he's smiling.

CHAPTER 6

WE LEAVE the house and go to the driveway, where his vehicle is waiting. The guard opens the door and Soren waves me in. I slip into the seat in the back and he slides in beside me.

When the car drives off, I sigh.

"You have to know that people won't want you to have too much power and rule over us like a god," I say, not caring that he knows what I think. He has access to my every thought so I might as well be open.

"I know," he says, glancing out the window of the vehicle as we drive down the street. "I'll be there for religious purposes, not to run their lives. But religion will once again play a more central role in the day-to-day life of the people. I'll see to it."

"Why?" I ask. "So you can have more power? Is power that important to you?"

He turns to me, an expression of tolerance on his face. "People need to have something to believe in. Death is such a scary prospect. That's my role. I'll be their focus. A pope is a mere human, but I'll be a true god."

"Not a god," I say, stubborn. "Truth and reality are better than myths and fables," I say, atheist to the end.

"Oh, such a Doubting Thomas," he says and touches my cheek. I pull away, not wanting him to touch me or show me any affection. "You may not need religion, Eve," he says and sighs. "But I guarantee humans need something. Without God, they're lost."

"They need knowledge so they can make the right choices," I say, unwilling to concede anything to him about religion. "They have to come to some kind of peace with life. God doesn't have to be part of that."

"Such a hard heart," Soren says, shaking his head at me. "Can't you feel sorry for the poor mortals who must face their own deaths? They need God to get them through their days."

I don't say anything. I know it's hard to face mortality. But I was never one of those who wanted to hold onto some fantasy of another life after this one as a way of consoling myself. I just couldn't believe in one.

"I don't think people should believe in fantasies."

He sighs and watches out the window as we drive through the streets, which are growing darker by the minute as the sun sets. The streets are really dark now with no power to the street lights. Occasionally, I see a hint of light in a window, in a storefront, or in one of the buildings. People using candlelight like we used to a century earlier. This is what we've come to – living like we did before electricity.

Some of the better connected people have solar panels that were produced by Blackstone's scientists and are unaffected by the plague, but most are reduced to burning wax candles, or wood for their light and heat.

I'm one of the lucky ones, who lives in Soren's compound where there is both heat and warmth and food. I wonder how many people have died because of the plague.

Some died right away, due to the loss of electricity – like Sarah. Some died when vampires started to hunt again with no restraints to hold them back. Others have died in street battles over resources.

I don't want to be a part of any of the deaths and violence, yet I was one of those who led to the deaths of dozens of people.

"Are we going back to the cathedral?" I glance around, trying to get my bearings in the dark but it's hard. I don't recognize this part of the city. "I'd think people would refuse to come to the cathedral, given what happened before."

"No one knows about what happened before," Soren says quietly. "Their families think they were caught outside the plague zone and they'll meet up again, once the plague stops – or should I say, when I stop the plague for them."

He turns to me and smiles.

"So you compelled their families?"

"I couldn't let it get out that there was any death connected to the resurrection of my brethren. They'll forget all about their family members once the plague has stopped. To them, it will be a given that they must have died in the aftermath. They'll all feel sad but they'll come to mass and feel better after, their sadness waning with each passing mass they attend, each confession they give."

I think about those family members and part of me is glad Soren gave them that kind of closure but of course, it does nothing to bring the dead back to life.

"Those people still died. How do you reconcile that?"

"They'll find their own heaven," he says quietly. I want to push him, but don't want to get into a real religious debate so I shut up and we drive the rest of the way to the cathedral in silence.

Once we're there, I see a stream of parishioners going into the cathedral. They walk right over the freshly leveled mound of dirt that buries their dead relatives. I wonder what they'd do if someone told them – would they scream and flee?

"They'll never know, Eve. Even if someone told them, their minds wouldn't hear it. That's the sweet thing about compulsion. I can compel a person to not hear anything contrary to what I command them to believe. So, if someone told Mrs. Jones that her husband was really food for Kael? Her mind wouldn't register the words, although her ears would hear and her brain would receive the signals. So, don't go thinking you can tell these people the truth and turn them against me."

"I wasn't thinking that. I wondered how they'd respond to knowing they were walking on the graves of their missing family members."

A guard opens Soren's door and he slips out and stands on the path leading to the rear entrance to the cathedral. He stretches as his wings spread out behind him and I hear a few ooohs, and gasps from those among the parishioners who are taking the steps up to the cathedral's ornate entrance.

He did that on purpose, of course. He's such an attention whore…

"Eve," he says and his voice is chiding. "The people want to believe. All I do is feed them what they most desire – to see one of God's angels in the flesh?"

I catch his grin and follow him down the path to the rear doors, where another set of guards stand holding the doors open for Soren.

What a showman.

We enter the familiar alcove and go to the room where we'll prepare for the ceremony. Julien joins us and my heart squeezes to see him dressed in priest clothing, a white lace surplice covering his white vestments. A large wooden cross hangs around his neck. He really does look like a priest – a devastatingly beautiful priest and I hate that I'm caught up in this religious ceremony when I'm such an unbeliever. At this point, I'll comply so I can stop the plague.

It's a small price to pay to end that horror. It may take years to recover, but if we stop the plague before it hits the oil fields, we might be safe.

Julien smiles at me softly when our eyes meet.

"Julien," I say but he shakes his head.

"Can't I even speak to you anymore?"

He puts his hand on my shoulder but it's not like two lovers touching. It's like a priest trying to comfort one of his flock.

"I have to prepare for the ceremony," he says softly. "I haven't done the whole ritual for a long time and I'll be a little rusty." He smiles at me, his eyes closing.

Soren comes over. "You'll do fine," he says to Julien and claps him on the back. "It's like riding a bike. Once you learn, it's in you for life. All you have to do is get back up and ride."

He turns to me, his expression changing. "And don't worry your little head, Eve. In my church, celibacy is optional, so you'll get your Julien back. I need his services for a while, but then he's yours to do whatever you want with, as long as you cooperate."

I nod and look in Julien's eyes, but I don't see a lover in them any longer. I see a priest who is all about self-sacrifice.

I wonder if Soren will re-compel him to be my lover again. It makes me sad to think of the uncertainty I now must live with, never knowing what is real with Julien and what is false.

Julien goes to the side of the room with Soren and they bow their heads together, while Soren speaks with Julien quietly. Even with my vampire-sharp ears, I can't make out what they're saying, because there's sound coming from the doors which open to the cathedral. A hundred or more parishioners arrive and take their places in the pews and in the background, someone is playing a huge organ.

It sounds like Handel, but I can't be sure.

I take in a deep breath, trying to remember what we did last time. Michel took a chalice and slit each of our wrists so that our blood mingled, then he took a drink after passing it to the rest of us. It linked our minds and then, the awe that the parishioners felt when Soren performed his works of wonder were fed through me to him. He used that power to raise Kael from stasis.

I glance around and see that Kael has arrived, followed by his own small entourage. He looks well-fed and satisfied, dressed in a long white robe, and while I watch, he flexes his wings. He catches my eye and smiles, his eyes narrowing. He must know that I disapprove of him and what he did when he was resurrected, but I'm glad that he can't read my mind the way Soren can. I think he's the most vile creature in existence, the way he gleefully killed all those poor people who came to their church thinking they were going to witness a miracle only to die a horrible death.

Oh, Eve... so dramatic! They will get their reward in heaven.

I don't believe in heaven. So, of course, I don't believe they'll get anything except decomposition into soil and bone.

Soren comes over to me, and grabs hold of my shoulders. "You've witnessed wonders, Eve. You've learned that there are vampires and angels and resurrection and a power beyond what you can explain. Why can't you believe in something as simple as an afterlife? There is more to this universe than your mortal physics know. Have some faith that the wonders you have seen are only a small piece of the puzzle."

I shake my head. How I'd love to believe there was something – some existence after death – but I can't. It's worms and earth and dried white bones polished by time, that are eventually petrified and will become a future archaeologist's objects of study.

That's as far as I can believe.

"Such a limited belief system is science."

Soren seems truly sad that I can't believe and his eyes have this expression I find condescending. Like I'm a child and he's an adult, tsk tsking that I still believe in Santa Claus. Except to me, it's the other way around.

Soren turns to all of us. "Let's get this show on the road, shall we?"

He opens his arms like some uncle and ushers us to the door.

"Julien, you know what to do. Eve, you don't have to do anything but drink the blood from the chalice once it's passed to you. All of us will combine our strength to raise Procel from the dead. It will astound and amaze the congregation and we'll all of us be infused with their power."

We enter into the nave and stand at the rear of the altar. Beside it, I see one of the tanks containing Procel. The lid has been removed and Procel is buried under a sea of tank gel, that keeps his body alive but in stasis. He's very similar in appearance to Kael, with pale skin and platinum hair, a perfect jaw and well-muscled body. He could be a sculpture in a Greek temple, he's so perfect.

The congregation quiets when they see us emerge from the room and the organ stops. Finally, after a few coughs in the parishioners,

Soren sits on the throne behind the altar, his wings still spread out behind him.

I check the faces of the congregation and they are definitely in awe, their eyes wide. I wonder what they think is going to happen... Are there any among them who have fears? Or are they certain that what is going to happen is a miracle?

Julien goes to the altar and begins the ceremony, doing what an ordinary priest does when they hold mass, blessing the chalices that will be used to perform the resurrection.

We go through the entire mass, with the congregation repeating Julien's words and responding properly. They already know what to expect, and watch with awe the tank that holds Procel inside.

Finally, Julien holds the cup up high and speaks in Latin, asking for God's blessing. He comes to me and holds up a small dagger, which he will use to take some of my blood. He slices through the skin on my wrist, and my blood drips into the chalice. When he feels there is enough, he leaves me, his eyes distant when they meet mine like he's in some other headspace. He goes to Soren and repeats the bloodletting, and after cutting his own wrist and adding his blood to the chalice, he cuts Kael's wrist and he bleeds as well into the chalice. We then each share the blood. I am the last to get any blood, and so there is only a few mouthfuls left. As soon as the blood hits my stomach, I feel it – the connection to the others – to Soren, to Kael and to Julien.

Our minds unite and I feel each of them separately before we blend together into a single mind and heart.

I am overwhelmed once more at the bliss I feel, at the pure unadulterated joy Kael and Soren feel at being reunited once more. They always shared this bond when they were in their former incarnations, but that was taken from them and they were forced to be individuals, and the loss was so great...

The congregation sighs with awe when Soren stands before them, his wings outstretched, Kael beside him. Light streams off him like from the sun, and the congregation's love and awe and fear stream into me, and from me into Soren and Kael. Together, the two of them become even more powerful, their bodies enlarging, the light coming off their faces almost blinding. I remember vaguely, as I am filled with this sense of awe and bliss, the Bible talking about angels being blinding with the light that emanates from their faces and I know now that is what the Bible was speaking of. I see it with my own eyes and tears stream down my cheeks from the wonder of it.

I still don't know what Soren and his brethren are, but now I am sure that they are what the authors of the Bible wrote of when they described angels.

I know that they can be terrible as well as beautiful.

While I watch, both Soren and Kael go over to the tank where Procel lies in the gel. They stand on either side of the tank and glance down into its contents. Soren reaches in, his hand sliding into the gel, and he lays his hand on Procel's chest the way he did to Kael. Kael lays a hand on Soren's shoulder. The congregation leave their pews and surround the two as they stand by the tank. I feel their awe as they watch the resurrection. Soren allows them to watch, and I know that he wants them to feel awe and reverence as they watch, so their power will flow through me and into Soren and Kael and from them into Procel.

While we all watch, a white light flows from Soren into Procel. From Soren's hand on Procel's pale chest, the light spreads down his perfect naked body, infusing Procel with whatever life-giving power Soren possesses, a power which increases as the congregation's awe increases.

Soon, Procel's eyes open and he sits up in the tank, blinking to clear his eyes of the gel. He coughs and spits, and then Soren offers him a hand, to assist him out of the tank.

People in the congregation step back and I see their faces – filled with wonder, awe, reverence, and some fear. Have some of them remembered what happened before? Or is it just fear of such unworldly creatures that are before them?

Soren keeps his hand on Procel and soon, the tank gel dissipates like steam coming off melting snow on a warm spring day. His body is dry in a mere moment and he takes in a huge breath, his arms raised above his head, his eyes staring up at the ceiling, his wings manifesting behind him, spreading out fully eight feet on either side.

When he returns to a normal stance, Soren takes a huge silver chalice from Julien and hands it to Procel. It's filled with blood and Procel takes it and stares into its contents.

So it will be like this?

Procel turns to Soren, speaking with him directly in his mind.

Soren nods. *It must be like this. Soon, we will all be reunited. It's the price we must pay to be together.*

Procel raises the chalice of blood high up over his head.

So be it.

The audience is once more awed at him and he remains in that position as if soaking up their adoration. Then, he drinks down the chalice of blood, careful to drink every last drop. When he does, he grows even larger, and Julien brings yet another chalice of blood and Procel drinks that as well. I wonder how much blood he'll drink as chalice after chalice is handed to him and he drinks it down.

I wonder how he can take so much in – I'd be vomiting by now, but he's unaffected, his body growing even larger with each chalice. He's almost blinding now, the light so white that it hurts my eyes and the congregation cowers a bit.

Finally, Julien hands Procel the tenth chalice of blood and when Procel drinks it down, some blood spills down his chin and drips onto his chest. He finishes, and hands the empty chalice to Julien who takes it and bows, then returns the chalice to the altar, placing it next to the other chalices.

Did that represent ten human's worth of blood, I wonder as I watch Procel. He wipes his mouth with a pale white hand and then glances out at the congregation, who are now on their knees. First one man in the front knelt, and then the rest followed suit and now, they are all kneeling at Procel's feet, their hands clasped in prayer, their eyes closed.

Julien is standing at the altar, his eyes closed as he too recites some prayer in Latin. I don't know what the words of the prayer mean, but I understand its meaning.

Soren and Kael stand together with Procel and the three of them drink in the awe of their worshipers. It's then I realize that Soren wants a critical mass of his fellow angels back so they can revive the rest without the need for an audience. They need only one more to be resurrected in this manner and then the four of them can do the rest on their own without our help.

I wonder whether Soren will kill me at that point. He won't need me anymore.

I still need you, Eve. You unite us. We can't do it without you. So don't fear death. Not yet...

I calm down a bit from that. I realize that for these angels, or whatever they are, being united is what they consider to be heaven. They need me to unite them. When we share blood, we share a single consciousness in which everyone's thoughts and emotions are united. This will be my job from now on – to reunite them the way they were before they lost their previous form.

That is something I still don't know completely or understand. What were they before? Where did they come from?

I still don't accept religious explanations for who and what they are, but they are clearly powerful beings that science has not yet explained.

Are they aliens? Are they beings from some other dimension who are trapped here?

What I can't accept is that they are God's angels, even fallen ones. That will never be something I can accept, but I can accept that they are beyond our current understanding of what is possible.

I will keep helping them as long as they need me, for it is only in this manner that I will know what they really are and what they want of us.

Yes, you will, Eve. You'll get everything you want, but I have to get every-thing I want as well. I want my brethren back. I want us united as one. I need you for that, and you need me – you need us -- for the rest. As for who and what we are, it's up to you to decide what to believe. You'll never know for sure so it will come down to belief. I know that's hard for you, but that is all you have. Just like you'll never know whether Julien truly loves you or whether I have compelled him to love you. Even if I tell you I did or I didn't, you'll never have the scientific proof of which you demand. In the end, you will have to accept one or the other on faith alone.

I frown, despite the endorphins rushing through my body from the blood bond I share with Soren and his brethren. Julien shared blood with us as well, but I can't feel him because of the power of Soren's, Kael's and Procel's joy at being united once more. I try to search him out in my mind, but fail, as if his mind is too dim for me to reach.

I want to know if he truly loves me the way I love him and it upsets me that I can't sense him now.

Finally, the ceremony ends with Soren and the other two angels leaving the nave and going to the small anteroom at the rear of the cathedral. Once we are there, Soren hands Procel a white robe similar to the one he himself wears. Over top of it, Procel puts on a white breastplate that looks like something out of a Roman army, with gilded edges and a washboard abdomen. He girds himself with a huge sword in a white leather scabbard and white and gold greaves and gauntlets. He looks like an avenging angel out of some Botticelli painting.

The three stand together, their foreheads touching, hands on each other's shoulders, and I feel their bond from across the room. Whatever they are, they do love each other and their emotions are so powerful, I weep from it.

They re-experience the sadness at being torn apart, and incarnated into bodies that have so little ability to join together except when they share blood. Then I understand why they became vampires – so they could at least join with humans while drinking their blood. They can't stand to be separate consciousnesses.

It feels like death to them.

When they are reunited, it is life itself for them.

So whoever and whatever they are, and from wherever they came, they are only happy when joined as one consciousness.

That's why I've been so strategic to them and to my mother and

Michel and Dylan. I can both unite the thirteen of them or deny them that capacity.

Whatever my mother has planned, I suspect it doesn't involve the thirteen angels being united. I know that sooner or later, Soren will want me to find my mother, and find Michel and Dylan. Only when I'm with them will he know what they plan.

They probably won't let me be with them again, I think to myself and to Soren.

Perhaps, Soren replies. *But perhaps Michel will be unable to stop himself. One can always hold out hope that true love will prevail.*

True love, I scoff. I feel certain that Michel *doesn't* love me. He loves the Church. He loves the priesthood. Like Danielle before me, I was just something he used to help him give up the pleasures of the flesh. To remind him what he was giving up for God. I am, Danielle was, a pleasure to renounce to prove the strength of his love for God and for the Church.

Perceptive, Procel replies. *Julien loves you. That should be enough.*

I frown as we leave the church and enter the vehicle. Is he admitting that Julien truly loves me?

"He truly loves you," Procel says out loud. "Soren likes to keep things uncertain, to keep you off center, but I'll tell you the truth."

My heart skips a beat at that, and when Soren sends Procel a mental knock, I know what Procel says is true. I relax back into my seat and watch the road as we drive off. Outside the vehicle, the congregation lines the street, their faces peering inside the vehicle to catch a glimpse of Soren and the other angels. I can still feel their adoration, and it continues to feed the three of them so that I am adding to their powers.

That's why we'll keep you around, Eve. As long as you cooperate, you'll get your wishes. The three of us will resurrect one more of my brethren and then the rest. Once we're all resurrected, we'll stop the plague. Then, we'll eradicate vampirism. We won't need it any longer because we'll be united together once more.

I frown, for something has just occurred to me. "What about me?"

I say quietly. "You need me to share blood with you, for you to be united…"

Soren shakes his head. "You'll always be our priestess, Eve. That's your fate."

Does he mean that I'll always be a vampire?

That prospect fills me with grief.

"What are you saying? Are you saying I have to remain a vampire?"

Soren frowns. "It's key to your gift. You were gifted before you became a vampire, but it was limited. We'll always need you to unite us. None of us will ever go back to being what we were before."

A weight of dread fills me. I don't want to remain a vampire. I want to be free of this terrible hunger for blood. Yet, I want Soren to end the plague and stop Dominion – stop Blackstone. I want him to cure vampirism. Will he do it if I don't cooperate?

"Your cooperation is key, Eve. Like I say, you have a choice. You can cooperate and get everything you want, or you can fight me and get nothing. It doesn't matter to me if Dominion happens, although I hate the idea that Blackstone will be a tyrannical ruler and that so many humans will die… Plus, industrial society was pretty decent, all things considered. It's Blackstone who wants to take us back to the steam age, if not before that. He's the one who thinks that the destruction of industrial society will usher in a new age of dominion for vampires, not me."

So the price of stopping Dominion is that I become the one thing I've hated all my life. I shake my head and stare out the window at the empty storefronts, the dark streets, the bare sidewalks, the broken windows of the city now ruined by Blackstone's plague.

Is this what Michel didn't want me to know? Is this fate that I must choose the reason why he wouldn't tell me the truth?

I sigh. Soren isn't answering nor is Procel or Kael. They're lost together in some kind of orgy of recollection, and it seems as if they can tune me out so I can't hear what they're thinking. It makes me feel incredibly helpless.

What I want is to speak with Michel and my mother – and Dylan

– so I can see how they respond, what they will argue to stop me from going along with Soren.

Michel left. He's left Soren and is therefore in outright rebellion against him. I wonder what his plans are and now, I feel incredibly alone. Julien is Soren's creature and the fact that he truly loves me doesn't negate that fact. I can't rely on Julien to tell me anything or offer advice. It could all be tainted.

The vehicle finally arrives at the compound and we file out and walk up the stairs to the entrance. The other vehicle drives up and out steps Julien, still dressed in his white robe and surplice. In the light from a solar lamp, his hair is shiny and black. He looks so much like Michel at this point, it makes my heart skip a beat.

Michel... Come back.

I know the three angels can read my mind and know what I'm thinking but at that moment in time, I don't care. At that moment, I want Julien's arms around me, and I want to know where Michel is. I want him to be safe.

I love him, despite everything.

WE GO to the huge library and are served more blood in tall champagne flutes as if we're toasting some special occasion. I drink my blood down because I want it to wipe away my sadness and confusion. I also hope it will dampen the effect of our shared blood so that I will have some peace from Procel and Kael, who I don't particularly like or want to share minds with any more than I must.

Oh, Eve... so mean to my brethren...

I turn to Soren, frowning. "Can you please give me some peace?"

Soren smiles and turns away, meeting Procel's gaze. I finish my glass of blood and then turn to Julien, who stands beside me, drinking his own glass. I take Julien's hand.

"Let's go. I'm exhausted."

Julien resists. "Not just yet," he says. He glances at the three angels and waits as if he won't leave without Soren's approval.

I turn to Soren. "May we leave?"

Soren shrugs. "Suit yourself. Julien, you stay."

I dig my nails into my palms. "Why does he have to stay? I want him with me."

Soren turns to me. "He's not yours."

"He's not yours either."

Soren smiles. "Willful child. I'll send him to you when I'm done with him."

Then Soren turns to Procel and they drink a toast to each other and I'm forgotten – or ignored. I look at Julien but he shrugs as if he's helpless to resist.

"I'll come to you later," he says and forces a smile. Then he turns away from me as if he's dismissing me.

I get the sense he really wants to stay with them. It upsets me to see Soren manipulate him so blatantly. He's nothing more than a puppet to these angels – someone to use for their amusement or to stand in for Michel.

I leave them and go back to my rooms, glad to be away from them. I strip off my robe and stand naked in the cold bathroom, taking a washcloth and washing off my body with cold water from a carafe. When I'm done, I brush my teeth and slip into a nightgown, before crawling into bed and crying myself to sleep.

CHAPTER 7

JULIEN RETURNS LATER in the night while I'm asleep, but he wakes me when he starts to undress, removing his vestments, the large wooden cross knocking against the dresser top when he removes it. He stands naked before the window for a moment as if he's deep in thought, and I wonder what's going through his mind.

He's been eight hundred years away from the priesthood, and now has held a mass. The first one I bet he's done since he left the church.

I turn over and watch him stalk to the bathroom and listen as he splashes water over his face and then returns, slipping into bed beside me. He doesn't touch me, his back to me.

"Julien," I say and reach out, laying my hand on his back.

He turns over and in the light from the window, I see his cheek-bones, his blue eyes, and dark arched brows.

"I can't be with you tonight, Eve," he says and yawns. "Not after all that."

"You can't even hug me? I need some reassurance."

He moves closer and pulls me against his body, my head on his shoulder, my arm around his chest.

"How are you feeling? Was that your first mass since you left the church?"

He sighs heavily. "No," he says and I feel his heart beat under my cheek. "I did it once before today, when I was the only person available. But it feels wrong."

"I'm sorry," I say, feeling bad for him, wanting to comfort him. I try to let the walls down between us, but he's blocking me for some reason.

"Julien," I say, rising up on my elbow so I can see his face better. "Why won't you let me in?"

He lies back, his arm behind his head. "I can't be with you, Eve," he says once more. "I need distance. I need to process everything."

I lie back down on my back, several inches of space between us and it feels like a million miles. Without being able to connect with him, I have no idea what he's thinking or feeling. All I know is that I need him and want him. I want to lose myself in him, but he won't let me in.

It only adds to my sadness, my throat closing, tears brimming once more in my eyes.

"I'm sorry," he says softly. "I wish you could understand…"

"Show me and I will understand," I say, but I know it's no use. This thing he has with the church is beyond my understanding. I was never a believer. I can't be one. I accept that he has faith, but it's a divide that neither of us can cross.

That doesn't make it hurt any less.

"Good night," he says and I want to lash out in anger, but I hold myself back. He doesn't need me being difficult.

"Good night, Julien," I say softly and roll over so that my back is to him.

I barely sleep the rest of the night.

⁓

THE NEXT MORNING when I wake up, Julien is already up and dressed, sitting on the edge of the bed, pulling on his socks.

"You're up early," I say and yawn, stretching. Usually, I look forward to the day, but not today. Today, we'll likely resurrect more of Soren's brethren. I don't want to do it, but I see no alternative.

"We have to get busy. We're doing an early mass because Soren wants to raise the rest of the Twelve as quickly as possible. We're going to do three at a time until they're all back."

He turns to face me, his eyes haggard and I suspect he didn't sleep well either. "You'd better get up and get ready. You'll need to have some blood to prepare yourself. It's going to take a lot out of you."

I nod and slip out from beneath the warm coverlet, and pad to the bathroom. I feel Julien's eyes on me, and some of his longing for me slips through whatever barriers he's put up between us – or Soren has put up for him – and it sends a thrill through me. It heartens me to think that whatever has happened, at least he still wants me.

But it must be confusing for him, this priesthood without the celibacy clause that Soren has instituted. It must be so against his grain.

I wash and dress, and soon, the two of us are ready for the day. We drink down a glass of preserved blood, clinking our glasses together before we do.

"Here's to getting this plague stopped," Julien says, his eyes meeting mine, his expression serious.

"Yes," I say. "And to the cure."

"To the cure."

We drink and then place our glasses on the sideboard. Some servant will arrive later when we're out and clean up, so now that we've both fed, it's time to go to the Cathedral for mass.

OVER THE NEXT TWO WEEKS, Soren resurrects the remaining members of the Twelve, one after the other. Julien is still a priest and although we sleep together in the same bed, he doesn't make love to me. It frustrates me, but I understand that Julien can't. Soren's way of giving me reason to cooperate. On the final night, I'm exhausted by the time we arrive back at the compound. I'd like to go right to my rooms, but Soren invites us for dinner and he makes it clear it's an invitation we can't turn down. While I'm tired and want a hot bath and bed, I know I need real food as well.

We sit around the table and eat the venison, roasted root vegetables, and dark bread, drinking in some burgundy wine as accompaniment.

Julien sits beside me, still in his vestments, and we are silent, listening to the resurrected angels speaking to each other. They caught up mentally after each resurrection, our connection through the blood still strong, and now they are busy talking about the strategy moving forward.

So as much as I would love to be back in my rooms, I know this is important to know and don't want to leave.

Soren relates how far the plague has spread to the latest who we resurrected and the other angels murmur about the human cost, and how long it will take to recover. I am surprised at their expression of remorse for how far the plague has spread. For some reason, I thought that they didn't really care too much about the human cost, and cared more about what it meant for them and their position in the new post-apocalypse world Blackstone has created.

But I can sense their real concern, their real heartbreak, at the stories we hear from several of Soren's lieutenants, who report on the death toll, and of Blackstone's factory farms where humans are both slaves to work the fields and continue producing food, while at the same time, donating blood.

Some are chosen specifically for blood, while others are chosen for labor and spend their days in backbreaking work, tilling the fields using rusty old machinery that has sat idle for a century once the era of fossil fuels was ushered in.

Farms are once again running on brute animal power – horses, oxen, and men – pulling tillers, sowing seeds – whatever. It seems as if Blackstone and his people enjoy the return to pre-fossil fuel era, but to me it means back to a pre-technological era where humans were not much more than oxen.

Now, we're – *they're* – not much more than blood bags for vampire overlords.

That's true, Eve. That's what Blackstone has brought humanity down to. I don't want it. But it will take some more finessing on our part to stop this plague.

I drink my wine and don't respond. It's enough for me to feel the emotions and know the thoughts of the Twelve as they sit around their leader and discuss the coming battle with Blackstone.

Soren believes that a lot more humans will die before the plague is stopped and before Blackstone breathes his last breath. I also know that Soren wants to be the one to stick a stake through Blackstone's heart and that of his son. The hatred I feel from him is so much stronger than I imagined.

I think that Soren's been preparing for this battle for years. That was why he established all his training camps, teaching humans how to fight vampires effectively. Taking the brightest and best soldiers, turning them into vampires, and gathering them for a huge battle he anticipates will come all too soon.

I sit at my seat, a few chairs down from Soren, and watch him speaking with his soldiers and the other Twelve. He is the serious general now, talking strategy, and how even if they stop the plague, which they plan to do very soon when Dylan brings the cure to them, they will be fighting a war for ascendance over Blackstone.

Of course, I didn't think of that – I thought that they would defeat Blackstone, get the cure to the plague and it would all be over. It seems the reverse will be the case. Dylan will turn over the cure, the plague will be stopped, and then the war with Blackstone will start.

At that moment, Dylan and another of Soren's lieutenants arrives in the room and takes a seat. Dylan is wearing a cloak and has a broadsword in a scabbard on his hip. He shrugs the cloak off before sitting at a spot beside me, leaning in to kiss my cheek.

"Sister," he says softly.

The man with Dylan is young, strong, and has scars on his face as if he's seen many battles.

"What news?" Soren says and motions to the servant to pour wine.

"We've heard tell of Michel on the road to New York City," Dylan says, his voice low and deep. "He's stopped in at several churches along the way, giving sermons, holding mass and communion."

"And? What was the gist of his sermons?" Soren says, his brow knit. He turns to the other and shakes his head. "Not that I have any doubt."

"Not good," the lieutenant says and drinks down some wine. "Mostly that you're a false god and that you'll lead them all to sin. He's trying to undermine you at every turn."

"*Damn* him," Soren says and motions to his own glass. The servant moves slowly to his side to pour but Soren is impatient. He grabs the flagon of wine from the man, shoving him out of the way, his eyes flashing in anger. He pours his own wine and slams the flagon onto the table. "Damn him to *hell*," he says and glances around at the other angels. "The last thing I needed was a rebellion on Michel's part. What the fuck did I do to lose him?"

He looks in each of our faces but no one has anything to offer.

"He has to be found. He has to be brought back into the fold. Or, he has to die. There's no other option."

The others discuss Michel's rebellion, their voices rising and falling but I can barely listen, for I'm filled with dread at the prospect of Michel dying.

"This is war, Eve," Soren says out loud. All eyes turn to me. "Even if we stop the plague, humanity is still in it for a long bloody time. People will die. Perhaps Michel will as well, if he won't cooperate." Soren's eyes are filled with determination.

"Yes, Eve," he says quietly, but his voice carries, and everyone listens raptly. "The coming battle will be very bloody. We'll need everyone to pull together. That's why I want you to find Michel and bring him back to me. I need him on my side, not fighting against me and Blackstone. If he thinks that will solve anything, he's wrong. It's a choice between me and Blackstone. There is no other way. He has to realize that truth or die. I can't afford to have him fighting against me."

"And you think I can change his mind?" I say and shake my head.

The others turn to watch me. "I don't have that kind of influence over him."

"You alone can bring him back," Soren says. "I'll send you soon. But first, we have food to eat and wine to drink. And something special on the agenda."

He raises his glass to Dylan and to me, but I refuse to toast with him, for my dread is so heavy on my heart that I can't imagine toasting anything.

I glance at Dylan, whose color is high, his cheeks flushed. He stands and holds up his glass.

"I want to make a special toast to the coming battle. I've been working with Blackstone for the past month, while they've been perfecting the plague virus and trying to ensure they can control it more effectively. Lucky for me, I have a few friends among the scientists working there – old professors who I worked with at college. We've been working on the antidote. I think we have a version we can test and if it produces the results we've seen in the lab, we'll have this thing licked in no time. It's just a matter of producing as much of the antidote as we can as quickly as we can."

"Can you show us?" Soren says, leaning back in his chair, his expression open and calm now.

"I've brought along something to show you, so you have proof. Note that this is only on a small scale. We barely have any of the antidote produced and will need to get a lab up and running immediately if we want to have any quantity to stop the plague before it reaches Ghawar."

"Consider my vast wealth at your disposal," Soren says with a smile. "Please, continue on with your demonstration."

Dylan leaves the table and goes to a bag he left beside the entrance. From inside the bag, he pulls out a glass vial with a clear amber liquid in it. He returns to the table and moves his plate, cutlery and glasses out of the way so that he has an empty spot in front of his seat.

While we watch, he takes the lid off the vial and pours it out onto the tablecloth. At first, we see nothing except the viscous liquid pooling on the linen and then soaking in, spreading out from the original spot. He quickly returns the stopper into the mouth of the vial and puts it on the table.

"Watch," he says and as we do, the liquid, which I assume is petroleum oil of some quality, soon starts to grow dark, as if it's changing state.

"You can see that there are still nanoviruses in circulation even now. They've found the oil and are starting to denature it. It shouldn't take too long."

A moment passes and the blob of oil grows darker and the surface starts to dim, turning from the shiny amber to a dusty-looking grey-black. It changes shape before our eyes, and is now more of a pile of dark particles, like dust.

Dylan reaches into the pile of dust and rubs his fingers in it, lifting them up so we can see that the oil has been completely transformed into some kind of useless carbon dust.

"See how quickly it is destroyed?"

He takes a linen napkin and wipes his fingers off. Then, he reveals a small dropper with a clear liquid in it and sets it aside. He repeats the previous actions, pouring out an amount of petroleum oil from the vial onto the linen tablecloth, but before it starts to turn grey, he empties the dropper of clear liquid onto the oil.

Nothing happens except the oil seems to absorb the even more viscous liquid into it. No greying of the surface, no darkening of the oil. It remains amber.

He takes a candle and dips the flame towards the oil, and it burns.

Everyone oohs and ahhs at the sight for we've witnessed the cure to the plague. Dylan holds up the vial and smiles at Soren.

"So there you have it," he says and turns to me, smiling. "A cure for the plague."

Everyone claps and Soren stands and raises his glass high. "To Dylan and the scientists working with Blackstone for their treachery. It wouldn't have been possible without you, Dylan. You'll be well rewarded."

"When?" Dylan asks, and his tone seems impatient.

"Why not right now?" Soren says and glances at the others. "We're all here. Eve's here. We can work a little resurrection magic amongst the fourteen of us, don't you think?"

The other angels nod and Dylan turns to me. "Eve," he says, his face hopeful, his eyes wide. "Will you help?"

"Help what?"

"Sarah..." he says, as I remember that Soren promised to resurrect Sarah if Dylan succeeded in bringing him the cure for the plague.

My God...

CHAPTER 8

"Of course!" I say and hug him when he comes over. He squeezes me and presses his face into my hair. "Thank you, sister," he says, and I hear the emotion in his voice, which is close to breaking. He was afraid I wouldn't comply but of all those we resurrected, Sarah will be the only one I really want to bring back to life.

We end our embrace and Soren motions to us to sit back down.

"Bring her in. We can do it now," Soren says and two guards leave the room. Dylan sits back down and his hands shake visibly even from where I sit. My own heart starts to speed up in excitement. The thought of resurrecting Sarah is a happy one and I turn to watch as the guards roll in one of the containment tanks.

Soren stands and goes over to the tank, resting his hands on the side. He looks down at Sarah, and I can just see a peek of red hair from where I sit. Dylan stands and goes over to stand beside Soren. His eyes are already wet, his face flushed with emotion.

"Come, Eve," Soren says. "Let's do this. I need you to share blood with us all so we can combine our powers. Julien, you can do the honors."

Julien stands and goes over to the sideboard on which a silver chalice sits. I see now that there is a sharp knife beside it. Soren had this planned all along – did he know that Dylan was coming with the cure?

Julien brings the knife over to me and I hold out my wrist, allowing him to cut the skin, my blood dripping bright red into the silver chalice. After a few drops have filled the bottom of the chalice, he moves on and repeats this with Soren and the Twelve and then returns to me so I can take a drink. We all drink from the chalice, all fourteen of us and instantly, I'm assaulted with their combined consciousness, all at once and I don't know how they can do it. I don't know how they can bear the weight of so many minds joining at once. It's far more than I have ever experienced and I feel dwarfed by their minds, ageless beings who have been in existence for thousands upon thousands of years...

Still, they seem to coalesce around a single goal – resurrecting Sarah. Soren places his hand on her chest, and the Twelve gather around and watch, with Dylan standing close by Soren. Dylan turns to me and motions to me to join him. I go to his side and he puts his arm around my shoulder and pulls me close so that the three of us are standing, staring down into the tank where beautiful pale Sarah lies naked in the tank gel, her hair floating so peacefully, her lips slightly bluish, her eyes closed.

In their minds, the Twelve and Soren debate whether to restore her to immediately before the event or earlier. It might be harmful for her to remember those moments before she died. They go inside of her inert body, their minds searching out hers as life is restored to her flesh – how, I have no idea -- but I can feel it as they feel it. A bright light similar to previous resurrections surrounds her. Her heart beats slowly at first, lub dub, lub dub. She doesn't need to breathe for the gel contains an extremely high oxygen level and so it passes into her lungs and into her blood even as she is lying there, her chest unmoving. It is enough to keep her from dying completely, to keep her brain from dying. They search out her memories and find the moment, the last moments she laid down in memory as she struggled for breath but none came, and the look of panic on her parents faces as they realized that they couldn't save her...

That's too painful and so they go back farther, to the hour before she died, and how she was sitting in her room, admiring the shells that Dylan had collected for her, the spiral of the conch, the tiny cockle shells, the oysters, the clams. How she loves the ocean, the smell of the salt air, its taste on her lips, the feel of the moist air on her skin. She looks forward to Dylan returning home so he can take her down to the beach, leaving her wheelchair at the end of the path that's been worn down in the sand, picking her up gingerly and removing the portable ventilator so he can carry her to the water's edge and dip her toes in the surf.

Such a loving brother, and a warm wave of emotion floods through us all at her memory and emotions...

I feel a sob building in my chest, the emotions are so intense and magnified by each of us joined by sharing of our blood. Julien takes my hand and squeezes and his empathy for me makes me even more emotional. Our minds touch and I feel his love for me. It's real. Procel said it was, and now I know for sure.

The Thirteen decide to stop there so that when she wakes up, she will feel that peace, that contentment. She won't have any memories of her death or the panic that ensued in the brief time before the last conscious moments, when she thought to herself *this is how I die...*

But they do more than resurrect her as she was...

They reach into her body, and search out the damage done to her genetic code that led to the damaged part of her brain, and they *heal* her, removing the lesions that led to her progressive deterioration. Her eyes finally blink open and she sits up on her own, panicked at having her mouth full of tank gel, but they hold onto her mind while she struggles to breathe and calm her while she clears her lungs, coughing and gagging, wiping off her face, spitting the tank gel out over and over. Finally, she takes in a long ragged breath and looks up. They take her back to that moment of peace and she blinks. Her expression moves from panic to calm and she sees Dylan and smiles.

"Dylan," she manages, then clears her throat once more. "I was just thinking of you..."

"Sister," Dylan says with a gasp. He reaches out and takes her hand

and she grips his, staring at her hand like it's foreign. She smiles, but makes a face of confusion, her brows knit together, her green eyes quizzical.

"Where am I?"

Dylan takes her hand in both of his and squeezes, bending down to kiss her wet knuckles. "You've been healed."

She glances down and sees her nakedness, but the thirteen minds swoop in to calm her and she shrugs it off as part of the procedure. A servant comes over with a white terrycloth bathrobe and holds it up and before our eyes, Dylan lifts her up and out of the tank, onto a step that's been placed at the side. She slips on the robe and ties it and then holds up her arms and the expression on her face is one of rapture.

"I'm cured," she whispers, moving her arms around in amazement. Then, she falters, her knees buckling. Dylan puts his arm around her and helps her stand. Together, they take a step and then two, Sarah wavers a bit because it's been so long since she walked on her own – a decade since she stopped walking and had to use the wheelchair.

"You're cured," Soren says and there's an expression on his face that shocks me for he is emotional as well, his own face flushed. The Twelve are similarly affected, and I feel their satisfaction that they've done this, and returned a sister lost of a brother who grieved.

Dylan embraces Sarah and they stand together for a while, hugging each other. Dylan is overcome and I see his face scrunched up with emotion, like he's fighting so hard to maintain his composure, but finally, he gives in and weeps, great sobs coming from him as he rocks Sarah in his arms.

Sarah is surprised, but seems delighted by her newfound abilities and she rocks him and speaks softly to him, rubbing his back.

"It's okay, I'm okay, Dylan..." she says, resting her cheek on his shoulder, her eyes closed.

The Twelve all look like they're eating this up, like it's food for them, this scene taking place before them. They love that they've done this, and restored Sarah's ability. I can feel their emotions, and I know that this is what they look forward to – when they're all joined like this, sharing their minds and emotions, and when they've done some-thing good like this.

They're proud.

Soren's proud.

Finally, they return to the table and leave Dylan and Sarah to themselves. I stand with Dylan and lay my hand on his shoulder, wanting to connect with him and feel his joy. He lets me in and the three of us stand with our arms around each other's shoulders, our heads together.

"I'm better," Sarah whispers, smiling widely. "I feel like I need to cough again, but I'm better."

"You are," Dylan says and wipes his eyes. "You can cough if you need. You can have a bath, and get any remaining gel off."

He releases our shoulders and motions to one of the servants. "Can you please go to my rooms and prepare a warm bath for my sister?"

The servant leaves the room. The three of us go to a set of couches over in the corner and sit down, waiting for the servant to return and let us know that the bath is ready.

"Tell me what happened," Sarah says. "Where's mom and dad?"

"You'll see them soon," Dylan says. "A lot has happened since you went into the tank to be healed. We'll see mom and dad in a few days."

"Where are they?"

"They're safe," he says and I wonder how he's going to handle telling Sarah about the plague, and about everything that's happened.

It's bound to be shocking.

"Where are we?" she asks and glances around. "Is this a hospital?"

Dylan takes her hand and squeezes again. "We're at Soren Lind-gren's compound outside of Boston. He and the other Twelve healed you."

She looks around in wonder. "The Twelve?" She glances over at the huge table where the Twelve all sit, with Soren at the head of the table. They're busy drinking wine and speaking in low voices. They're also connected at another level, and the talking is like a lower order of connection.

"They're angels, Sarah," Dylan says.

"Angels?" she says and frowns. She turns back and examines them. "Are you serious? What happened to my *scientists believe nothing but evidence* brother?"

Dylan shakes his head. "I saw the light, so to speak." He smiles and continues to hold Sarah's hand. Then his expression changes and he becomes serious. "I have a lot to tell you," he says. "While you were in the tank, a lot happened."

"How did I get into the tank? I don't recall getting into it or coming here…"

"It's part of the process. Sarah, you died when the power went out and the battery died."

"What?"

Dylan recounts what happened, telling Sarah about the plague, and how it spread, destroying all fossil fuels in the process.

Sarah sits silent for a moment while Dylan explains. He tells her about Blackstone and his plans for Dominion.

"I knew you were different," she says. "I could tell, but mom and dad told me that one day, I'd understand. I thought you were just a genius."

She smiles and Dylan smiles back. He chokes up again and has to look down, clearing his throat to get control over his emotions.

The servant returns and comes over to us. "The bath is ready, Sir," he says, his eyes downcast.

"Let's go get you cleaned up," Dylan says and stands, keeping Sarah's hand in his. She stands as well and wavers a bit, still unsteady on her feet. "I'll help you. I can carry you, if you want."

"No way," she says with a laugh. "I spent a decade in that chair. I want to use my feet now that I can."

They leave me sitting on the couch. I don't follow, allowing them the privacy of their new relationship, now that Sarah's healed.

I glance over at the table where Soren and Julien and the Twelve sit talking about next steps in their plan to stop the plague. I wander over and take my place at the table, not that I want to spend time with them, but I think it's a good idea to listen to what they're talking about. I may get some hint of an overall goal for all this. Soren has been very careful not to say too much to me. I have a sense he wants to be worshiped as a god, but not much else.

Whatever the case, I doubt that Michel likes the idea and so I want to know why.

I still want Soren to save the world from the plague and I still want him to eradicate vampirism, so as long as he doesn't kill millions of humans, I want him to succeed. I've given up trying to understand Michel's game, for I know now that he can't let me know. If I know, Soren's knows.

Soren turns to me as if he's been reading my mind.

"I have been," he says with half a grin. "I want you to go and find Michel. Of all the bait in the world to capture Michel, you are the most desirable. If anything can capture him, you can."

"What makes you think he'll come to me? He takes his vow of celibacy seriously."

Soren laughs. "You kissed him and he practically fell on top of you. Tell me another one, Eve. He'd make love to you in a moment if you offered yourself."

I frown and glance at Julien, whose face is passive like he didn't even hear.

"He's gone," I say. "He's on a mission. I doubt if I can take him away from his mission. It's everything to him."

"*You're* everything to him," Soren says. He takes a sip of his wine and eyes me over the rim. "All I want you to do is go and find him. We're going to be busy here getting the antidote ready to stop the plague. I don't need you for anything right now but I do want Michel back. Julien's great, but this is for Michel, not him."

"What's for Michel?"

Soren smiles. "Oh, a lot of my plans are meant for Michel."

"Revenge?" I say, anger filling me at his desire for revenge against Michel for Marguerite's death. "Shouldn't someone as powerful as you be unconcerned with petty matters of revenge? It happened eight centuries ago."

"I feel time differently than you do, Eve. I feel it as if it happened only yesterday. I remember everything. *Everything.*"

He finishes his glass of wine and pours himself another, one knee bent up on his chair. He looks quite relaxed, as if he's confident that everything is going his way – except for Michel. It makes me wonder if he truly can see the future. He didn't see Michel leaving…

"I knew it was a possibility," Soren says and sits upright. "I didn't think he'd take this route. I'm surprised." He glances at the Twelve who are seated all around him at the table. "Well, I didn't think he would choose this path. I thought he'd try to preserve things as much as possible the way they were. I was wrong."

I have no idea what he means by this so I say nothing. Finally, Soren stands and stretches, his wings folding out behind him.

"You can leave in the morning," he says. Then he points to Julien. "You'll stay. She can go on her own with a guard."

Julien sits up straighter. "I should go with Eve," he says. "She needs someone older and stronger to protect her."

Soren shrugs. "I'll send her with one of my men. Older than even you, Julien. You're staying behind."

Julien shakes his head. "Please," he says, his voice low. "Let me go with her."

Soren shakes his head and lays a hand on Julien's shoulder. "I need you here, to say mass daily until Michel returns."

"What makes you think he returns?" I ask, standing up from my place.

"Oh, he returns. I know his game now. He'll have to come back."

With that, he turns to go and the Twelve rise and follow him out of the dining room and into the study. Julien turns to me, his face wary.

"I don't want you to go without me," he says, his voice low.

"I'm a big girl," I say, trying to be one. "Soren won't let you go and there's no way you're getting out of here unless he wants you to go. We both learned that lesson the last time we left on our own."

"Eve," Julien says. "I don't like this."

I squeeze his shoulder. "Neither do I. But I have faith now that I know Michel is invisible to Soren. He has a plan, and I trust him. If it suits him to come back with me, he will."

I smile at Julien. He stands and takes me into his arms. "Be with me before you go," he says, his voice husky. I'm surprised. Has Soren now lifted the compulsion preventing him from making love with me?

"Come with me now," I say and take his hand, leading him toward the door. If Soren wanted to stop me, he would have so I take it that he doesn't mind that I'm going to spend the night with Julien.

I wish he would stay out of my mind though.

Oh, none of us can or will stay out of your mind. Not after today and all the blood we shared. Get used to it. Being in your mind, Eve, is part of what makes us happy and why you're so valuable to us.

I sigh. *Voyeur.*

Julien and I leave the dining room, taking the hallways to our rooms in another wing of the compound.

When we enter the bedroom Julien wastes no time and pulls me into his arms.

"I don't like this," he says and runs a hand over my hair, pulling it out of the clip that's holding it up.

"I have to go," I say, pulling him down to me. "I'll be fine," I say and kiss him. He fights me, wanting to protest against me agreeing to go so easily.

"You'll be at risk," he says and his voice is shaky with desire as I run my hands over his chest and start to unbutton his vestments. I feel strange, undressing a priest, but of course he's not a priest to me. He's my lover. I can't think of him as a priest.

I pull him over to the bed and we strip our clothes off, eager to get naked together for one last time before I go away. I'm not worried about myself. I know that right now, I'm too strategic for Soren to allow anything to happen to me. I am curious about whether Michel will fall for the bait. I almost hope he doesn't.

I don't want to force Michel's hand in any way, but I realize that I don't have a real choice. I've seen into the hearts and minds of the Twelve and Soren. I'm starting to believe that he will stop the plague. He will eradicate vampirism.

If so, my wishes will be fulfilled.

Whether I have either one of the twins at the end is a whole other question. It's of lesser importance so I have to do what's best for humankind, if not myself. In fact, if I have to die in order to stop the plague or end vampirism, so be it.

Then, I lose myself in Julien, not caring any longer whether Soren and the Twelve can peek in and experience what I do. All that matters is that I create more memories with Julien, in case these are the last ones we make.

CHAPTER 9

LATER, when we're finished and lying together on the bed, our arms and legs entwined, I feel secure in the fact that everything will work out. Julien, on the other hand, is very anxious. He doesn't like it and lets me know.

"I wish you could say no," he says, running his fingers over my cheek and down to my lips. "I hate being here and you being out there, without me to protect you."

I nod, but don't share his concern. "Soren's sending someone older than you with me, so I'll be fine. We'll go looking for Michel and hopefully, he won't find us, but if he does, it will be because he chooses to."

Julien leans on his elbow and looks in my eyes. "What happened to make you so full of faith all of a sudden?"

I smile. "When I realized that Soren can't read Michel. That's why Michel has been so secretive. That's why my mother left me. They knew that if I was with them, Soren would know what they were doing. When Michel found me, he did so because it was strategic for him to do so. It was the same with Dylan finding me. And my mother showing up. They only did so because it fit their plans. I used to hate not knowing everything. Now, I understand why I can't."

I run my fingers down Julien's scar to his jaw, which is covered in a light dusting of stubble. An onlooker would never know how tender hearted Julien is by his outward demeanor. He looks like a warrior but he's soft inside. Able to love completely. Show me his vulnerability.

That's why I love him. As much as I wish he could come with me on this journey, I know that he has to stay.

I pull him down to me and we kiss once more. Julien lies on top of me and I wrap my legs around his hips.

"I don't want you to go…" he whispers, kissing my cheek, my forehead, my lips.

"I don't want to go, but I have to. I love you, Julien."

"I love you, Eve," he says, his voice breaking. "I'll wait for you, even if it's until the end of time."

We lie like that, my heart swelling until it almost bursts with love. Time passes, and soon, I feel myself drifting off, but before I do, I watch Julien, hungry to memorize every detail of his face and body, just in case I never see him again. While I don't think I'll die on my trip, it is always possible that someone miscalculates and one of us dies.

So until sleep takes me, I watch Julien, who has fallen asleep almost as soon as he finished speaking.

I WAKE UP MUCH LATER, when the light from between the heavy curtains is starting to make its trip across the floor and particles of dust hang in the sunbeam.

I rise and go through my morning routine of washing and brushing my teeth, dressing and brushing my hair. I braid it, so that I can keep it under control for our trip.

I leave the bathroom and see that Julien is sitting up on the side of the bed. "Why are you up so early? Come back to bed." He pats the bed and looks dejected, his mouth turned down, and a frown on his face.

"Have to get going."

I throw a few items into my travel bag. I know Julien wants to make love once more before I go but I don't think we have time.

"I don't like this," he says softly. "Not one bit."

"I know," I say and go to him, standing between his spread thighs. I pull his head against my chest and he wraps his arms around me. "I don't like it either. Michel will or won't find me, depending on his plans. I'll be back before you know it, either with him or alone."

He glances up at me and his eyes are imploring. I bend down and kiss him tenderly, running my fingers through his hair, which is slightly messy, now that it's longer than he usually keeps it.

Finally, I pull away and continue to pack a small bag with a few changes of clothes. I don't know how long we'll be but it will be pretty rough going for the trip to New York. We will likely have decent accommodations, given that Soren has people everywhere and technology on top of it. But I have to plan for a pretty low-tech time of hotel rooms with little or no heat and pretty basic food.

A knock at the door draws my attention away from my bag and I answer to find one of Soren's guards.

"My Lord Soren will see you in the dining room in five minutes," he says and stands at attention.

"Tell him I'll be right there," I say but he shakes his head.

"I'm to escort you. Please prepare yourself."

I nod and close the door. When I return to my bedroom, Julien is dressed and sitting on the bed beside my small bag.

"I'm going to have breakfast with Soren," I say with a grin. "Are you going to join us?"

Julien grabs my hand. "The only thing I wanted to eat was you, but I guess I'm out of luck considering you're all dressed..."

"You are insatiable," I say with a laugh, hoping to lighten his mood.

He smiles. "With you, there's no other option. You make me insatiable. I'm going to miss you. More than you can know."

"I'll miss you. Now, I have to go. Please come have some breakfast with us."

"I will."

Julien gets up and joins me at the door. I open it and the guard eyeballs Julien but says nothing so I take it Julien is invited as well.

The guard leads us down the hallway to the dining room where Soren and the Twelve and a half-dozen of Soren's lieutenants are seated, chatting and eating breakfast. Soren sees us enter and smiles.

"Come in, come in," he says and points to a couple of chairs beside his seat. "Oh, Julien, please go to the sideboard and fix the table several carafes of juice will you?"

I take my seat while Julien goes to the sideboard where there are glasses and jugs for juice and coffee. I think it's strange that Soren has asked Julien to do this when there are waiters there who could do it, but I shrug and take my napkin, opening it and laying it across my lap.

At that moment, the door opens and the guards drag in a young vampire dressed in a black uniform. He has a sword in a scabbard and looks like one of the guards patrolling the compound.

Julien stops where he is and watches, as do the rest of us.

The guards take the man to the center of the room and hold him there.

"Ahh," Soren says and stands at his place. "The main event. This is the guard you found with the dead girl?"

The guard on the left bows his head. "Yes, My Lord," he says, his tone dark. "He drank her dry and left her outside her home. The neighborhood is in an uproar. There are petitioners outside demanding to speak with you because you promised to keep them safe from vampires."

"So I did. And this guard broke those rules and killed a young woman in the prime of her life. I suppose," he says and turns to me. "I suppose, Eve, that I have to punish him. Do you concur?"

I look at the young vampire, who still has blood on his chin. "I suppose you do," I say, although I don't like being part of this little performance.

"Yes, we must keep the order and those who break my laws must be punished. So be it."

I glance over and Julien is still standing at the sideboard, pouring juice from a larger carafe into a smaller one.

"Julien, you watch as well."

Julien puts down his carafe and turns to watch.

Soren remains where he's standing and wipes his mouth with a napkin after drinking down the rest of his juice.

"So, Aaron, you've been accused and found guilty of taking the life of a mortal without proper and lawful order. Do you have any last words before I pass your sentence?"

The vampire named Aaron glowers at Soren.

"Under what authority?" he asks, his voice a direct challenge to Soren.

"Under the terms of the Treaty of Clairveaux, under which all vampires operate."

"The treaty's dead," Aaron says and shakes his head. "It has no power anymore."

"Under my rule, the treaty is in force. All those who break its terms will be punished."

I turn to watch, frowning, surprised that Soren is going to mete out justice right here in the dining room.

"If you have nothing else to say, so be it. Aaron, I sentence you to death."

Aaron gasps and struggles in his chains as if he wasn't expecting a death sentence.

"Did you forget that the punishment for unlawful death of a mortal is death? Perhaps you should have paid more attention to my decrees about the Treaty for I clearly stated to all my staff and to all those who operate in my territory that mortals will no longer be open season. That as the terms of the Treaty indicate, only those with permits that have been officially sanctioned will be able to take a mortal's life and then only with just cause."

I don't remember hearing Soren's decree about the Treaty and at that moment, I doubt that he made one, or made it very public. Besides, I was in a state of shock the night he showed his powers to the congregation so perhaps I missed it.

Regardless, Aaron is certainly not prepared for his death sentence and fights with the two guards that take hold of his arms.

"Silence!" Soren yells and his voice is so loud and so deep that everyone stops and stands still.

Soren turns to me and winks. "Watch this, Eve," he whispers.

Then, he reaches out his arm and points at Aaron. "I sentence you to die." Then Soren snaps his fingers.

Before our eyes, Aaron frowns, his mouth opening as if he's struggling to breathe. His shackled hands grip his throat like he's trying to pull open his windpipe. Soon, his face becomes extremely gray, his eyes bugging out, and he falls to his knees.

Soren keeps his hand out, watching while Aaron falls forward, his body limp. I assume he's passed out due to lack of oxygen.

"Check him. See if his heart has stopped."

One of the guards bends down and places his fingers against Aaron's neck. He kneels like that for a moment and then rises up, shaking his head.

"He's dead."

Soren lets his hand drop and he walks over to the fallen vampire, standing over him for a moment. Then he turns to the rest of us.

"I don't take the life of a vampire lightly," he says. "For an immortal to lose his life is a grave punishment. But if we are to win the hearts and minds of the populace, we have to ensure they feel safe. I am not yet ready to cure vampirism entirely, but when I do, mortals will no longer live in fear of being killed or rounded up and enslaved for their blood. It is my promise to mortals that if they follow me, if they hold me above all others and obey me, I will keep them safe. Anyone who breaks my laws, and who disobeys my orders, will be punished."

Soren then walks back to his place at the table and sits down while the guards drag the dead vampire away.

"Burn his body," Soren says before they leave the room. "Bury the ashes somewhere and leave the grave unmarked."

The door closes behind them.

I sit quietly, trying to process this show of power on Soren's part. I knew he could resurrect mortals and vampires, but I didn't know he could kill at a distance like that. His powers must be magnified now that the Twelve are all restored and after sharing blood the way we did in the cathedral.

"So, Eve," Soren says as he holds out his empty glass. "You can see that I have the ability to kill at a distance. For example, I could kill Julien where he stands pouring juice into a carafe for the table."

I turn and see Julien still pouring juice. He frowns and turns to face Soren and the rest of us.

"Why would you?" I say, alarm building in me.

"If I had reason, I could. I just wanted you to know that."

Julien comes over and pours some orange juice into Soren's glass, which he holds out. Obviously, Soren enjoys showing how much power and authority he has over us all, that he can order one of the oldest and most powerful vampires in existence to be a servant to him.

I begin to realize that this whole business with passing judgment and sentence on Aaron was part of Soren's way of warning me that I had better obey his orders or he'll kill Julien just as easily as he killed Aaron.

Precisely.

I glance up at Soren, who smiles at me.

"I'll obey your orders," I say with a shaky voice. I know that Soren wouldn't think twice about killing Julien. I've always known that he cares less about Julien than Michel. He wants Michel to return and be his high priest. He will use Julien as a bargaining chip to ensure that I cooperate and bring Michel back.

I take a sip of my juice, my throat suddenly dry and a feeling of dread heavy in my gut.

Julien goes around the table, topping off everyone's juice and coffee like a servant. The servants stand at the side of the room, their hands clasped in front of them, with nothing to do while Julien takes over their duties.

"Yes, Eve," Soren says, his voice sounding so self-satisfied. "I am the law now. You have to obey me if you want to return and find your beloved Julien in one piece, still slavering after you the way you like."

I watch Julien's face to see how he responds, but he says and does nothing. He continues to go around the table, still refilling everyone's coffee and a few glasses of blood. Finally finished his little display of power, Soren smiles and turns to one of his lieutenants and starts to talk about the security arrangements on our trip.

Julien returns and sits beside me, drinking down his own glass of juice. He turns to me.

"What do you think of that? Nice warning," he says and leans in closer to me.

"He made himself pretty clear," I say. "Although I didn't need to see him execute someone before our eyes."

"It's war," Julien says and digs into his meal. "You have to get used to summary execution. Happens all the time on the battlefield, or used to."

He seems unconcerned and eats his meal with gusto. It really must be different to have seen so many battles over the centuries. To have killed so many and to have seen so many dead. Does it make them immune to death?

I push my own food around on my plate and wonder what the day will bring. It's quite a trip to New York and I don't look forward to it, but there is no choice, so I try to resign myself to my fate.

When we're done, I stand to leave, to finish packing my bags. Soren stands as well and surprises me by joining me before Julien and I make it to the door.

"Eve," he says and opens the door. "I thought we'd walk together and talk about this little trip you're taking."

"Of course," I say.

"Julien, please stay behind and speak with the others about our plans for the week."

"I want to see her before she goes," Julien says in protest.

"Oh, for Heaven's sake, you will," Soren says and makes a face of impatience. "Did you really think I'd force you to not see her off?"

Julien leans in and kisses me on the mouth before he returns to the table and sits down, craning his neck so he can see us before we leave the room.

"Don't worry about Julien," Soren says and escorts me out into the hallway. "I'll make sure he doesn't miss you too much. I'll keep him busy."

I frown, not really trusting Soren to keep Julien happy. Besides, keeping Julien busy could mean a lot of things, and of course my mind goes immediately to Gabrielle and how Soren pushed Julien and Michel at her to make me jealous. I wouldn't put it past him to do it again.

"Oh, Eve, you know me far too well," Soren says with a laugh. We arrive at my suite and he comes in with me, watching while I finish packing my bag.

"So," he says, sitting on the bed, watching me rifle through my drawers in the chest against the wall. "I know you're now cooperating, but you have to know I want Michel back here, and compliant. I'll do what I have to in order to get him back, but never fear," he says and crosses his arms. "I want you both back. Nothing will happen to you."

I fold a sweater and push it into the bag on the bed beside Soren.

"I hope so, but you're taking a chance," I say.

"I have a pretty good idea of how things will go," he says and taps his temple. "Prescience, you know." He smiles at me.

I zip up my bag and stand with it. "I'm ready," I say, not wanting to acknowledge anything.

"Good," Soren says and leads me out of the room. A guard is waiting there and the three of us make our way to the front entrance, where a tall vampire in full SWAT gear stands speaking with Julien. Relief floods through me that I'll be with someone who at least looks strong. As well, I see that Soren has come through with his promise to allow Julien to say goodbye, but neither Dylan or Sarah are in sight.

One of the servants takes my bag and goes out to the waiting vehicle in the driveway. Soren takes me over to the vampire I'll be traveling with and introduces us.

"Jan," he says and points to me. "This is Eve Hayden, whom you have heard so much about. Eve, this is Jan Clermont. He'll be your guide and guard on this trip. He's from Marguerite's homeland so you know he's one of the oldest vampires in existence. I trust him with my life and I trust that he'll be able to take care of you. Now, go find that damned rebellious Michel and bring him back to me."

I nod at Jan and he extends his hand for a shake. I take his hand and his grip is firm and strong, but not too strong. He is aware of his power, evidently. That's good.

Then I turn to Julien, who stands beside us, his face flushed.

"Julien," I whisper, and lean into his arms, not caring if Soren is watching us. "I'll miss you. I'll think of you every day. Every night at midnight, think of me."

He buries his face in my neck, kissing the skin beneath my ear and sighs. "I'll think of you more than you'll think of me. You'll be so busy, traveling, finding Michel..."

I pull away and look in his eyes. "I love you," I say and hold his face in my hands. "You. Do you understand?"

"Yes," he says finally and we kiss once more, deeply. I hate to leave him, and I'm angry at Soren for not sending Julien along with me, but I'm sure it's for strategic purposes.

What those purposes are, I have no idea, but I have to trust that Michel knows.

I pull out of Julien's arms with reluctance and follow Jan down the stairs and into the waiting vehicle, a large black SUV, which is running, its electrical engine barely making any sound. We get strapped in and as we drive off, I turn to see Julien standing there beside Soren and a few of Soren's lieutenants.

Julien waves, and I fear in that moment that I'll never see him again.

CHAPTER 10

THE TRIP out of Boston and Cambridge is slow and tedious, as we have to carefully navigate through streets clogged with broken down and abandoned vehicles, their doors open, hoods popped, and tires nothing more than a grungy muck on the street below the rims. Often, there is too much debris and we have to find an alternate route entirely. The streets themselves are empty and devoid of life, the shop windows broken and the provisions already raided long ago by roving bands of robbers.

Here and there are burned out buildings, razed to the ground because there's no functional fire service. Whole blocks have burned, and the blackened hulks are stark against a winter sky.

When we finally leave the city limits on the road south to New York, I feel the weight of the city leave and the open country is more refreshing. We drive through a forested area on a narrow road that has been cleared of all vehicles so travel is relatively quick. I'm sitting in the front passenger seat and Jan is beside me in the driver's seat. Between us, on the console, there are a couple of weapons – a revolver and a stake, in case anyone tries to attack us on the open road.

Behind us in the back seat, my bag is next to several boxes of provisions for the trip. I see earthen crocks for water, glass vials of blood in boxes of ice to keep them cool, and cans of food, paper bags filled with bread and other dry goods. We have enough to eat for the several days it will take to get to New York. We should be able to make the trip in a day, in the times before the plague, but with the main interstate being impassable, we're forced to take US Route 1 and that makes for a longer journey. As well, our vehicle goes only one-third of the speed of a car before the plague struck, so even with clear roads it would take us three times as long to make the trip. Jan tells me that we'll likely stop for the night in New Haven, Connecticut and then drive on to New York tomorrow.

I settle back into my seat and watch out the side window, examining the scenery, trying to enjoy the trip along the coastal road. Now and then, when we have to bypass a blocked section of Route 1, we take a road that borders the Atlantic and I can see glimpses of the ocean and it makes me happy.

Our first stop is several hours later, to sit by the side of the road and eat a light meal of fruit and bread, with honey. It feels rustic and like something you'd read about in a book about a medieval fantasy. Merry and Pippin might eat such a meal, and I smile to myself, thinking how my life has become part horror story, part fantasy.

Jan is very quiet as a traveling companion. I try to get him to talk about himself when we first set out, but after a few monosyllabic responses to my questions, I gave up. Instead, we have the sound of the road to keep us company and I try to keep my mind busy naming the kinds of trees and wildlife I see. It's surprising how much of nature has returned now that there are few vehicles traveling along the roads. Now and then, I spy a bird of prey high up in the trees, or some small rodent in the underbrush dart across the road ahead or behind us. Squirrels? I have no idea, but that's about the extent of my entertainment during the trip with Jan, who I now call Mr. Silent Type, to myself.

We arrive in New Haven, Connecticut late that night as the sun is setting, and find a small hotel on the edge of town. When we break open a door, we find a relatively clean room to bunk for the night.

The place is covered in a layer of dust, but it's otherwise clean. The room is cold, but there's nothing to be done about it. We can't light a fire, so instead, I unwrap several sleeping bags and slip inside one.

Jan stands guard.

"Should I take a turn at watch?" I ask, trying to be a good traveling companion.

He laughs to himself but doesn't reply, so I take that as a no. I suppose he doesn't want to put his life into the hands of someone like me – a young, newly-ascended vampire. I must seem like a pup to someone like him.

I close my eyes, and soon I doze off because, despite everything, I'm exhausted after a long day of travel.

JAN WAKES me up a few hours later, when the sun is still below the horizon. We have to get going, for Jan wants us to arrive in New York before noon. The drive becomes slower the closer we get to New York City, as we pass through the suburbs on the way down the coast. I grab some more fruit and bread, and drink an entire unit of blood to start my day, and watch the passing scenery as we travel through the small towns along the coast. It's picturesque and I wish I could stay at a few of the places I've heard about but never visited – Bridgeport, Fairfield, Norwalk. They're all names I've heard before and I think that one day, when everything has returned to some kind of normalcy, I'll return with Julien and spend some time traveling along the coast, visiting the small towns and walking the beaches.

Finally, before noon, we arrive in Queens, and stop at an old gas station so I can use the facilities. The water isn't running but it appears no one has used this washroom since the plague struck so I'm able to relieve myself without too much disgust at the smell.

Travel is even slower now that we're in the Bronx. The streets are much more clogged with old cars and so we have to push a few out of the way with the front of our vehicle. Luckily, it's quite a heavy vehicle with a truck chassis and so we are able to use brute force to clear a few streets and make our way through and on towards Manhattan. I get the sense that there are people in some of the buildings, watching as we drive slowly by. I feel their eyes on us, and hope that they're just onlookers, and not part of any organized group.

We take a road across the Bronx River and then cross over into Harlem, down narrow streets past old brownstones that line the blocks. We finally get to a street that's blocked on all three sides with vehicles.

"It looks like a barricade," I say, for the vehicles are lined up bumper to bumper and look like they've been placed there rather than simply abandoned.

"We'll make a run for it," Jan says and tries to plough his way through a line of smaller cars, their doors off, their hoods open. Unfortunately, we're unable to slam through the line and instead, our bumper gets locked into another back bumper of a light truck. Jan gets out and tries to pull our vehicle off the other, but it's no use. Even with the two of us trying to lift the bumpers up and apart, we can't budge them.

"Damn," Jan says and wipes his brow of sweat. He runs his hands through his long hair and shakes his head. "Looks like we're on foot the rest of the way unless I can find someone to help."

We glance around, but these streets seem empty. Doors hang open on their hinges, windows are smashed. The only sound is a few dried leaves crackling in the wind.

Jan retrieves our bags and stuffs a few vials of blood into his and a few into mine, and we shoulder the backpacks and start on foot.

"Do you know where you're going?" I ask, following Jan down a street.

"South and west," he says, simply. "That's all I know. South and West. Get to Harlem and find our way to Central Park. Keep going all the way to Battery Park."

I nod and we set out, and after a day and a half of driving, it feels like a relief to walk for a change. I wonder if we do find Michel whether he'll return with us. I can't imagine Jan thinks he'll just find Michel and convince him to return. I doubt I'll be able to convince him either. Still, I have to assume that Soren has it all planned out and somehow sees this in his plans.

I gave up trying to figure everything out. Instead, I've decided to go with the flow as much as possible. Trust my gut.

Right now, my gut says that the streets here are empty and I wonder where all the people have gone. Perhaps they've fled to the countryside where there might be food. Perhaps further south, where the weather is warmer. The city would run out of food very quickly unless there are shipments coming in on a daily basis. It's easy to forget how reliant we all were on the transportation system to bring food from the south and from other countries. Now, all that's gone. With the world falling apart little by little, mile by mile as the plague spreads, everyone is facing the same prospect of starvation and death by diseases that used to be easily treatable.

After about an hour of walking, we reach Central Park and skirt along the exterior, down to the southwestern edge and over to 5th Avenue. On the way, we stop to have a bite to eat, sitting on a bench in a little side street park that must have been quaint once upon a time, when the city was full of life and teeming with pedestrians and tourists. Now, it's quiet except for the wind. Old newspapers float in the breezes between buildings, the eddies of air lifting up some dried leaves. It's mournful.

We walk on farther south, along Park Avenue past Washington Park, and at long last, we near Battery Park, past City Hall and the 9-11 Memorial. I never did visit after the attacks, and now we stop briefly near the empty reflecting pool, filled with wet leaves and trash. With no pumps to empty out the water underground, the subway system has been filled with seawater. I wonder how long before the ocean reclaims this part of Manhattan and it makes me so sad to be here, now.

As we get closer to Battery Park, I start to feel as if someone is shadowing us, walking down side streets, just out of eyesight, but every now and then, it's like my blindsight kicks in and I have this weird sense that there are people all around us, watching, waiting.

"Do you feel like we're being watched?" I say quietly while we walk down Broadway Avenue.

"I felt it too," Jan says, his voice barely above a whisper. "Remember that vampires have excellent sense of hearing."

I nod and say nothing more. If this is Michel and his people, I won't feel too afraid, but if it is just a lone gang, we might have to fight.

"Do you have your weapon handy?" Jan says in a light voice.

I grip the handle of my blade and touch the stake that rests in a pouch on my other hip. "Yes," I say softly. "I'm as ready as I'll ever be."

"Stay close," he says and I do, keeping up to him, shoulder to shoulder, although he is much taller than I am. We keep walking down the street and I can see the river so we're getting close to Battery Park and the ferry. When we take a side street, three men step out at the end of the road and wait for us, their swords drawn.

"What do you want to do?" I ask, my heart rate increasing even more than before.

"Let's see whether they're friend or foe."

We continue on down the street and Jan holds out his hands, empty of weapons, and speaks to them in a loud voice while we're still half a block away.

"Ahoy there," he says in a friendly voice. "We're travelers looking for old friends."

One of the three men, older, heavy set with greasy clothing that resembles SWAT gear, steps forward, his sword held out in front of him.

"This is our territory. If you have no permission from our Lord to be here, you're going to have to leave."

Jan stops, leaving a distance between us. "And who is your Lord?"

"Braxton," the man says. "He holds this territory. If you have not been invited, you must leave."

"We will," Jan says and holds out his hand to stop them. "Before we go, I want to say that we're looking for a priest named Father Michel," Jan says, glancing at each man in turn. "We hear he works out of a cathedral around these parts. We're old friends, so if you know this priest, please tell him that we're here to speak with him on urgent business. We'll go farther north, closer to Central Park. He can find us there."

The three men look at us suspiciously but don't respond.

"Let's go," Jan says and we turn and begin walking down the street. I glance back and the three men are standing together, speaking, watching us as we leave.

"That feels too easy," I say, not sure I trust that they won't come after us.

Sure enough, before we've even reached the end of the street, I hear them running towards us and so Jan and I take off running, taking alleys and side streets as we travel back north and east, trying to get away from our pursuers.

"Down here," Jan says and we take another alley, running down the narrow passage between hulking buildings, the scent of rotten garbage and grease behind a restaurant making my stomach churn. We take another alley and find ourselves in a small street that has only one exit. We're trapped, and I turn back and see the three men enter a few streets back.

"In here," Jan says and motions to an old parking garage with a high cement fence. He jumps up and stands on the wall, then reaches down to me, but before he can, an arrow whizzes past my head and bounces off the cement. Then another strikes Jan in the shoulder and he falls backwards, losing his balance because of the force of the impact. I turn, ducking as I do, and see one man has a crossbow out and is nocking another arrow.

I have nowhere to run and so I stand up straight, my blade in one hand, my stake in the other.

I won't be taken easily. If they shoot me, there's nothing I can do but if they don't shoot me, I can at least use my sword to defend myself.

"Stay where you are," one of the men says. The other with the crossbow points it at me. "He has a wooden arrow. It would kill you instantly if it hit your heart and believe me, he's an expert marksman."

I stand my ground. "I'll leave, we'll both leave. We don't want any trouble."

"You won't get any, as long as you cooperate. You say you want to see the Priest? Well, it might be worth our while to have you for a while. We might be able to use you to get some food and provisions. A trade, if you like. The Priest has a lot of followers. If you're truly his friend, we'll see how much he values you."

Jan struggles up and leans against the cement wall that lines the car park.

"The Priest will want to see the girl," Jan says and jumps over the wall to stand beside me, his voice strained from his wound. "Tell him her name is Eve. He'll pay you whatever you want and if you hurt her, he'll make *you* pay."

One of the men motions to me to come towards them, but Jan puts a hand on my shoulder.

"She stays with me until the Priest comes himself."

"We tell you what to do, not the other way around," the man in the middle with the sword says. "Eve is to come with me. I'll take her to the Priest. You'll stay here."

I turn to Jan and he shakes his head. "I don't like it. There's no telling if they even know Michel."

"We have no other choice. That guy with the crossbow could kill us both."

"I'll go with you," I say and step forward. Jan tries to grab me, but he's shot immediately in the other shoulder and he groans, staggering back from the force.

"Stay, Jan," I say firmly, and leave him by the wall. I go to the man in the middle, aware that crossbow could shoot me as well. He nocks another arrow and holds the bow pointing towards me.

I stand in front of the men and the one in the middle grabs my arm and turns me around while another one grabs my backpack. Then the man ties a black blindfold around my eyes and ties my hands behind my back. I'm pretty much helpless at this point and can do nothing but walk along with the three of them down the street. I can see my feet as I walk, so the blindfold isn't completely blocking my vision, but

I can't see much else. We walk on for about ten minutes, and soon, we enter a building, taking a hallway into a room that echoes as we walk along the marble floors.

I'm pushed down onto a chair, my hands over the back.

I sit in silence, waiting for whatever is going to happen to me.

The three men – or two now, I can't tell – speak in soft voices a distance away from where I sit.

"Okay, Eve," the man says. "We're going to contact the Priest and let him know you're here. It'll be up to him as to what you're worth."

I shrug. At this point, I'm sure that Michel will pay whatever they demand and I feel badly that it's come to this. I don't want him to be forced to rescue me if it somehow thwarts his plans.

He'll know what to do. I don't think he'll let me die, once he knows I'm here.

It's quiet now, and all I hear is the sound of a guard breathing. My arms ache, and I feel the ties chafing at my wrists, but I can bear it. Waiting for whatever happens next gives me time to think. I wonder how Jan is and whether he's even alive. Even though I barely know him, and he is one of Soren's men, I don't want anything bad to happen to him. And I can't help but wonder what Michel's been doing all this time away from Soren.

He's developed a following during the past few weeks that he's been gone. He's got access to food and provisions, or so the man seemed to think. He has influence.

I wonder if this isn't all part of his plan – to leave me and fight Soren from the outside. The only way I'll know is if he does actually come for me.

He'll come for me, I hope…

Time passes. I estimate about an hour or more, before I hear footsteps in the room.

"Take off her blindfold, for God's sake," Michel says. I hear his footsteps come nearer and then my blindfold is removed and I'm staring up into his face, and I have never been happier to see him before.

"Michel," I say, a constriction in my throat. "I'm sorry about all this. Soren sent me. He threatened to kill Julien unless I complied. I didn't want—"

"Shh," he says and personally cuts the ties on my wrists and helps me up, pulling me into his arms for a warm embrace. He's dressed in a black cassock and has a large cross around his neck. He looks like a monk from some medieval era instead of my Michel, the first man I fell in love with.

"I'm sorry it came to this," he whispers in my ear. Then he pulls back and holds me at arm's length. "You look no worse for the wear. I hear they shot poor Jan with two arrows." Michel shakes his head. "I'll make sure he gets some blood so he can heal. We have him at the medical facility and will keep him there until we send you back to Boston."

"Soren wants you back," I say. "He said he'll kill Julien if we don't return with you."

Michel shakes his head. "He won't. He's just bluffing."

"How can you be so sure?" I ask, alarm filling me. "He showed me that he can kill with a thought, from a distance. I believe he'll kill Julien if you don't return."

"Think about it, Eve," Michel says and escorts me out of the room, throwing a small leather purse of money over to the large man who brought me here. "Soren needs someone to say mass for his followers. He wants me, but he'll make do with Julien. He wants one of us, so he can make us pay for what we did to Marguerite. If he kills Julien, he knows I'll never willingly return to help him. He's bluffing."

"He sent me to get you to return."

"No, he didn't," Michel says and leads me down the street. Flanking us are six guards in SWAT gear, their weapons drawn. I can see how much power Michel has amassed in so short a time. He has loyal followers willing to protect him.

"What do you mean?" I ask.

Michel turns to me, a half smile on his face. "He wants us together," he says. "He wants to push us together, to tempt me from my vows. He's not going to succeed."

I want to respond that he's right, but I don't.

"Where are we going?"

I glance around the street, trying to figure out where we are, but I don't know Manhattan and so it's all just big city to me.

"We're going to my offices."

"You have offices?" I ask, wondering how he was able to get so powerful so quickly. "You did all this in the past three weeks that you've been gone?"

Michel smiles, but doesn't meet my eyes. "I've been planning this for a very long time, Eve."

"You and your plans," I say and smile.

We continue to walk to an ornate building wedged in between two others. It looks like a church in the middle of the block.

The guards open the doors for us and we enter the cool dim interior. There's a hush inside and I see that it is a church, with ornate flying buttresses and gilded features. At the altar is a crucified Christ on the cross. Everything looks like it came from thirteenth-century France...

"This is your church?" I ask, running my hands on the polished wood of a pew.

"Yes," Michel says and leads me past the altar to a small room off the rear. It is an office, with a huge desk and walls of bookshelves. It feels old, like a study that has been used for decades. A huge stained glass window arches from the floor to the high ceiling, featuring angels looking up to heaven.

Michel points to a small sitting area with two couches facing each other, a coffee table between them. I take a seat and wait. He sits beside me.

"So, tell me. How are you?"

He looks so earnest, like he's truly concerned for how I've been.

"I'm fine," I say and smile.

"I was worried about you. I suppose you cooperated with Soren and the Twelve are now all resurrected?"

I nod. "I know you disapprove of them, but Soren promised to stop the plague and eradicate vampirism. I knew if I helped him, you'd disapprove but I had to put humanity above my own desires."

"I understand. I would never blame you for resurrecting them. There comes a point where we all face difficult choices. Sometimes, we just have to make them even if they're hard."

I sigh, glad he doesn't hate me for doing it. "I've learned that I have to just accept and try not to understand everything."

"Yes," he says and takes my face in his hands. His expression is so earnest. "Finally, yes. You finally understand."

I nod, smiling, tears filling my eyes for some reason. "When Soren came into my room and almost strangled me, I realized that he can't read you. Or my mother or Dylan. But he can read me. That's why you could never say anything."

"*Yes*," he says and his expression is so sympathetic. "I could only tell you so much. I couldn't tell you why. I knew that whatever I said, he'd have access to that information once you shared blood with him."

He strokes my hair and I wait for him to take his hands off me, but he keeps them on me, touching my hair, one hand on my arm.

"So it was only after I shared blood with him that first time that he could read me?" I ask. "You mean when I resurrected Kael?" I frown. "I thought he could read my mind much, much earlier.

"He might have been able to read you earlier, but only if he slipped something into your food or drink when he met you that first time. That's the only way he had access to you much sooner."

"Could he have given me some of his blood much sooner? When I was a child?"

Michel shrugs. "Perhaps. I tried to keep a close watch on you, but you were out of my control for a long time when you lived in Europe. Then, when you were with Franklin..."

"So he could have slipped me some of his blood far earlier – maybe right from the start."

Michel finally takes his hand off my arm and sits back, watching me. "It's possible that he's known where you were since you were born."

I shudder at the thought. "I felt something strange that first day I saw Soren in the Sheriff's office in Helena, as if he could read my mind from a distance. Maybe he was."

"Perhaps," Michel says. "Regardless, you're here now. I thought he might choose this path, but I wasn't sure. I wouldn't know until we all played out our parts in this game."

"It's a *game* to you?" I say, surprised to hear him say such a thing as that. I always figured it was more of a life-and-death struggle.

"It's a game to Soren. When you've been around for thousands and thousands of years, it's *all* a game. This is just a more interesting game to him because it's more complicated than previous games, because of technology and the possibilities it provides."

"So he's been doing this kind of thing for thousands of years?"

Michel shrugs. "As far as I can tell. He's been vying for power throughout his existence. It's his downfall."

"He seems pretty powerful and not at all in any kind of downfall."

Michel leans back and runs his fingers through his hair as if he's tired.

"His original downfall, I mean. He's always had such ambition." He smiles at me but then his expression goes back to dark in an instant. "Anyway, I'm glad you've finally understood why I can only tell you so much."

I exhale. "I do," I say and reach out to touch his arm briefly. "I'm sorry for how much trouble I was. You should have told me why you couldn't tell me."

He shakes his head. "Couldn't. Not proper timing. Even now, I have to watch what I say."

A man enters the room, dressed in vestments – is he another priest? "You wanted some tea?"

Michel nods. The priest waves at someone outside the door and a servant enters with a tray bearing a teapot and cups. He places it on the coffee table across from us. When the servant and young priest leave, Michel pours me tea.

"We have a bit of a battle going on over territory right now so I'm going to have to keep you here for at least a week," he says softly. "His timing was impeccable. I'm sure Soren hopes that I'll somehow succumb to your charms because I have to keep you here with me, which would give him an advantage, but I won't succumb." He hands me the cup, and his expression is dark. "I won't be deterred from my path. Not even by you."

I take the cup and set it down on the coffee table. "Did he really think he could tempt you onto another course by sending me here?"

"Yes." Michel takes a sip of his own tea. "He knows this is the harder choice for me. I could accept his bait. It would be the easier solution. It would be the sweeter solution all around. But that would leave him in power, and I just can't have him in power. He has to know that. No matter what the personal price for me. I can't accept it."

"What personal price?" I ask, alarmed now that he's taking a course that I won't like. "Don't tell me you die in this scenario of yours?"

He forces a smile. "I can't say whether I die or not. But in the scenario Soren wants, you and I are lovers again and we return to Boston and help him. I can't have that, which is why I left. He wants me to know that if I cooperate, I'll have you to myself again, but as much as that is tempting, I won't take his bait."

"I told you we would never be together again, Michel," I say, angered that Soren and Michel think I'm so easily manipulated. "I came here not to be your lover again but to bring you back so Soren will stop the plague and end vampirism. Us being lovers again is impossible. Nothing could happen that would change that."

He glances away and smiles sadly. "If only that were true, Eve, but you don't see all the possible events and circumstances that could push us together. Soren does and so do I. Or at least, I saw them before I became mortal again. But you don't have to worry about it," he says and sits back, turning back to face me, the cup in his hand. "I'm strong enough to refuse."

There would be nothing that could tempt me into going back into Michel's bed. Even though I know he lied to me to prevent Soren from knowing his plans, and about my mother and Dylan, it doesn't mean I want to be his lover again. That died when my mother came back and even though I know the truth now, my feelings are dead.

"So, you're going to send me back to Boston alone and you're sure Soren won't kill Julien?"

Michel sighs. "Yes, Eve," he says softly. "That's exactly what I'm going to do. This trip was all for nothing. Soren hoped that me seeing you again would make me fall again, but it won't. I know he won't kill Julien because Soren still needs me if his plans are to come to fruition and I would never help him if he killed Julien. He won't kill you either because if he delays his final game plan again for another generation, things will have gone too far to recover. No, this is the time for Soren to make his final move. So I have to make mine as well."

"That sounds ominous," I say and put down my cup of tea, no longer really happy with what Michel is proposing. I have a sense that Michel is going to sacrifice himself and that he will finally get his way and die a mortal.

Can I go along with that? Even if it means that the plague will stop and vampires will be history?

We sit in silence for a moment and I feel a weight of dread come over me. I was so happy that I finally understood the reason for all the lies and deceit. That it would all be okay now that I knew why it had to be that way. Now, I feel like my heart will be ripped out of my chest no matter what happens. Michel's going to die – that's what I fear. I fear he's taking the option that preserves my life but at the expense of his. I don't want that.

"I hope you aren't planning on sacrificing yourself so that I live," I say, turning to him, examining his expression for the truth. When he says nothing, I know he will. "If you think I'll go along with it willingly, you're wrong. There has to be a way that all of us survive."

He shakes his head. "No, Eve, not all of us will survive. That's all I can say. Now, finish your tea. I have a room made up for you where you'll stay until it's time for you to go back. We're going to repair your vehicle so you can return to Boston once this little disruption is over. Your place is there, not here."

I sigh heavily. I promised myself that I would just trust my gut and go with what Michel chose because he knew best what course to take. Now, I'm not so sure. I have to remember his death wish. He wants to die a mortal. He wants to save the world and then exit stage left.

Is there anything I could do to stop him from succeeding?

I finish my tea while Michel goes to the door and speaks with his guards. So, all of this was for nothing. Soren didn't get what he wanted. Michel may get what he wants, which is not what I want.

I have to admit to myself that I don't want Michel to die. I don't want us to be lovers because that would be too complicated, trying to manage both him and Julien, their jealousies.

What would it be like to live with them both, but in peace?

Soren pops into my head, even at this great distance and I know his powers are strong.

Keep out of my mind, I think to myself but of course, it's useless. I've never found anything to keep Soren out of my mind that I know of.

And a damn good thing because if you did, I'd have to kill you. You'd be of no use to me if you could block me, so don't even try to find a way, Eve.

I watch Michel speaking with his guard, his head bent as they make arrangements.

All you have to do is go to him, and he'll be yours. One kiss, Eve, and you can prevent him from dying in this scenario.

I consider. If I did go to him and kiss him, would he really succumb? Am I that much of a temptation?

Come on now, Eve... You and Danielle are the only women who have ever tempted Michel. The only two he has been weak for. The others he was with meant nothing to him but temporary solace. Go to him. You can have it all... All of it.

In the end, I can't do it.

I think you're wrong. He won't respond to me. He's made his choice.

Soren doesn't respond and I hope he's leaving me alone for a while.

"Come, Eve," Michel says. "I want to take you to your room before it gets too dark."

"Is Jan okay?" I ask as I stand up and go to the door.

"Of course," Michel says and frowns. "I'll send one of my guards to take you to the apartment. You'll be safe."

"How do I know Julien won't be dead when I get back to Soren's compound?"

"Because Soren knows that will mean he loses."

We walk back out to the street and Michel remains standing at the top of the stairs, his hands behind his back.

"Go," he says and waves towards the street. "I'm staying here tonight. Consider my apartment your home until it's safe to leave."

I stop and turn to look at him. "Will I see you again before I leave?" I ask, my heart suddenly squeezing.

"We'll have meals together. You can always come to mass, but I'm busy trying to organize a rebellion," he says but it sounds non-committal and not like he really believes it. "And just right now, I have a small insurrection on my hands I have to quell."

"Michel, even though we won't be lovers again, I still love you," I say, my voice breaking. "Don't do anything reckless. Don't die."

He smiles, and I can see his demeanor change. He softens, as if he's been holding himself so tightly under control this whole time.

"I don't plan on dying. I love you as well. Always."

I turn away, and my vision is blurry.

CHAPTER 11

THE GUARD TELLS me his name is Brent and that he's originally from Philadelphia. He's been there since the founding of the city and so is one of the older ascended vampires in existence.

I feel comforted that at least he's probably able to protect me in case any humans come after us, looking for whatever they can steal.

We walk through the empty streets, back to a vehicle and get in, driving down the dark streets to a tall brownstone. On either end of the street, city buses block access and are pulled apart when we arrive to admit us. Armed guards line the street.

"Is this Michel's headquarters?"

"This is his residence. It's just a block away from the cathedral. He likes to be close by."

He leads me into the building and we pass a sentry who looks me up and down. He checks me for weapons and finding none, motions to me.

"She can take the guest bedroom on the left."

The guard walks me to the bedroom and unlocks the door. "If you're hungry, I'll have the cook bring you a tray."

I nod, and go inside. It's small but well-appointed and there's an en-suite bathroom. I sit on the side of the bed and look out the window. Sheer curtains filter the light, giving the room a bit of a gloomy atmosphere. There's a lantern on a table and a fire in the hearth.

I sigh and lie down, staring up at the ceiling while I wait for my tray of dinner to arrive.

When a knock comes at the door, I sit up and rub my eyes. I fell asleep, and am surprised to hear my stomach rumbling.

"Here you are," the young man in a cassock says. "Cook prepared a sandwich and some fruit and tea. That's all we had. Father Michel is pretty frugal so there's nothing fancy."

He smiles at me and he looks so young.

I sit beside the fire and eat the sandwich – roast beef with lettuce and real butter. The tea is hot and there's even some honey, which pleases me. There's even a small carafe of preserved blood, which I drink down to quench my thirst. The meal is delicious and I glance around the room, wondering what I'll do every day until it's safe for me to return to Boston.

There's a bookshelf against one wall and so I spend the rest of the evening examining volumes of literature – most of it old, dusty and from names of authors I've never heard of before. Some of it is in French. I wonder if this isn't one of Michel's apartments from his years of life before I met him. I half expect Michel to come by before bed to say something, but he doesn't. Perhaps he thought better of being alone with me. If so, his faith in his own commitment to celibacy may not be as strong as he thought.

I go to sleep when the old grandfather clock in the entry strikes midnight, after washing my face in a basin of cold water and giving my teeth a quick brush with the personal supplies I brought with me.

Then I crawl into bed and sleep almost immediately.

THE NEXT DAY I wake early, and for a moment, I forget where I am. The room is unfamiliar and it takes me a while to reorient myself.

Then I remember I'm in Michel's residence in New York City. I check the clock. It's early and still dark out. I rise and get dressed and then sit alone in the room, after stoking the fire to build it back up again.

It's then I remember that Michel said I could come to mass if I wanted. Of course, I don't really want to go to mass, but I do want to see what Michel is doing here in Manhattan. He spoke about organizing a rebellion, and so I want to find out what I can.

I go to the door and speak to the guard posted outside my room.

"Michel said I could go to mass if I wanted."

The guard takes me down to the vehicle.

"He's at St. Patrick's today," the driver says and takes me through the streets to a gothic cathedral all the way north in Midtown Manhattan. As we walk to the entry, we join a stream of people who are also going to early mass. They look tired, their eyes weary, but they seem intent on going despite the early hour. We enter St. Patrick's and I'm awed by the beauty of the old building. Inside it's warm and hushed, the only sounds are of the people taking their places and whispering their prayers.

I sit alone in the back, watching Michel and his assistants go through the mass. Once, I would have taken part, but not now. Now, I'm only here to watch Michel and try to understand why he is so devout. Why is he doing this? He must think that this is the only way to preserve his church, the church of his faith, against Soren's usurpation. I know that Soren wants to harness the power of the Catholic Church's millions of believers. That must really upset Michel, so much that he's willing to die to preserve the church.

It feels strange to watch him deliver the mass, dressed in his vestments, his altar boys at his side. I only feel sadness. There is no solace for me in watching.

Then, he gives his homily and I listen to him speak about false gods and I know he's talking about Soren. Michel talks about power and how it corrupts those who have it, using it for their own ends, and not the ends that would be best for humanity. He's trying to set Soren up as a false god so that when Soren does his feats of wonder, not all believers will be converted.

When mass is finished, I leave without interacting with anyone, for my heart is heavy at what I've seen. I've lost Michel and even though I love Julien and chose Julien, I still feel a deep grief that Michel is lost to us both.

My guard next takes me to a small park near the memorial in Battery Park, and a crowd has gathered, waiting for Michel, I assume. Are these the non-religious, the non-church goers? When Michel arrives, they whisper amongst themselves and I examine those gathered more closely. They're workers, and rough men with scars and work boots, looking like they've had hard lives. Michel gives them a simplified version of his sermon at the Cathedral. Instead of God, and false gods, he talks about despots and tyrants, who use men and throw them away when they're finished.

It's cold and I shiver as I watch Michel deliver his speech to the crowd. Then, he finishes, to a round of applause. People crowd around him when he leaves the podium and goes into the crowd. He shakes hands and speaks with people individually. For a moment, he catches my eye and smiles, before turning back to one of his followers. For they are followers – of that I am sure.

He's planning an insurrection.

This is why Soren sent me – of that I am certain. Soren wants to know what Michel's up to.

Now he knows.

I'm surprised Michel showed me this, knowing as he does that Soren can read my mind. When Michel is finished, he enters a vehicle and is driven to some other location. We don't follow. Instead, my driver takes me back to the residence in Battery Park and I spend the day alone with only the bookshelf and a tray of food to keep me company. I grow impatient the second day, and knock on the door. When the guard opens the door, I ask him to take me to Michel's office, but he shakes his head.

"The Bishop said that you were to stay here until he called for you." He shrugs and so I'm forced to remain alone for yet another day.

I make a face. "He's a Bishop now?"

The guard looks insulted and closes the door, leaving me alone for yet another full day and night, during which time I wonder if Michel isn't punishing me. Or avoiding me. Most likely, he doesn't want Soren to have a window into all his operation here in Manhattan, but he must have wanted Soren to see him preaching against him.

So why doesn't he just send me back? On our way to the cathedral, I didn't see any discord on the streets. There was no military presence outside of the usual armed guards. No danger I could see, despite what Michel told me.

I sigh and resign myself to spending my days alone and completely in the dark about what Michel is doing.

Don't worry, Soren says. *I'm still gleaning a lot. Every bit helps me understand his game. He won't win, no matter what he does. Tell him that for me. Tell him I win in the end. I've won for this long and I'll keep winning. He'll always be playing a guessing game.*

I don't respond. Instead, I try to focus on the book in my hand, pushing thoughts of Michel and Soren out of my mind until Michel decides it's time to send me back.

FINALLY, on the fourth day that I'm in Manhattan, Michel sends for me, indicating that I'm to return to Boston. The driver takes me back to St. Peter's Cathedral, a few blocks away from City Hall. I enter the vaulted interior to find Michel sitting in his office, one of his fellow priests bending down over the desk, pointing to some document before them.

Michel looks up when I walk into the room and gestures to the other priest. The older man with grey hair and fine metal rimmed glasses, examines me, his gaze moving up and down in a judgmental manner, before leaving us alone.

I sit on the old wooden office chair across from Michel's desk, impatient for an explanation.

"What took you so long?" I say, unable to hide my frustration and being kept alone for four days.

"Do you even have to ask?" he says, exhaling heavily. He stands and comes around his desk, leaning against it across from me, his arms folded.

"Yes," I say, frowning, not sure what he means. "I do have to ask."

"I'd think you understood why, given our past relationship."

I laugh despite myself. "Did you think I'd try to seduce you or something?" I ask, indignant.

He shakes his head, his expression hurt, his eyes dark under a furrowed brow.

"Of course not," he says softly. "You made it clear enough that you *love* Julien. You *chose* Julien. Still, seeing you, having you here, vulnerable, and under my care… You have to understand how it would affect me. I'm weak, Eve. I…"

He turns his head away as if he can't bear to even look at me. It's then I understand. He was afraid he'd want to try to seduce *me*. Protecting me, having me in his control, needing his protection… it would bring out the alpha male in him. The man he tries so hard to keep in check with his prayers and self-denial.

The man he tries to keep in check through the priesthood.

"I'm sorry," I say, glancing away when he meets my eyes finally. "I didn't think…" I sigh, sad that it has come to this between us. Him afraid of still wanting me. Seeing me as a temptation. As a sign of his weakness.

"You really must despise me," I say, a pain in my chest that makes me almost sob. "To see me as a weakness. Something to avoid. That your feelings for me make you bad."

"No, *no*," he says, and reaches out to take my hand. He squeezes it. "It's not that way at all. Our love was the most beautiful thing I've ever experienced. Those were the happiest days of my existence. In all my eight hundred years, I have never been happier than when you and I were first together. But you have to know that Soren would be able to see into me, into my memories, my plans, through you if we were to make love. He'd see into me through our connection."

Finally, I look at him and meet his eyes. I see no revulsion in them. Only love and understanding.

Regret.

I shake my head. "I'm sorry. I should have realized…"

"Don't be sorry," he says, and kneels at my feet. He takes both my hands and kisses my knuckles. "I'm not sorry for the time we had together. It was precious to me. Every moment."

He smiles up at me, and in his eyes I see love and sadness and regret. I see the conflict he feels between his love and desire for me and his sense of duty to his god.

How I wish…

You wish he'd smarten up and give in to his true desires…

I want to scratch Soren out of my mind, but I don't let him upset me. This moment with Michel is too important to let Soren ruin it for me.

"I risked everything to be with you," Michel says, stroking my palm with his thumb. "I thought I could keep you out of my mind, and for a while I tried to keep control over our connection, but the deeper I went with you, the more you were able to penetrate my mind and then you were able to block me out completely. And yet, you could easily get into my mind when I was vulnerable."

I remembered the times I tricked him, using sex to get into his mind and find out things he wouldn't tell me. At that moment, I feel incredibly guilty, but it was only because I didn't understand… I couldn't understand.

"Michel, no matter what happens, I still love you," I say, my voice breaking as regret fills me for what happened between us that broke us apart.

"I know," he says and kisses my palm, his lips lingering over my skin the way he did that very first night I met him at the university. Although I have no personal memory of it, I do remember reading about our first meeting in my journal – how he tried to compel me to forget and how he almost threw me down the stairs in his desperation to have me forget. In his haste, I fell and scraped my palms. I read how he licked my wounds and tasted my blood, thus cementing our bond. How I saw his vampire nature come out – his fangs, his eyes blood-red…

Oh, Michel…

My heart breaks once more as I remember seeing him on the beach and how he found me in the rain when I twisted my ankle and cut my lip on the boulders lining the beach. How he sucked the blood from the cut on my bottom lip and changed once more before my eyes. How he ran from me, once again trying to be honorable but being weak.

Kiss him now and he's yours...

I could. I could kiss him and I'm sure he'd be mine.

But I don't.

Finally, Michel stands up and lets my hand drop.

"My driver will take you back to your vehicle. Jan's well enough to travel and it's time you went back. We've managed to quell the mini-rebellion in the Bronx, so you'll be able to travel safely through that territory.

I stand up and try to look in his eyes, but he avoids mine as if looking in them would be too much. Michel motions to the guard standing at attention by the door and he comes over to take my bags.

"Michel," I say, wanting to have some kind of closure between us, but he waves me off.

"Just go," he says, his voice breaking. "No goodbyes for us."

I turn and follow the guard out of the room, feeling like I need to cry my eyes out, but instead, I take in a deep breath and swallow back my pain.

The guard leads me to the street where our vehicle is parked. Jan is sitting in the driver's seat waiting for us. I thank the guard when he opens my door, and I get in the passenger side of the vehicle, wondering what's going to happen and whether Soren will really kill Julien if Michel doesn't show. I imagine he could let me know right away if he does, but Michel seemed so sure...

We drive through the streets back to the highway and I feel like this has been a total waste of effort, but at least I was able to see Michel and get some idea of what he's doing. He's trying to start a rebellion against what Soren may become, if Soren has his way. Michel's building a foundation of doubt in order to fight Soren if and when he does try to assume some kind of overarching power.

Michel wants an end to the plague, as I do. He wants an end to vampirism. But he can't support Soren in his quest for total power in the church.

Michel wants the church to remain pure – whatever that means.

I don't know if Soren will do what we want unless he gets what he wants in return. I don't believe any of it – not really – not the religious part. I believe Soren and the Twelve have powers that humans don't understand. I believe that they could act as gods, and I suspect they have in the past claimed to be gods. But of course, I know they aren't. They aren't the creators of humanity or the universe. They merely possess immortality and the ability to manipulate matter and affect minds.

That doesn't give them the right to have power over humans.

Humans have the inherent right to self-determination.

Yes, and if they choose to be ruled by powerful beings, what right do you have to deny them that choice, Eve? Freedom means the right to choose your oppressor as well as liberator.

I squeeze my eyes shut, hating the fact that Soren has dipped into my mind. I don't want to answer him in my mind. So I don't. I merely watch out the window and try to forget that Soren's there. I won't give him the satisfaction of responding psychically.

We drive north and east and my anxiety grows as we leave Manhattan. I want to find Julien safe and alive when I return to Soren's compound in Cambridge. My mind wanders to the punishment I'll receive when I return and how exactly Soren will torture me... Force me to watch Julien be with Gabrielle? Deny me Julien's affections? It's hard to know what to expect...

It's when we're leaving the city that a truck pulls into the street ahead of us, blocking our exit.

Jan slams on his brakes and comes to a halt about twenty feet from the other vehicle.

"Get down," he whispers, reaching out a hand to push me down onto the seat. Before I can, something crashes through the windshield and I feel an intense pressure in my chest, the pain blinding for a moment. I glance down and see a wooden arrow protruding from my chest right in the middle of my left breast.

I reach for it but before I can grab it, a cold numbness spread through my body and my vision dims.

I realize that I'm dying...

CHAPTER 12

THE LIGHT IS BLINDING in intensity.

I try to shade my eyes, but my body feels like lead, my arms limp beside my body. I don't know where I am but it's too bright so I have to keep my eyes closed, but I also feel a need to understand where I am.

The last thing I remember...

The last thing I remember is being in Manhattan and saying goodbye to Michel.

When my eyes finally adjust to the brightness, I'm able to focus and I see Soren's face. He's leaning over me, frowning.

"There you go, Eve," he says, and holds up an arrow. It's covered in blood and I remember that I was shot before Jan and I were able to leave Manhattan...

Soren's resurrected me.

I try to sit up and find that I'm not quite back to normal. I'm dizzy and have to cover my eyes for a moment as I catch my breath.

When I open them again and glance around, I see Michel sitting on a chair beside my bed, his head bowed as if he's been praying. When he looks up and meets my eyes, I see resignation in them.

Of course, it's then I realize what's happened.

I turn to Soren. "*You* did this," I say, anger filling me. "You had someone shoot me with a wooden arrow so Michel would have to come to you and ask you to revive me."

Soren smiles at me, but I see anger in his expression, despite the gloating look in his eyes. "I have ways of getting what I want, Eve. Never doubt that I'll use them in the end."

I turn to Michel, who finally looks up at me. His eyes are red, as if he's overcome with emotion. Despite everything, he takes my hand and kisses my knuckles.

"I'd pay any price to keep you alive, Eve."

"What price did he make you pay?" I ask, turning to Soren and giving him a frown. I know it's pointless. I have no power over him but at that moment, I hate him for manipulating Michel.

All Michel wants is for the church to remain what he believes it to be. He wants to be a mortal priest and die as one.

Soren is so bent on revenge that he can't let Michel have his one desire.

"Oh, stop with the mental theatrics, Eve. Michel made a choice. He had the opportunity to let you die, but he didn't. He *chose*."

"I did," Michel says, and kisses my hand once more. "I made my choice."

I look around the room and see Julien standing by the door. He's glancing down at the floor and his face is unreadable.

"What about Julien?" I say, and at that Julien brightens. He lifts up his head and looks at me, our eyes meeting. My heart leaps to see him for I was afraid that Soren would have killed him when he knew I'd failed to bring Michel home.

"You did fail," Soren says quietly. "But luckily, I *didn't*. I knew how to get Michel back here even if you didn't."

"By blackmail," I say.

"By any means possible," Soren says. "I have an agenda and I'm going to do everything I can to see it through. If that means I have to force Michel's hand, I will. I did."

Soren leaves us and goes to Julien. "Come," he says and places his hand on Julien's shoulder. "You might as well leave the two lovebirds alone. Unless you want to stay and take part," he says and glances back at me. "I've always wanted to see the three of you together."

"You never will," I say and pull my hand out of Michel's grip. He looks upset that I have, but I don't want Soren to think that somehow, this means Michel and I will be resuming a sexual relationship.

"Never say never, Eve," Soren says and grins. Then he pushes Julien ahead of him out the door and closes it behind him.

I look at Michel. "What did Soren make you agree to?"

"That I wouldn't leave again until everything's finished – the plague and the end to vampirism."

"That's it? Nothing about you and me?"

Michel shakes his head. "Nothing about you and me."

I frown. "I find that hard to believe."

"Soren thinks that if he pushes us together, we'll fall into each other's arms and he'll get to be all smug and say he told us so."

"We won't," I say, pulling up the sheet to cover my naked breasts. Already whatever wound I had from the arrow is gone, healed through Soren's powers.

"This is what Soren did to Julien to get you to obey him and ascend when I first met you, right?"

"Yes," Michel says. "Soren wants the three of us together. He'll do whatever he thinks will work."

"It won't," I say.

"It won't," Michel replies.

I sigh and lie back on the bed, closing my eyes. "Did you see this as a possibility?" I ask, too tired now to open my eyes and watch him.

"No," Michel says softly. "I knew he might try to use you to convince me to come back, but I didn't see this. It was a shock."

I open my eyes. "I'm sorry he used me as a pawn. I don't know what your plans were, and I won't ask, but I'm sure they didn't include coming back here."

He takes my hand in his again and kisses my knuckles once more. "It's all right, Eve," he says and his voice is thick with emotion. "I couldn't let you die. You're necessary to the final endgame. Soren knows that, too. He wants to torture us, Julien and me, by dangling you out in front of us, like a piece of ripe fruit. I spoke with Julien and we agreed that neither of us would be with you until this is all over."

I frown. "I don't suppose you might have considered asking me what I think about that," I say angrily. "I never agreed to give up Julien. I don't see why I should."

"Soren wants to use you against the two of us. We decided that it would be best not to let that happen. Beat Soren at his own game. Sorry, Eve. This is the way it has to be."

"For how long?"

"As long as it takes."

I pull my hand out of his and close my eyes once more. I'm angry, because I want Julien with me. I want to feel his body next to mine in bed. I want his comfort.

Take Michel. He'll cooperate, if you give him a push...

I fist my hands and grit my teeth, frustrated that Soren can just pop in any time he likes and comment on my thoughts.

One of the perks of being a god...

"You're not a god," I say out loud, refusing to speak to him in my mind.

"Of course I'm not a god," Michel says, frowning. "Why would you say that?"

I shake my head and smile. "No, not you. I was responding to something Soren said to me in my mind. He does that whenever he feels like it."

Michel grins ruefully. "Sorry. It must be annoying."

"It is. I refuse to answer him mentally so if you hear me say something out of the blue, it's probably in response to something Soren's said."

I close my eyes once more and say nothing for a moment.

"You should rest for a while," Michel says. "Someone will wait in the anteroom in case you want anything."

"What will Soren do to try to force us all together in one bed?" I ask. "I know that's what he really wants. He thinks I want it as well, but he's wrong so don't worry."

"Oh, I don't worry about it, Eve," Michel says and I think I detect a slight bit of hurt in his voice. "It's not something I want either, nor does Julien."

"Good," I say and close my eyes again, pulling the covers up around my neck.

Me thinks you and Michel doth protest too much...

I can almost see Soren's grin in my mind's eye, but I refuse to follow through with the visualization. I won't give him that satisfaction.

Michel leaves me alone on the bed and I turn over, my back to the door.

In a very few moments, I can't keep my eyes open.

LATER, I wake when the grandfather clock in the corner of the room chimes softly, indicating the half-hour. I feel rested but have no idea how long I've slept. A female servant dressed in a maid's uniform is placing a robe at the foot of my bed. She smiles when she sees me sit up.

"I've come to give you a bath," she says and she's really very sweet looking, with dimples and her hair up in a bun. "Then you're to get dressed and join Lord Soren for dinner."

I grab the robe that she hands me and pull it on. I glance at the mirror to see the place where the arrow pierced my chest, but now all that's left is a small white scar. I'm sure the next time I drink blood it will go away completely.

I follow the servant into the washroom where the tub has been filled with warm soapy water. It feels good to slip into it, and I lie back and close my eyes.

While I'm lying there, I wonder how my staking and resurrection will screw up Michel's plans.

I hope a lot.

I frown and splash water on my face, trying to distract myself from Soren's words. I don't want to even think in response to him, but it's impossible. My mind can't help but go there and I wonder how much my being in Manhattan has changed the future.

You have to keep me happy if you want me to end the plague sooner rather than later. Humor me, Eve.

"What will it take to humor you and get you to stop the plague?"

Sleep with Michel, at least once more before this is all over. I miss you two. So passionate in a very controlled way but you make Michel almost lose control for a change. I like that. You and Julien are just so cute but I prefer you and Michel, personally. I'm rooting for you to pick Michel, but I'd be happy with a threesome.

"I told you before that I won't sleep with Michel again. He's chosen celibacy, and I've chosen Julien."

Not even to stop the plague <u>this</u> week?

I slam my fist down on the surface of the water. "You should stop it this week because you can, not because I sleep with Michel or not."

I want what I want.

"I'll tell you what," I say, trying to think of a way to win. "You stop the plague and I'll make a pass at Michel."

I can almost feel Soren's glee.

Deal.

"If he doesn't sleep with me, it's not on my head. You still have to go through with the rest of the plan and eradicate vampirism."

Deal.

I feel like I've won a small victory with Soren. I'll offer myself to Michel after Soren releases the antidote to the plague. Once I see that it's taken affect, I'll go to Michel and offer to sleep with him. He'll refuse and Soren will have no recourse.

I smile to myself.

Don't get too smug. He might say yes.

I laugh to myself. "Back at you," I say. "He might say no."

After my bath, I dress in something conservative and go to the dining room, where I see everyone has gathered, including both Michel and Julien. I check for an empty seat but of course, Soren has taken it upon himself to place me beside Michel, with Procel on the other side. Julien is seated between two of the other Twelve and so I have no choice but to sit where Soren's placed me.

I move to my place and Michel and Procel both stand up. Michel holds my chair for me and I sit down. He helps move my chair in and his hands brush my shoulders for a moment and I know he's done it deliberately.

Is he being tempted by Soren as well? Is Soren playing the both of us or is it just me?

Why don't you and Michel have a nice little chat after dinner and find out?

I take a drink of water and don't reply, either in my mind or out loud. Instead I try to ignore his suggestion. However, I *am* interested in talking with both Julien and Michel – separately – to find out what happened and what their stories are.

Of course, I can't believe anything either of them tell me anymore, but at least I'll get the sense of what stories they feel they have to tell me, whether out of compulsion or to protect me.

The meal is delicious, and I eat my fill of the roasted game and vegetables, plus there's blood and wine. I don't speak to Michel and he doesn't speak to me. Instead, we listen to the Twelve discuss their plans for the aftermath of the plague and how to restore things, but with them at the helm.

I want to intervene and argue against them taking power because I don't approve but I realize I'd just be an annoyance. To them, their own dominion is a fait accompli. Nothing I can say will divert them from their course, so I amuse myself looking at each one in turn and wondering what kind of being they are.

Are they aliens who came here eons ago and decided they liked this place and incarnated in our form to blend in and take over? Are they just mutated humans who possess powers that science has not yet been able to measure and describe? I have no idea which it is so until we have more evidence, I'm going to be agnostic on their origins and just accept that I don't know what the hell they are.

Finally, dinner is over and everyone leaves the table and goes to the study with Soren. There, they sit in clusters or stand together in small groups and discuss different topics. It's like some salon one might find during centuries past in France or perhaps Vienna. The conversation is elevated to issues of free will and the nature of freedom, and they genuinely seem interested and focused on being good shepherds but also not treating us too much like sheep.

Part of me feels a bit in awe of them but another part is extremely wary.

I grow tired soon and yawn. I've been sitting alone, in a chair by the huge bookshelves next to an arched window, looking at a volume of 18th Century anatomy, examining the drawings of the interiors of various animals. Michel sees me yawn, and comes over to me.

"Can I walk you back to our rooms? You look tired."

I glance up at him, wondering if this is something Soren has planned or whether it's on Michel.

"Our rooms?"

Michel shrugs. "Soren has decreed that the three of us will continue to stay together. Julien and I have the two rooms off yours. We'll share the main living area."

"And what Soren decrees, we must obey."

Michel slips his hands in his pockets and looks around, perhaps to see if Julien or someone else is in earshot, but no one seems to be paying attention to us.

"We don't have to obey," he says softly. "But it's unlikely that we can entirely resist and be successful. You have to decide what hill you want to die on, Eve."

I nod, but don't know exactly what hill I choose to die on. I don't want to give Soren any satisfaction by letting him see the twins act jealous over me in public, but at the same time, I want the plague to stop and vampirism to be eradicated.

Those are the hills I want to die on, if I have to die.

I stand up, rejecting Michel's hand, and we leave the room. Julien is in deep conversation with one of the Twelve, their heads bowed in the corner. I want to speak with him – I want to *be* with him – but I don't want to cause a scene so I leave with Michel quietly and leave Julien to his conversation. If he wants, he'll come to our rooms.

"So has Soren been trying to tempt you into sleeping with me?" I say to Michel.

He seems shocked at my words and says nothing for a while, walking beside me with his hands behind his back.

"Soren wants the three of us together. He wants a threesome, but I told him he'd never get one."

"Why?" I say, angry at Soren's doggedness about the threesome. "Why does he want it?"

Michel turns to examine my face. "Because he knows it would tear us apart and he wants both our pain. He'd relish it because he knows we'd be too jealous and would grow to hate each other. That's why it won't happen."

"It won't," I say firmly. "You're brothers. I love you both, but I don't want you at the same time." I shiver. "That would be incestuous."

"I agree," Michel says. "We had it much easier with Marguerite, but we never did a threesome with her. We always were with her separately. Soren wants to push us to demean us and make us suffer."

"He really should get over his need for revenge. All these years later and he's still wanting to make you two suffer..."

"He's eternal. His emotions and desires are as well," Michel says and shrugs.

We arrive at our suite of rooms and enter. I go over to the window and look outside at the darkness, then up to the sky to see what stars are visible. The moon isn't up and so there are quite a few visible even through the glass. I wish I could go out and stargaze for a while, but I'm too tired.

"I'm going right to bed," I say to Michel. "I'm sorry I don't feel like talking. But while I get ready, maybe you could tell me about what happened – from your perspective," I say and then add, "What you can say, of course."

Michel follows me into the bathroom. I pour water into a basin and wash my face, and then brush my teeth.

"You were shot while you and Jan were leaving the city limits. From what Jan said, a truck pulled in from an alley and blocked your vehicle and someone used a crossbow to shoot a metal tipped wooden arrow into you through the windshield. They drove off, so you were the target. Jan went on foot to the first guard he found and carried you to us. I knew when I saw the arrow that this was Soren's work. He knew that I'd have to come to him to resurrect you. There would be no one else who could bring you back."

Michel's voice breaks at the end and I'm surprised at his emotion even now.

"You knew I wasn't dead permanently, though," I say and turn to examine his face. "Soren was just manipulating you."

He looks as if he's struggling for a moment. I reach out and touch his arm, squeezing it softly.

"I'm fine, Michel," I say and smile. Then, I remove the clips from my hair and brush it down, before turning to him.

"I don't know what your plans are, but I know I can't ask any longer. I'm fine knowing that the plague will stop and that vampirism will end. What you do about Soren, I'll leave to you. I trust you to do what's right."

Michel nods. "Thank you," he says softly.

"Just don't get yourself killed," I add, remembering that one of the futures involves the death of one of the twins. "I don't want to pay that price. Whatever future you fight for, make sure it includes you both, okay?"

I smile and he forces one, but I know he doesn't feel it right now. I can tell that he feels on the edge of breaking down, his skin flushed, his voice throaty.

"Michel," I say and against my better judgment, I slip my arms around his neck and squeeze him against me for the briefest moment. It's not meant in a sexual manner, but just to comfort him and reassure him, but he responds far more fervently than I planned. He pulls me against his body and squeezes so hard, his face pressed into my neck.

"Oh, Eve, I was so afraid he'd decide to create another one of you and let you die, I couldn't bear that future."

"I know," I say and pat him on the back, wanting to assuage him.

"I'm fine. He still needs me and he got you back as well. Everything's going to be okay. Or at least, for now."

I pull away and he lets me go with reluctance.

"Now, I really must sleep, considering I spent most of the last two days technically dead-dead."

"Of course," Michel says and lets me go, but before he does, he strokes my hair and smiles, his eyes wet. "Go to bed. Rest. You need your sleep."

I leave him in the bathroom and go over to my wardrobe to remove my robe from the shelves. Michel goes to the sitting room, where he picks up a daily hand-printed newspaper. I return to the bathroom and change into my nightgown and then slip quickly under the covers, but I catch him looking above his newspaper at me in my little babydoll.

He can't help it, I think to myself. He's just a man after all.

He is. A man who still loves and desires you, despite his vows. Offer him your hand, Eve, and he'll willingly take it. Do it.

"Go to hell," I say out loud, not caring what Soren thinks.

Over at the couch, Michel stirs and folds down his paper. "What?"

"I wasn't speaking to you," I say softly. "Just Soren plaguing my mind. Sorry."

I pull the coverlet up and sigh. "Good night, Michel."

"Good night, Eve. Sweet dreams."

I close my eyes but I fear they won't be sweet.

CHAPTER 13

I WAKE up hours later when Julien arrives in the room and I them speaking. The problem with vampire ears is that you never sleep very deeply and any loud noise can wake you, despite how soft it might be. I sit up and Julien sees me and comes right over. He sits on the side of the bed and leans in to kiss me but I hold out my hand and stop him.

"No, Julien," I whisper. "Not when Michel is in the room. Remember what you two agreed to."

"Fucking Soren," Julien says petulantly.

"I know," I say and touch his face briefly. "There's nothing to be done about it. One day we'll be free to be together."

"I hope so," Julien says and looks in my eyes. "If not, I'm going to be pretty damn pissed about all the sacrifice for nothing."

I frown. "Julien, it won't be for nothing if we stop the plague and end vampirism. That's bigger than us both. Bigger than our relationship."

"I still have to live in that world and if I don't have you, it won't be worth much."

"You'll have me, if I survive."

"You *must* survive, Eve," Julien says and leans in, his eyes dark. "I can't stand the thought of living without you. If you die," he says and shakes his head. "I will, as well."

"Don't you dare say that."

Julien kisses me, despite my admonition against showing any affection in front of Michel but luckily, Michel's otherwise occupied with his paper and doesn't see it – perhaps he's studiously ignoring us so he won't be jealous. Whatever the case, Michel doesn't turn to see us and so I let Julien kiss me more deeply, because I miss him. I want him.

"Listen, Eve," Julien says when we finally end the kiss. "I have some bad news," he says, avoiding my eyes.

"What?" I say, a bad feeling starting in the pit of my stomach.

He purses his lips and then meets my gaze, his eyes intense. "Soren's sending me on patrol, along with Procel and two others of the Twelve. He's going to be releasing the antidote soon and he wants us to reconnoiter the area before sending a force to be near Blackstone's residence, to ambush him and take him out. Once we have that set up, we'll be back. But you have to know that eventually, Blackstone will try to come after us. When that happens, as one of the oldest ascended vampires, I'm tasked with the job of capturing him, with the assistance of Procel. Of course, I couldn't be happier."

"Julien!" I say, alarm filling me at the prospect of him leaving. "Why?"

"Once Blackstone realizes that we've got the antidote, he's going to want to retaliate. We have to stop him before he can. That falls to me, as the most seasoned warrior besides the Twelve."

"What chance do you have against his forces? He's very strong..."

Julien shrugs. "Soren's been building his forces for years. All his compounds across the country, all the ex-soldiers he's hired and has been using to train his forces. He's as ready as he'll ever be to fight Blackstone."

I nod, and of course had already realized that Soren was preparing long before the plague struck. I still don't want Julien to go.

"I thought Soren wanted us all together." Even when I say it, I realize that it's just me being upset that Julien will be gone and possibly will die in battle.

"He does, but he's pushed his agenda up and will release the first antidote in a very short time – maybe this week. If so, I have to be prepared. We have to get ready to hit Blackstone before he's able to respond. Today's mission will be in preparation for that eventuality."

I slip my arms around Julien's neck and pull him against me. "I don't want you to go," I say.

He puts his arms around me and kisses me, his kiss hungry and desperate. "I can't be with you, Eve," he says, despite how much he responds to me. "I have to just say goodbye and go now, but I'll be back in a few days."

"I don't like it that you're the one who has to capture Blackstone," I say. "He's older than you and could potentially kill you."

Julien shakes his head. "Soren's promised me that you and I will be together once this is all over, if I bring Blackstone back. I have to believe that's true. It's all that keeps me going."

I kiss him back deeply, my tears starting, a darkness welling up inside of me – fear that Julien will die to capture Blackstone. He said he didn't want to live without me, but now I have to face the prospect that he'll die in battle and I won't want to live without him.

You get everything you want, Eve. Just do what I ask. That's all.

I want Julien, I think to myself.

He's yours, if you comply. It's that simple.

I kiss Julien again and again, not caring if Michel sees us. He has to understand that I must say goodbye. Michel knows I love Julien and that Julien loves me. I know he'll be jealous, but I can't stop myself, and tears run down my cheeks.

"I don't want you to go..." I say, wiping my eyes. I get out of bed when he stands up, and I quickly pull on my robe.

"I'll be back soon," he says and smiles softly. "Just a day or two." We stand beside the bed and he runs his fingers over my cheek, slipping through my tears. "Capturing and then killing Blackstone is what I've been waiting for all these years. To finally get revenge against Blackstone for what he did to me and my men. For using us and then trying to kill us. And to stop him from retaliating and releasing more of the plague."

"I know," I say, for it's true. Julien has wanted revenge against Blackstone for what he did to Julien and his unit. It was what motivated him when we first met and became lovers. Julien has been a fearless warrior, for so long and if anyone has the ability to capture Blackstone and bring him back to Soren's compound, it would be him. There were few who would have that knowledge of tactics and experience with special ops. Just a few older ascended vampires and the Twelve.

I'm glad that Procel is going along with Julien. Of course, I'm sad that Julien is going at all but I know I have to let him go. Julien kisses me once more and then leaves me beside the bed. He goes over to the sitting room and sits in a chair next to Michel. The two speak in soft voices and I try to get control over myself but my heart feels incredibly heavy and I fear I won't see him again.

Calm down, Eve. You get everything your heart desires. Just cooperate.

I'd like to believe Soren, but I can't. I can't trust him, but there's nothing else to do, so I do nothing. Instead, I go to the bathroom and splash water over my face, then dry my eyes off with a clean towel.

I'm staring in the mirror at my swollen eyes and red nose when the door opens and Michel pops his head in the room.

"I'm sorry, Eve," he says, and I can see that he means it. "I don't want Julien to go either."

I nod. As much as he's jealous of Julien, there can be no doubt that Michel loves his brother and doesn't want him to die. Still, I'm overly emotional and cover my eyes, trying to hold back a sob, but I fail.

He comes closer and wraps his arms around me and despite everything, despite how I've promised that I won't be with him, how I decided to never be with Michel again, at that moment, I can't resist him. He rocks me gently in his arms, whispering in my ear, "It's okay, Eve, it's okay..." and when I finally get my sobs under control, we stand like that, our arms around each other, our bodies touching. "He'll be back in a few days. This is just a routine mission to scout out positions. He won't be in very much danger."

I know I shouldn't do it, but I think of getting all my wishes, of having what I want to come true. I think of what Soren promised and all I have to do is offer myself, and I will get it.

Do I trust Soren?

Will he deliver on the goods?

I know I have to wait until I see his plague antidote work so although I could very easily right now kiss Michel and see if he takes it further, I don't.

I extract myself from Michel's warm, very human and very tantalizing embrace and wipe my eyes.

"I'm sorry," I say and turn to the basin so I can wash my face once more to get rid of the tears. "I'm just so overwrought because of everything that's happened."

"I know," Michel says and his voice is so soft, so warm and sympathetic. "You've been through so much. Finding out about your mother, becoming a vampire, meeting Dylan, your death and resurrection. It's a lot to take in during a lifetime, let alone in a year."

I straighten my robe and then we leave the bathroom and go to the sitting room. I take a seat and Michel sits across from me.

"What's going to happen now?" I ask him, and then I shake my head. "I mean, with Soren. What's his agenda? He promised to release the antidote this week in return for Julien joining Procel to capture Blackstone."

Michel leans forward, his arms resting on his knees, his hands clasped.

"When the antidote's ready, we're going to go to Soren's research facility and inspect the premises so you can see what he's been doing – what Dylan and Soren have been doing. Then, he'll release the antidote in a specific area to show the world what he can do. It will be timed to get the most audience for him and the Twelve so people will know it was them who stepped in and saved humanity, of course."

"Of course," I say. "He wants to get maximum results. Where will he release it? How will people know? Haven't all the telecommunications systems fallen?"

"Not all," Michel says. "The military has some communications via satellite and there are old Ham Radio operators and telegraph operators out there who keep communications up. But you're right," he says and shakes his head sadly. "The world has fallen, due to the disruption along the Eastern Seaboard and Western Europe where the plague was released."

I sit there and consider what he's said. I expected that very quickly the world would fall due to the destruction of so much of the fossil fuels and petroleum products in the fallout zones, not to mention the utter disruption in services. How many people have died?

It's impossible to tell. It makes me hate Blackstone more and more. It also makes me hate Soren for not stopping it sooner.

Patience, Eve... Even I have limitations. I didn't see everything coming. I didn't have the ability to stop it. That's why I resurrected the Twelve in the first place. Then you had to come along and put us all in stasis or this whole process would have been much farther along...

Don't put the blame on me, I think. *No one cared to tell me the truth or I would have been fighting Blackstone sooner.*

I turn to look at Michel. He must wonder what happens when I zone out.

Fair enough.

I don't respond to Soren. Instead, I smile at Michel and reach out to take his hand.

"Thanks for being here for me."

Michel smiles. "Of course," he says softly. "Always. You can count on me." He lets go of my hand, as if he's reluctant to touch me. "Now, you must be hungry. Let me get you a tray with something to eat."

I nod. "Thank you."

Michel goes to the door, and speaks with a guard outside. He returns to the room and I decide to get dressed. I go to my wardrobe and pick something warm – a nice sweater and a pair of jeans plus some warm socks and an undershirt. I won't look very fashionable but it's cold in the compound and since my 'resurrection', I can't seem to get warm.

Michel leaves me alone for a while and I wait for the servant to bring me my meal tray, reading over the print papers that come in the morning. There's one that summarizes all the news for the affected zone and whatever information can be obtained at the barricades, shouted over the tops of the barricades lined with barbed wire.

It's pretty grim, with little foreign trade taking place due to fears of contaminating any fossil fuel supplies or products made with petroleum. As a result, many of the countries that used to trade have become more insular, keeping their resources to themselves and making do. It's been only a very short time since the plague was released but already people are starting to cope. Those with the most basic skills have become the new power brokers in society – carpenters, plumbers, and anyone with any experience in medicine or farming are now the leaders, while those who were educated in the modern technology have become redundant. They've had to start learning the old skills that previously were replaced by machines run on fossil fuels.

Countries lacking an internal system of farming and food production have suffered, from all accounts, as trade between agricultural producers and consumers have all but stopped. Hundreds of thousands are starving in some of the wealthiest nations on earth.

We're lucky here, only because Soren knew what was coming – or had an idea. But it will be a long lean winter.

CHAPTER 14

SOREN pretty much leaves me alone for a couple of days, and I spend my day doing much the same thing – reading news papers, and spending time in Soren's huge library, reading old books, and being impatient for something to happen. I try to keep my mind occupied because Julien's gone and in danger, but I find myself thinking of him almost constantly. Each time I push Michel for information, he shrugs and tells me we have to wait until everything's in place before we can go to Soren's laboratories where the plague antidote is being manufactured.

I wish I could be there now, but there's nothing I can do without Soren's leave.

Instead, I wonder if Soren isn't hoping that Michel and I will somehow fall into each others arms just because we're spending time together day in and day out.

Instead, we tend to keep our distance. Michel is polite and helpful, but he doesn't push me and spends a great deal of time away from our rooms. I don't know what he does, but as the priest for the parish, I imagine he has priestly duties to fulfill.

So it's with pleasure that on the third day since my resurrection,

Soren calls for Michel and me to pack a bag for our trip to the facilities south of Boston.

As I'm finishing packing, Michel returns to the room and hands me the morning paper. In it, I see mention of a meeting of rebels, held outside Boston at the Cathedral, who are promising to find a way to stop the plague's spread. Some have said that it's Soren who is leading the group of rebels. I find it surprising that Soren is trying to drum up support for himself by publicizing his impending works of wonder. It's as if he's deliberately inviting Blackstone to retaliate.

"Why is Soren letting it slip out that he's planning on stopping the plague?" I ask Michel as we sit at a table together and have our breakfast.

"It's a rumor," Michel says and points to the headline. "He's making sure to keep it stated that way. He and Blackstone have agreed that Soren will do some kind of miraculous event that will get Soren the power in the churches. Soren probably will deny it and point to his plans to protect church goers from roving bands of vampires…" Michel rolls his eyes as if he can barely stand the subterfuge.

"Blackstone plans to let the plague go completely around the world, right?" I ask. "He doesn't want it to stop."

Michel shakes his head. "No. He wants it to be total. Soren has provisionally agreed, but will stop it before that happens. Blackstone knows this, or should know it, but he also has his endgame. However, it's in Soren's interest to make people think he's planning on stopping it. When he's ready, he'll do the public event and own up to it. Then, it will be the final battle between them – Soren and Blackstone. Blackstone thinks he'll beat Soren. He won't."

"Why do you say that?"

"He's underestimated who and what Soren is."

I don't say anything for a moment. "You want Soren to win," I say, watching Michel's face. "But you don't want Soren to be as powerful as he wants to be."

"I want a lot of things, Eve," Michel says. "Let's hope I get them."

I nod, understanding that he can't tell me what he really wants. I know now that Soren can't read Michel, as much as Soren wishes I didn't know it.

When we're finished eating, one of the servants takes away our trays and then a guard pops his head in the room.

"Lord Soren says to tell you that we're ready to depart."

Michel stands. "I guess it's time to go and see what wonders Soren has in store for us."

I grab my bag and follow Michel and the guard out the door, wondering if what Soren promised will really happen. I have a hard time believing that Soren will stop the plague but I want it to be true.

We enter the large vehicle, and Michel sits beside me while Soren and Kael sit across from us. I don't like being in the same vehicle as Kael, but I have no choice. He seems to be Soren's best friend among the Twelve so I take in a deep breath and try not to let my distaste for him come through in my behavior.

We drive west from Cambridge to a facility in Worcester that looks like an old telecommunications warehouse. There's a huge fence surrounding it with barbed wire and numerous guards pacing back and forth with weapons slung over their shoulders.

A guard at a gate waves us through after glancing at the driver's credentials and peeking into the rear of the vehicle. We drive up a long driveway to the side entrance, where several guards stand at attention. In a field beside the facility, hundreds of solar panels are tilted to face the sun. On the roof, hundreds of other panels, their metal faces glinting in the dim winter light. One guard meets the vehicle and opens the door for Soren, who nods at the man and then gets out, waiting for us at the entrance.

A man with round horn rimmed glasses and a lab coat greets us. Soren introduces him to us as Dr. Mark Wu, a professor of bioengineering who once worked for one of the largest genetic technology companies in the world.

Dr. Wu takes us through the facility and I'm curious about how they are able to run a biotech lab, given the challenges they face due to the plague.

He stops and turns to us. "Everything has been re-engineered to require no plastics or fossil fuel-based technology."

"How long have you been preparing for this?" I ask. "You must have known for some time to re-engineer everything to have done all this."

"We have been anticipating some kind of event that would knock out the grid for at least eighteen months. We did all the redesign a couple of years ago and so when the plague struck, we were ready."

I glance at Soren. "That was great foresight."

Dr. Wu shakes his head. "Scientists have long thought that the grid was far too vulnerable to cyber attack or to some kind of solar event. It was only good business to prepare."

I nod but don't say anything. I can't really blame Soren for preparing, if he's know all along that this or something like this was in the works, but still... I can't help myself. As we walk down the long hallway behind Dr. Wu, I pull up beside Soren.

"Did you know all along that this was going to happen?" I say, glancing at him from the corner of my eye to see his response. If he's surprised I ask, he doesn't show it. "I mean, do you already know the outcome or was there always the possibility that something different from what you plan will happen?"

"That's the sixty-four-thousand-dollar question," Soren says and turns to me as we walk down the hall. "I can see many ends and have to decide which one I want to see through. It's a game of chess, Eve. A game of chess."

I nod and fall back beside Michel. "When did you start seeing the future?" I ask, having a vague notion that his prescience came on when he ascended.

"I think I always had the ability to see various futures, but I thought I was conjuring them up in my own head. Once I became a vampire, the ability seemed to heighten, but I was never able to use it for any end. It was only my ascendance that seemed to solidify the power of seeing various threads of the future and how decisions might change it."

We finally enter a large production facility where there is a large glassed-in lab with all kinds of technology that looks like it came out of a chem lab somewhere. Workers dressed in full hazmat suits mill around, moving from one table to another, looking at computer screens, and microscopes.

"This is our lab," Dr. Wu says. "Here, we've been working on the virus, analyzing its structure and function, trying to replicate it, figure out its capabilities. We want to harness it and turn it on itself, cure the plague by reversing its ability to denature petroleum products. We're using retroviruses to do so, and will insert a sequence of RNA into the plague's genome to halt its ability to destroy hydrocarbons."

I nod and it's then that one of the hazmat suited workers comes over, stands in the anteroom where his suit is blown by some liquid to clean him off. He's dried by powerful blowers and then he removes his suit.

It's Dylan. He smiles when he sees me among the group of visitors.

"There you are," he says and comes right over to me, giving me a hug. "Soren said he'd bring you for a visit and demonstration."

Dylan turns to Soren and gives him a shake and pulls him closer for a hug and it surprises me. I would never think that Dylan is fond of Soren, but perhaps getting his sister back alive and cured is the price of Dylan's love and loyalty.

"We're doing more than a mere demonstration," Soren says and pats Dylan on the back. "We're pushing the schedule up and will be releasing the first batch of antivirus inside the red zone."

Dylan looks surprised. "How come so soon?" he says, frowning. "I thought we were on schedule for next week."

"I have some PR issues to deal with," Soren says with a smirk and glances at me. "Gotta prove I can do it to some of my very tough customers."

I don't say anything. It surprises me that Soren is so determined to push Michel and me together. Why does he want it so badly? Purely to satisfy his desire for revenge?

Soren says nothing to me in reply, either mentally or out loud so we move on, with Dylan joining the group. Next, Dr. Wu escorts us outside the main building to a hanger that is hidden behind a grove of tall trees. Outside, tethered to the ground, is a dirigible. A zeppelin. As well, there are several weather balloons lying on the ground.

"This is how you'll disperse the agent?" I ask.

"Precisely," Dr. Wu responds. "We are going to use the same dispersal methods that Blackstone used – an aerosol, sent to the upper atmosphere and released so that it falls out over a wide expanse. There only needs to be a small amount spread per hectare of land, due to the self-replicating nature of the nanobot. Once it gets to a certain altitude, it starts to replicate, using energy from the surrounding environment. If it comes into contact with the plague virus, it will stop it from replicating."

Dr. Wu smiles proudly.

"That's what we plan on doing once we have all our labs working at full capacity," Soren says, and he sounds so pleased with himself. "Next week will be the full launch, but today, instead of a demonstration, we'll be releasing it in the red zone."

Soren waves his hand and the technicians start to load machinery onto the dirigible's undercarriage.

"That's the dispersal mechanism," Dr. Wu says, pointing to the machine. "It will release the antidote once it is in the stratosphere. The wind and jet stream will take the particles and spread them over a wide area. We should start seeing it's effect within twenty-four hours."

Hope wells up inside of me that perhaps Soren can actually do what he claims – and will do it. I'll know within a day whether it works. It looks like this is all coming together and Soren means business.

I can hope.

"You don't have to hope, Eve," Soren says out loud. "I'm a man of my word about this. I want to stop the destruction of all fossil fuels. I happen to like modern technology, but we have made some amazing technological breakthroughs and so while the age of fossil fuels will linger on for a few more decades, the age of clean energy will surpass it very soon."

I nod and if what he says is true, I'll be happy. The age of fossil fuels needs to come to an end, but not abruptly the way it has, with hundreds of thousands of people dying and starving.

Soon, the technicians have the dirigible loaded and ready to go. They turn on the engines that power the propellers and up it rises, the sound a soft hum compared to an airplane. It keeps rising, still tethered to the ground until it reaches a certain height and the technicians release it. It bobs up higher and sets off, increasing altitude with each passing moment. Then, while we watch, it starts to deploy the antidote.

"Isn't it kind of low?" I ask. "It's not in the stratosphere yet."

"This is just the demonstration we already had planned for today," Dr. Wu responds. "The weather balloons will take the agent into the stratosphere and release it over the next few hours and the agent will start falling back into the lower atmosphere over the next few days. It will take a week of such releases coordinated across the affected zone to nullify the existing plague and stop it from spreading."

As we watch, other white-suited technicians inflate the weather balloons, which are released once they are filled and go high into the atmosphere to the edge of space. Their sleek silvery fabric shimmers in the winter sunlight, the material rippling as the balloon inflates and rises up. Gusts of helium fill the balloons and they start to lift off the ground, pulling the machines meant to disperse the agent beneath them.

It's all very exciting to watch and know that the plague will be stopped. I'm starting to feel good about this cooperation with Soren, as much as I dislike him.

Dislike me, Eve? I'm crushed...

I don't respond, but frown for it's too easy to forget that he can access my mind whenever he wants. Then, I do respond.

That's why I dislike you, Soren. If you understood humanity, you'd understand why.

Of course, he can't resist.

Oh, I understand humanity very well. I'm using that understanding to get what I want and give what humanity needs. Just watch me.

We continue to watch the weather balloons float off as a trio into the sky, pulled by the prevailing winds.

"We'll come back tomorrow and check whether the agent has been effective," Soren says, "but as I've already shown, we can stop the virus using our technology. It's just a matter of dispersing it widely enough."

Finally, when all the balloons are no longer visible, we troop back inside the facility and go to a boardroom where we sit and have some tea and coffee. Dr. Wu spends some time pointing to a map on the wall, which shows the earth's land masses. Areas where the plague has been released are colored in red. He points out where the various facilities are located, the labs that produce the agent and will disperse it once everything is ready.

Michel and I sit side by side, and I'm sure it pleases Soren to see us together. I'll have to follow through with my agreement to make a pass at Michel once I have actual physical proof that the agent is working and will be dispersed widely enough to stop any further damage to our petroleum supplies.

I glance at Michel from the corner of my eye and watch him as he drinks his tea. He's been very quiet the whole time, not asking questions or commenting. He looks very handsome in his vestments and I feel a bit bad that I find him attractive, even now when he's in his priestly garb. I can't deny my attraction to him – it has never waned. But no matter how I feel about him, I know that in the long run, Michel isn't happy sharing me with Julien, nor is Julien entirely happy with that prospect. I have to choose one of them and in the end, Julien is far more in tune with me about almost everything.

Michel turns and looks in my eyes. It may be just my imagination, but I get the sense that he's hurt by my thoughts. Can he read me as well? I thought now that he's mortal, he has no access to my thoughts, but perhaps his prescience and telepathy are still strong enough.

He turns away and places his teacup down. Soren abruptly stands up from the table and I figure it must be time to leave. We all follow him and Dr. Wu out of the facility to the vehicles that brought us here. I sit beside Michel once more, across from Soren and Kael. We drive off and I watch the facility disappear into the distance as we take the road back to Cambridge.

"Well, Eve?" Soren says, a self-satisfied grin on his face. "What did you think? Aren't you pleased that we're stopping the plague?"

"Of course," I say and nod. "Thank you. I wish it could have been stopped sooner."

"Never satisfied," he says and shakes his head. "I do hope you'll be satisfied tomorrow, in more ways than one." He winks at me and I know what he means. He hopes that Michel and I will make love so he can feel all pompous that he was right.

I don't believe Michel will break his vows again, but I could be wrong. Michel was very quick to lie on top of me that day when I kissed him. He would have probably followed through if I hadn't stopped him.

I sigh and look out the window as we drive back to Soren's compound, wondering what the night will bring. All I want is a glass of blood and to lie in bed with Julien and forget everything for a while.

We arrive at the front entrance and Michel escorts me to our rooms. Before he enters, he pulls me aside, and we stand outside the door.

"Have faith, Eve," he says softly. "If not in God, then at least have faith in me. You know I love you. You know I'm trying to do the right thing."

I smile at him. "I know. I understand now," I say, thinking about what Soren has planned, understanding why Michel has been so secretive all this time. "But I'm afraid I can't have faith. I know you'll do what's right because of your past behavior. I have evidence I can count on. I don't need faith." I reach up and cup his cheek, my heart filling with affection for him. Whatever else he is, he is a heroic man who is trying to do what is right and what is best.

"Thank you," he says and leans in to my cupped hand, his beautiful eyes closing. "I wish..." he says, his voice trailing off.

"Shh," I say, because I know what he wishes. He wishes that none of this had to happen. That we had been able to escape this fate that lies before us both.

Then he opens the door and I go inside. He doesn't join me and I frown, wondering why.

"Where are you going?" I ask.

"I have business to attend to. I'll be back later."

I nod and enter our rooms to find Julien sitting by the huge arched window reading the daily paper, his head bent over to read in the dim light of the cloudy day.

My heart leaps for there was a part of me that still worried something could happen to him. I go up behind him and wrap my arms around his neck, nuzzling his skin beneath his ear where his tattoo is.

"There you are," he says softly and puts down the paper. He turns his head and reaches back, pulling me around and down onto his lap. I circle his neck with my arms and we kiss, deeply and passionately. When he pulls away, he strokes my hair with one hand, his eyes moving over my face. "I was jealous that Soren didn't let me come along, but I suppose he was trying to do that, so I tried not to let it bother me too much."

"Forget Soren," I say and kiss him again. "Kiss me. I was so afraid something would happen to you. I want to lose myself in you."

I kiss him again and he responds, but then it's as if he has another thought and pulls away from me.

"I'm sorry," he says and shakes his head softly. "I don't think it's a good idea. Michel may come in at any time…"

"Michel said he had some work to do. Let's go into the bedroom and close the door. He'll understand what that means."

Julien shakes his head, and I see he's determined, and I wonder if Soren has compelled him to not sleep with me until I do my duty and try to seduce Michel away from his vows.

I sigh and give up, my head leaning on Julien's shoulder. "All right," I say and stroke Julien's very square jaw with a few day's worth of scruff that I find so undeniably attractive. "You can't fight City Hall."

"What's that supposed to mean?"

"You know what it means. Soren's probably compelled you not to sleep with me until I've done his bidding."

Julien frowns but doesn't say anything. I imagine he's not able to speak about Soren compelling him either. It's so frustrating, I want to pound something, but instead, I sigh and try to enjoy sitting on Julien's lap, our arms around each other.

That will have to suffice until I've done my duty.

CHAPTER 15

WE SPEND the evening reading and talking in quiet voices, waiting for our call for dinner with Soren. Finally, at about seven o'clock, Michel returns and pops his head into the room.

"Dinner's ready," he says. "Soren asks that you both come along."

Julien raises his eyebrows and I feel a bit of a jolt of adrenaline, wondering what Soren has prepared for us. What torture will he try to put us through? Probably sit me between Michel and Julien just to reinforce that he's the puppet master and we're all his puppets.

It makes me mad, but I have learned that I have to stop resisting everything and try to bend and be flexible. I have to try to go with my gut instinct more often.

My gut instinct tells me that all this posturing about Michel and Julien and me is really just amusement for Soren. He's lived an incredibly long existence and is bored to death. But since he's immortal, he can't die, so he has to do everything in his power to amuse himself. Seeing the three of us together amuses him.

I determine at that moment to amuse him.

"Just so the two of you understand," I say and lay a hand on both their shoulders as we walk down the hallway to the dining room, "I love you both. I always will."

Michel frowns and turns to me and I feel Julien's eyes on me as well. "Why do you say that?" he asks, his voice low and hesitant.

"I don't want to fight any longer," I say. "I spent far too much time fighting for the sake of fighting. From now on, I'm going to choose my battles and fighting with Soren over the two of you is not a battle I want to fight any longer."

We walk along and I can tell that they're both struggling with what I'm saying.

"That doesn't mean that we'll have a happy little *ménage a trois* or anything," I say, smiling at them both. "But I won't let it bother me any longer that Soren wishes we would. I understand why he wants it. Let's try to just enjoy each other's company and not be jealous or upset if one of us talks to the other. Can you both do that?"

I look in both of their faces, one after the other, searching to see if they understand and can accept my proposal.

"Let's not let him win," I say firmly. "Let's not let him decide how we will be with each other. Let's be the way we want to be. Let's be kind and considerate and loving, no matter what Soren tries to put us through. Okay?"

I turn to them both. We stand in the hallway outside the dining room.

"Okay," Michel says.

We turn to Julien and he shrugs. "I'll do what I can, but you know my situation. I can't make any promises."

I nod and touch his shoulder affectionately. "I understand. He's compelled you and there's only so much you can do that's completely free." I turn to Michel. "So Michel and I will have to be the ones to act responsibly and thoughtfully. Right?"

Michel opens the door. "After you," he says and ushers me inside the dining room, his hand at the small of my back to help me inside. Then he does the same to Julien, who walks beside me to the large dining table. A number of the Twelve are already seated and I nod to a few of them. I see there are place cards at each setting so I search for my name. There it is, precisely where I thought it would be, a few seats down from Soren, on the right side. Michel's place card is closest to him, followed my mine, and then Julien is on the other side of me. I smile to myself, for Soren is getting so predictable.

Julien pulls out my chair and then I sit, waiting while Michel and Julien are seated on either side of me. A servant comes right over with a carafe of blood and pours for us, while he pours wine for Michel.

Michel turns to us and holds out his glass of wine. "To the three of us. We started this journey together and let's hope we all end it happily, with the world saved from further ruin and on its way back to recovery."

"Hear, hear," I say and raise my glass of blood, clinking our glasses together. Then I turn to Julien and we touch glasses. I look in his eyes, wanting to make a connection with him so he knows I'm there with him, and our eyes meet. He smiles softly, his eyes no longer dark.

We drink and wait for Soren and Procel to join us. I note that Kael is missing as well. The two of them seem to be the most powerful of the Twelve and the ones that Soren spends most of his time with.

We listen to the others speaking, and I hear news of the day. How the agent has been released all along the Eastern Seaboard and will be released elsewhere in the next few days. How once it is proven to have stopped the progress of the plague, that there will be a big event that will announce Soren's accomplishments to the world. How their technicians have been working night and day to restore power to the communications networks so that Soren can broadcast on the old cable networks.

All of this has been undertaken in such a short time. I wonder if this wasn't in the works all along and Soren's and the Twelve's stasis was just a speed bump along the way. If so, I have to admit a grudging admiration for his planning.

Was he planning even back when we were in Jordan?

I thought he was trying to influence the wars, but perhaps he was trying to set up his networks to respond to the plague...

Why can't I do both?

I frown and then the doors open and in walk Soren, Procel and Kael.

They enter with a burst of applause from the Twelve and Soren smiles at all of us. Several of the Twelve stand at their places and so we do as well, ushering them in while they take their seats at the head of the table.

"Thank you, brethren," Soren says and he sounds so officious. He and Kael and Procel stand at their places and bow slightly while the rest of the Twelve clap. Finally, they stop and once Soren sits, the rest of us sit as well and the servants quickly fill their glasses with blood and wine.

Soren catches my eye and smiles, and I make sure I smile back. I raise my glass of blood to him, nodding in acknowledgement. It still irks me a bit to do so, but I'm determined to fight the right battles.

Our meal is delicious, of course, and I try to enjoy it and not think about the others who are going hungry because of the effects of the plague.

The talk is about the antidote to the plague and then the cure for vampirism. My ears perk up when Soren begins to speak about it.

"We're working on a way to disseminate the cure," he says. "The way we initially intended. We're working out the kinks right now but should have it ready to deploy very soon," he says and turns to me with a smile. "Dylan is my main man on that project. And then I expect to call in a few markers."

I nod but say nothing. I know what he means. He intends for me to help him do some feat of marvel so he can cement his rule in the Church. He wants to become the head of the Church in Rome. He wants to be worshiped as a god. Not THE God, but a god. He thinks humans need gods to keep them in line and keep them happy.

I don't even let myself argue with this goal in my head. It is what it is, but I find it an effort not to immediately go into why I reject that kind of future.

Still, I blot my disapproval out of my mind. It doesn't matter in the end whether I support Soren. He will do what he will do, and if it means Humanity will be saved – from the plague and from Dominion, and if vampirism will be eradicated – I'll accept what Soren wants. People who want to believe will believe. People like me who can't believe can go on our merry way.

We finish and after dinner is cleared away, Soren leans back in his chair and eyeballs the three of us sitting a few chairs down. I feel his eyes on me and I feel like my best move would be to leave now and get out of the room in case he wants to toy with us some more.

Toy with you? Moi? Eve... you have such a low opinion of me... I'm crushed.

Of course, I know he isn't crushed at all. He's smirking. He enjoys manipulating us all. We're his pawns in this game of power. And Pawns are notorious for being sacrificed to save the Queen and King.

Ahhh, but you are the Queen and King... So don't worry your little ass off.

I look over at him and he's frowning now, glaring at me from over his glass of blood. I don't understand why he's mad at me for being afraid of him. He's the most powerful being on the planet and could kill all of us with a thought if he wanted. I have no power over him. If I don't cooperate, he'll just kill me and then create another one, hopefully who will be more malleable than I am.

I wish I could know for certain that he'll follow through on his plans...

I take a final drink of my wine and then stand up. "Please excuse me," I say and a servant pulls my chair away from the table. "I've had quite a week."

"You have, poor girl," Soren says and stands, bowing low. "Go and rest. Have a nice hot bath," he says and snaps his fingers, pointing to one of the servants. "Go and make sure she has a nice hot bath in her room. Build up the fire so the room is nice and warm. Don't want my queen to be sick or too tired..."

I nod and then leave the room, noting his reference to 'queen' in response to my thoughts about being a pawn.

I wonder, as I leave, who will be coming with me – will it be Julien or Michel who comes back to the room? As I walk down the hallway, I check and neither of them follow me, which surprises me. I would have thought Julien would relish some alone time with me, but no. I thought Michel might come back to ensure I arrived safely and was taken care of properly.

I enter my room and sit by the window while the servants start to fill my tub with buckets of hot water. When it's finally filled, and the scent of eucalyptus fills my nose, I'm happy to remove my clothes and step into the tub, leaning back and sighing with happiness as the heat infuses my body, and the aroma of the eucalyptus soothes my senses.

I lie that way for quite a while, until the water begins to cool, wondering when Julien or Michel will return, but neither do. Finally, I get out and wrap a cotton robe around me as a towel and finish drying off in front of the mirror. I dress in my nightgown and robe before brushing my hair out and then brushing my teeth. Finally, I go over to the sitting room and pick up the newspaper but I've already scanned the headlines.

When I don't hear anyone coming down the hallway to the room, I turn out all the lights except for one by the mantle and then crawl into bed, pulling the thick coverlet over my head.

Sleep overtakes me before I can barely close my eyes.

CHAPTER 16

LATER, much later by the chiming of the clock, I wake up and see that the room is still empty and I'm alone. I expected to see Julien and Michel in the room, seated by the fire or sleeping in their own rooms, but nothing. I sit up and frown. Are they okay? Immediately, I worry that something's happened to them because I can't imagine they would stay away so long from the room. It's after midnight, and I've been alone and sleeping for a couple of hours. I rise and go to the window, checking outside to see what's going on in the courtyard. I see torches are lit and a crowd of people have gathered, but I can't tell what's going on.

Finally, I pull on my robe and slip on my shoes, before making my way down the hall. Before I get to the stairs, one of the guards sees me and bars my way.

"Sorry, miss, but you're not allowed to go any farther."

I frown and try to peek around to see what's going on but I can't make anything out. I hear shouts and the sound of metal clashing, but that's all.

"What's happening?" I say, my heart rate increasing. "Is there a fight?"

"I'm sorry, but I can't tell you, miss. You'll have to go back to your room."

"You can't tell me or you won't tell me?" I ask, indignant.

"Can't. Don't know myself. Now, please go back to your room."

He points down the hallway back to my rooms and I return, my gut in a knot about whatever it is that's taking place outside in the courtyard. Is there some kind of attack under way?

I try to search in my mind for Julien, but we haven't shared blood for some time and I get no reading from him. Soren isn't peeking into my mind to tell me what's happening, so I'm left to sit by the window, watching the shadows and light play off the wrought iron fences, and listen to the sound of men's voices. They sound upset, like they're angry, and I think there must be some kind of fight. Are they rebels, attacking the compound? Who would attack?

Blackstone… He must have discovered that Soren is releasing the antidote to the plague and is now here to pay Soren back for the betrayal. My heart skips a beat when I think of it, for surely he'll be angry with Dylan for helping Soren with the cure to the plague. He was supposed to be helping Blackstone not the other way around.

I close my eyes, and try to calm myself, because I don't want to think of anything happening to the brother I only just met and found once more, or my father, and I'm sure Blackstone will retaliate against us both. I want the two of us to be close for the rest of our existences, however long that may be.

Finally, I'm unable to stay in the room any longer and pull on a warm robe and my slippers so I can go to the front and see what's going on. When I arrive at the place where my usual guard is posted, he's not there, which makes me even more nervous. I think that perhaps I should go back and get my sword and stake, just in case, but since the house is empty, I tip toe down the stairs to the main floor and find the entrance. Several servants cluster around the great front entryway, peering out between the crack between the open doors, crowding around each other in an effort to see what's happening. I join them, but can't see a thing and so I go to the front reception room and look through the window. Outside, I see several soldiers with their weapons drawn surrounding a single man who has his hands fastened behind his back. Several other men lie on the ground and I see dark stains spreading out on the snow beneath them. *Blood.*

There's been a fight and there have been deaths. I want to run out and see if Julien is okay, but when I see him striding up the steps to the entry, my body relaxes and I sigh with relief. He's okay...

Then I glance at the remaining men standing around the bodies and see that Michel is there as well, dressed in his vestments, his hair blowing in the wind. He kneels down next to one body and is administering last rites, his hand resting on the dying man's shoulder.

Julien enters the building and the servants fall back, giving him room. I rush into the room and go to him, but when he sees me, he frowns.

"Eve, you should be in your room," he says and comes to me, taking hold of my shoulders and shaking me. I can tell his body is still tense from the fight so I wrap my arms around him and squeeze.

"I was afraid that you were injured or even killed," I say and close my eyes, my head resting against his shoulder.

"I'm fine," he says softly, then I feel his body relax. He wraps his arms around me and kisses the top of my head.

"What happened?" I ask and pull away, searching his face. He has a wound, from some blade, running down his brow to his cheek. Luckily, it's missed his eye and more luckily, he'll heal once he gets some blood.

"Blackstone's forces attacked, but it was really nothing. Maybe just a warning to expect more. We easily took them down. We have one captive and will interrogate him, find out what's going on and what they're planning."

I take Julien's hand and lead him up the stairs to our rooms. "You need some blood," I say. "And not just any old human blood."

Once we're in our rooms, I pull aside my robe to expose my neck and breast. "Here," I say and put my hand behind his head. "Drink my blood. You'll heal more quickly."

He doesn't hesitate, and I feel his cool lips on my neck and he bites down without resistance, drinking a few mouthfuls of my blood, which has more healing properties than ordinary blood.

Soon, he pulls away and closes his eyes. I know the feeling. It's ecstasy.

"Come over to the fire," I say and pull him to the two wing chairs beside the fire. "Have a seat. Let me clean you off."

I go to the bathroom and wet a washcloth, then return to find Julien removing his shirt, which is torn, sliced through by some very sharp blade. When his shirt is off, I admire his well-muscled physique even though I've seen it a hundred times or more. His washboard abs are stained with blood and his broad chest and shoulder have several stab wounds. They heal before my eyes, my blood working wonders on his injuries. All that's left in a moment or two are pinkish lines where the open wounds once were. I start to wipe him off, removing the blood that has run down and stained his perfect fair skin. I feel his eyes on me while I clean him off, and when I glance up into them, I see lust and love.

"I'm leaving right away," he says, his voice throaty.

"What?" I say in shock. "Where are you going?" But I know already. He's going to fight Blackstone.

I can read his mind now that we've shared blood. Soren has already given him his orders.

"Oh, Julien," I say and frown. "I wish you wouldn't go..."

"Just part of the job of Knight," he says and grins. "You know what they say – dance to the music, you eventually have to pay the piper."

"I know, but they also say that you live by the sword, you die by the sword..."

"I won't die. Only Soren can kill me."

"Or Blackstone," I say. "He's older than you."

He reaches out and strokes my cheek. "Stop worrying. Michel said we all survive and I believe him."

I sigh and return to my job. When I'm done cleaning his face and chest, I return to the bathroom and rinse out the cloth. I stand in the bathroom and stare into the mirror, upset that Julien will be going and I'll be here, helpless to know what's happening to him.

"I want to come," I say when I return to the fire and sit at his feet, my hands on his knees. "I can't stand for you to go and maybe die while I'm stuck here, helpless to do anything."

Julien shakes his head. "Not going to happen," he says softly and strokes my cheek. "Soren needs you here to work your wonders. Besides, you aren't really strong enough to go and fight Blackstone. You're too young, even as an ascended vampire. Blackstone has much older ascended vampires than you and you'd be a sitting duck. You have to stay here. Do what you were meant to do."

"What's that? Make Soren a god?" I say in disgust and shake my head.

"Save the world," he replies. "That's your job. Me? I'm just cannon fodder."

He grins at me and I can't help but feel my eyes brim with tears. I force a smile, for I know what he means. He's always been the warrior. Always been meant to fight and die for some lord or lady or king. Now, he can't die, except at the hands of someone older than him. Even then, Soren seems to have the final say in who lives and dies. He can resurrect any vampire as long as their body is intact and they haven't been burnt to soot and cinders.

Julien sits on the edge of the tub and pulls me onto his lap. He kisses me, then he pulls away and wipes the tears off my cheeks.

"Don't cry," he says. "You know how damn hard it is to kill me." He grins again and my heart swells with love for him.

"You better come back to me," I say and point my finger at him. "If anything happened to you, I'd give up."

He shakes his head. "Don't say that," he says firmly. "You have to continue, no matter what happens. You have to do your part, Eve, whether you have Michel or me or neither of us. You're meant for more than just being our lover."

I sigh for I know what he says is true, but still... "You're right," I admit. "But that doesn't mean I have to like it."

"Fate chooses us. We don't choose it. Your fate is to save the world from tyranny."

I run my hands over his chest and smile. "Tyranny?" I say playfully.

"I thought my role was to help stop the plague and eradicate vampirism."

"That, too," he says and pulls me back down for another kiss. We linger like that, our kiss intensifying and of course my thoughts go immediately to making love with him one last time before he goes and my body responds. I feel his body respond as well, but then he pulls back and ends the kiss.

"Sorry," he says, his voice husky. "We can't. I don't have time."

"Not even for a quickie?" I say, pouting. "Surely you have five minutes for a quick hard drive against the vanity…"

"Don't tempt me," he says with a grin. "No," he says and stands up, lifting me up as he does. "I have to grab a change of clothes and meet the others in the entry. I'm probably already late as it is."

I sigh once more, resigned to him leaving, and follow him while he collects up his fresh clothes, slipping on an undershirt and then a tunic over top of it. He pulls on clean jeans and socks, and then stuffs a few more items into a backpack that was in the wardrobe.

"That's about it," he says and glances around the room. "Maybe some shaving stuff," he says and goes to the bathroom, rifling through the drawer for his razor and a bar of soap. He tucks those into pockets on the side of the bag and then slings it over his shoulder. He turns to me and reaches out, a hand behind my head. He strokes my hair and his eyes move over my face. I see love in his eyes, and it's enough to make me tear up once more, but I bite my bottom lip to stop them. He doesn't need to see my overly emotional state when he has to leave for battle.

"No tears," he says, his voice low and deep. "I'll be back in a few days for the big event."

"You better be," I say and stand on my tiptoes to kiss him. We kiss deeply and then he lets go and turns away, leaving for the door.

He doesn't look back.

I want to follow him to the front entry but instead I sit by the fire and weep.

CHAPTER 17

In about fifteen minutes I hear a commotion at the front of the building and watch as the vehicles drive off, filled with fighters. I know Julien is in the company of a number of older ascended vampires and will be safe from all but the oldest of them. Still, I'm on edge for if he does get ambushed and staked, it will be solely up to Soren to resurrect him.

Soren could always decide not to resurrect him again. Except of course, Michel would probably rebel if he didn't save Julien.

That's my one consolation – Soren has to keep Julien alive if he wants Michel to do his bidding.

Finally, when my eyes will no longer stay open, I crawl back into my bed and pull the coverlet over my head. I need to sleep.

I feel like sleeping away the days until Julien returns but inside I know that Soren will never let me do that.

Later, when the sun has risen, I wake and turn over to face the window. I have no idea how long I've slept and crane my head to see the grandfather clock in the corner. It's already mid-day and I've slept for hours.

By the fire, I see Michel has returned. He's drinking some coffee and reading the daily paper. He glances over when I sit up in bed.

"Good morning," he says softly. "I let you sleep as long as you needed. I know last night was upsetting for you."

I don't say anything, but I nod in response. The scent of coffee is enticing and so I slide out of bed and wrap my robe around me, before going to the bathroom so I can have a pee and splash my face with water. I brush my hair once I'm done and then pad out to the main rooms, and take a seat beside Michel on the other wing chair.

"There's coffee and under the dome is some eggs and bacon, plus buttered toast if you're hungry."

"Thank you," I say and dig in, not realizing how hungry I am. It has been more than twelve hours since I ate and I didn't eat a lot the previous night so my stomach growls as I prepare a plate. While I eat, I watch Michel, who says nothing but keeps his eyes on the paper.

"Tell me what happened. I didn't have much time to get the story from Julien."

Michel folds up the newspaper and turns to me, his face composed. "Obviously, Blackstone learned about Soren releasing the antidote. We knew he would and have been mobilizing troops and deploying them around Blackstone compounds, but some of his men slipped through our defenses and attacked. They killed a couple of guards before we could stop them. Julien was injured but I saw him before he went and he was healed."

I nod, glad that we have this ability to heal as long as we get blood. I wonder what will happen once we're cured of vampirism. Will we remain immortal? Will we still have the ability to heal from terrible wounds like Julien?

"What's on the agenda for today?" I ask as I drink my orange juice, which is fresh squeezed and delicious.

"We're going back to the facility to do some testing of the antidote's effectiveness. Then, I expect Soren will want to do something public to announce that he's cured the plague. After that, we'll keep working on the cure for vampirism. Eventually, Soren will want to go to Rome and take his seat in the Vatican. Maybe he'll build another Temple of Apollo or something more suited to a god, rather than The God."

Michel says it with such disdain in his voice that I'm surprised he can still work with Soren. But, I guess Michel wants to be part of any effort to take over the Holy Roman Catholic Church.

He feels an ownership of it that goes beyond merely being a priest.

"I'll get dressed," I say and leave my seat, taking my coffee with me as I go to the wardrobe and select my clothes for the day. I pick some faded jeans and a t-shirt plus a wool sweater for warmth. I take my things to the bathroom and get dressed and brush my teeth, wondering whether Michel will be strong when I make a pass and offer myself or whether he'll succumb. Part of me hates having to do this, because I don't want him to fail. But Soren seems so convinced that Michel only needs a small push…

You'll see…

I squeeze my eyes shut, but of course that will have no effect on Soren's ability to pop into my mind any time he feels like.

Anytime, Eve. Remember that…

I press my fists against my temples and try to squeeze him out of my mind, but of course it's a silly response and soon I get myself back under control and take in a deep breath, determined to ignore him in the future when he pops in for a bit of sarcasm or an attempt to bait me.

Why can't he be reasonable and only go into my mind when it matters instead of any old time when I'm thinking private thoughts? Certainly, he can't be interested in my personal musings. Hasn't he got more important things to do besides invading my mind and getting titillated by my private desires and dreams?

That's precisely what I most want, Eve. Access to every little thing. It all matters to an omnipotent being…

"You're not omnipotent," I say out loud, frowning at my reflection in the mirror.

Not yet…

I say nothing in response, but can't stop thinking *Not if I can stop it...*

Strangely enough, he doesn't respond to that. I sigh and leave the bathroom, to find Michel standing by the window, his hands folded behind his back. He turns to me and the expression on his face when he sees me is tender.

It makes my heart squeeze just a bit to see that old look in his eyes and I can't help but feel desire for him – not in the purely sexual way I do for Julien, but a general love for him and affection. I'd like, if I could, to just go up to him and put my arms around him, squeeze him tightly, and enjoy his warmth for a while. I need it, but I hold back.

That would only complicate things, because eventually it would turn to something sexual – I know it would on my part very easily. At the drop of a hat actually, if I'm honest with myself.

Instead, Michel comes to me and offers me my coat. I slip on my boots and together we leave our rooms and walk down the long hallway to where our guard stands at the ready, his weapon in his hand.

"Ready to go?" he asks Michel and Michel nods.

The guard leads us to the main entry and we take the stairs to the waiting vehicle, in which Soren and his two lieutenants are already seated. Michel and I slip in across from them and we drive off, back to the facility. When we arrive, we exit the vehicle and enter the main research building where we saw the lab that produced the antidote.

There, Dr. Wu is waiting. He smiles when he sees Soren and bows low.

Soren smiles back. "Well, Dr., what have you got for us? I expect you have proof that the antidote has counteracted the effects of the plague, and petroleum and its products can now be used in this sector?"

"Precisely," Dr. Wu says, beaming broadly. "Come this way." He points to the center of the room and we go to a table where a lab-coated technician is pouring a dark viscous liquid from a flask to a plate. He then applies a flame to the liquid and it ignites and burns in front of us.

"There," Dr. Wu says and points to the flaming dish of petrol. "It's absolutely untouched by the plague and as you can see, is available for combustion. We actually have one of the old vehicles repaired and ready for you to drive back to your compound in Cambridge."

"Excellent," Soren says and rubs his hands together. He turns to me. "See, Eve? Just like I promised. The antidote has spread across the Eastern Seaboard, from Newfoundland in Canada to Louisiana. Soon, the oil will be flowing again and once we repair everything that's been degraded by the plague, the long slow recovery back to a workable economy and society will begin."

The scientists and those gathered to watch the demonstration all clap, and even I have to smile for if what Soren says is true, it means that we can now stop the plague in its tracks. It will be over and the remaining carbon-rich reserves will be available for us to use.

I should be happy of course, and I am, but a part of me wonders at the cost of saving the world's petroleum reserves. I don't mean worry about the climate or anything. That's been taken care of since the destruction of so much fossil fuel. It has reduced emissions by a considerable amount and will take years to get back to previous levels.

No, I'm thinking about the cost of having a god-like being at the helm of the Church and what that will entail. It's the cost I have to pay if I want the rest, but I hope humanity doesn't revile me forever because of it. Will Soren be some kind of terrible tyrant, ruling from his throne in Rome? Will Michel and I – and Julien – be the ones who enable him? Will Dylan be seen as the evil scientist who allowed it all to happen through his work on the plague?

I only hope History doesn't hate us for what we're doing...

Quit being so melodramatic, Eve. History will remember us as the ones who brought humanity back from the steam age. Chill...

I squeeze my eyes shut like a child, and then take in a deep breath. I have to stop fighting. I've made a decision and I am sure it's the only good one to make. Now, I have to commit to it and see it through.

Yes, Eve. You've made a decision. See it through and you'll get everything you want. Everything.

I want to believe Soren, so I force myself to just accept this fate and move forward.

To that end, I smile and clap with everyone else. The room is ebullient and the mood self-congratulatory. I see the scientists slapping each other on the back. Of course, this has come at a great price but the price humanity has already paid is great as well. At least the damage has been halted.

I hope…

We all receive a small glass of champagne to toast Soren and the science team and I drink down my glass, allowing myself a little thrill of excitement that we have accomplished one goal at least.

Now, I have to follow through on my promise to try to seduce Michel. Well, not exactly seduce as much as offer him the opportunity. I'm sure – I hope – that he refuses, keeping firm to his oath of celibacy now that he has taken on the persona as priest.

We put our glasses down and Soren gives us a speech about how under his guidance, we will change the world, and I try to keep a smile on my face as I listen. I am going to be a good compliant little pawn, so that I can see the future I want come to fruition.

We leave the facility to return to our vehicle and find an older vehicle parked next to it. The five of us return to the compound in style, in a stretch limo that has been repaired and is now humming. I barely see the landscape as we travel back to Cambridge, because I'm busy thinking about Michel and what is going to happen when we get back.

We arrive at the entrance of the compound and leave the vehicle, Michel first, then me and Soren last after Procel and Kael. The staff is lined up at the front door and claps as Soren walks up the steps. He smiles and bows to them with a flourish. I see that they are truly happy, their eyes bright, and real smiles on their faces.

They truly believe that Soren is their savior…

We all are, Eve. All of us.

I shrug his words off and we stand in the entry as the staff take our overcoats and scarves. I sigh and start up the stairs.

"Where are you going, Eve?" Soren says. "We have to have a little chat. I have some things I want to show you."

I turn back and follow Soren reluctantly into his study. He turns to me once we enter and points to the interior where I see my father and my heart squeezes to see him.

"Father!" I cry and rush over to him. I kneel at his feet and rest my hands on his knees. He looks much better than before, and there is no longer any madness in his eyes. He looks well-fed and clean.

"Eve," he says, his voice breaking. I stand up and put my arms around his shoulders, and he pats me on the back, for although the color has returned to his face and he has a bit of fat on him, he looks so much older than my memories of him. It breaks my heart that I've missed so much of his life and that so much of his life went down the drain in that horrible nursing home – prison that he was kept in.

I sit beside him on a chair and we lean together. He takes my hand.

"Soren has told me everything," he says and smiles. "I'm so glad that he's stopped this plague and will eradicate vampirism. He's truly our savior."

I frown for a moment, for I'm surprised that he's so willing to accept Soren, but perhaps he realizes that this is the only way to fight Blackstone.

"Yes," I say softly. "I'm so glad as well." I say nothing about Soren being our savior for that still irks me. He is doing the right thing. That's all.

Saviors are for Bible stories, not real life. In real life, there are only people doing the right thing or people doing the opposite. Or nothing. Soren is doing the right thing, as are we all who are fighting this battle.

I turn to Soren and stand. "Thank you," I say in a small voice. "Thank you for rescuing him."

He shrugs. "Like I told you. Everything. But I expect you to follow through as well. With conviction."

I sit back down with my father. A servant brings us a tray with a teapot and cups, as well as sandwiches and biscuits. My father is hungry and eats the food with relish. As he eats, I ask him how he's been since I last saw him and what happened during his rescue.

He tells me that several soldiers arrived and were able to fight their way to the rooms. That they told him Soren came to rescue him, and bring him to me so we could be together. When the servant finally leaves us alone, my father leans in and whispers, his eyes darting around the room as if someone might be listening.

"I don't believe it for a moment," my father says, his brow furrowed. "He's using me to manipulate you. I don't trust him, Eve. He wants to have too much power. He's the devil and Michel is his soldier. Mark my words."

I wish I could tell my father to be quiet, but I can't. Instead, I try to change the subject.

"Soren will save us," I say, patting my father's hand. "I've seen what the antidote does. It stops the plague from working. We can use petroleum now, in the affected territories."

"He's doing it so he can grab power, that's all," my father responds, shaking his head. "He and Michel – they want to rule the world. That's what Lord Blackstone told me. And they wanted to use you to destroy Blackstone and stop Dominion."

I nod. "That's right, father. I want that, too. Don't you want to stop Dominion, if you could? Do you really want vampire rule?"

"I don't want rule of either of them. Neither Soren or Blackstone. They should both go to hell for all I care."

I sit back and sigh, for I share his desire, but I doubt it's possible. "I want that too, but at this point, I think it's the lesser of two evils. Blackstone wants the slavery of the entire human race and is willing to destroy technological society to achieve it. Soren will stop Dominion, halt the plague's progress and turn it around, and he'll also cure vampirism. I've seen him, father," I say and squeeze his hand. "He can cure vampirism. He cured Michel."

My father looks skeptical. "I don't trust him. I never trusted Michel. He always wanted to use you for his own ends."

There's nothing I can say to dissuade him, so I give up. Instead, I talk about my trip to the facility to see the antidote at work. I tell him about the dirigibles and how they dispersed the antidote and it stopped the plague from working. I point out that we drove in a car fueled by gasoline.

"We'll start over, once the antidote has spread around the world and he's cured vampirism. He's going to use a principle of physics to achieve the cure. They're looking for something that all vampires share – something in our DNA – that will allow it to affect all vampires at once. It will move through the population and end our need for blood."

"Will you be mortal?" my father asks.

I shake my head. "From what I understand, the adamantine principle in vampire nature will remain. We'll be immortal, but I'm sure that at some point, we will be able to take that principle and provide it to all humans. Death will no longer have domain over us."

My father frowns. "What if he doesn't do that? What if he's merely exchanging one form of Dominion with another, more bloodless one? Maybe all of you immortals will rule over all mortals. Have you considered that?"

I sit back and think of what he's said. Soren never did say anything about taking the immortality principle in vampirism and giving it to all mortals. That was my mother's goal. And mine.

"That can be what we work towards," I say, not so sure anymore that Soren is interested in giving all mortals immortality. If not, that's a game changer for me.

It has to be on the agenda if I'm going to continue to cooperate with him.

I half expect Soren to poke his mind into mine and respond, but he doesn't and so my father and I sit, drink our tea and discuss the war and what we both hope will happen.

After a few hours, my father yawns and stretches. "It sure would be nice to have a sleep," he says and so I go to the door, where a servant stands outside in wait for a command.

"Please ask if there's a room prepared for my father so he can rest," I say and the servant bows his head briefly and leaves. I see a guard standing at the end of the hallway, keeping watch over me and close the door.

"I've asked the servant to find you a room so you can rest," I say. He smiles and finishes his tea, slurping down the last of it with relish.

"Blackstone has a nice residence, but they're much more vampire-like there than here for some reason. The place was always filled with vampires and I always felt like they were considering me for lunch."

He smiles at me, a teasing smile. "Sorry," he says. "I know it's not your fault."

We both laugh. "I know the feeling. It's hard not to look on humans that way. Don't worry though. Everyone here is pretty old and has lots of experience avoiding their more base desires, because most of the vampires here have supported the Treaty of Clairveaux. Plus, there's lots of blood available. Fresh and preserved."

I smile at him and he smiles back.

"Now, later, I want to hear you play," he says and folds his napkin, placing it carefully on the tray. "I hope you've been keeping your practicing up so you don't lose your abilities. We didn't get much time to visit when you were at Blackstone's so I hope we can catch up for lost time."

"Me too," I say and smile.

The door opens and the servant pops his head inside the room. "Your suite is ready," he says and my father stands, happy to be going to his own room for a sleep.

"I'll see you later," he says and kisses my cheek. "Then I want to hear you play."

"Okay," I say and smile, but of course, I have barely played piano since I became a vampire. It's not that I haven't wanted to, but there's been so much upheaval in my life I haven't had time to breathe let along practice.

I watch the servant walk him down the hallway. His rooms must be in a different wing, and I hope everything is okay.

I glance down the hallway and see Michel walking towards me. Now I know I have to live up to my side of the bargain with Michel.

CHAPTER 18

I SLIP BACK inside the study before Michel can see me, and rush over to the chairs by the fireplace, taking my teacup in hand, hoping to look nonchalant, but inside, my guts are roiling. It's nerves about how he'll respond. I don't want him to respond to me and I feel bad even trying to tempt him, but once we've finished the charade and he's said no, I'll explain to him that I was only cooperating with Soren.

Soren will know of course, but he can't stop me from letting Michel know.

Yes, I can. Don't tell him that I made you. I want him to believe it. I want him to think you truly love him and desire him. That you want the arrangement you had with him and Julien to start up again, even though he's a priest once more.

I close my eyes and take in a deep breath, wanting to argue with him in my head, but not wanting to at the same time.

Michel enters the room and closes the door. He looks pale, as if he's upset over something.

"Are you all right?" I ask, wondering what the problem is and why he looks so out of sorts.

He shakes his head. "Nothing. I'm fine," he says and forces a smile.

"Just the events of the last few days have caught up with me. That's all."

I nod in understanding. I'm sure it must have upset him greatly that Soren arranged to blackmail him with my resurrection. Of course Michel would ask for Soren to resurrect me. I wonder what the price has been, besides Michel coming back to Cambridge. What has Soren forced him to do in return for my life?

"May I join you?" he asks, stopping at my father's place and waiting.

"Of course," I say and motion to the chair. "Please do. My father was here for a visit and now has gone back to his room for a rest."

"How is he?"

"Fine, but a little frazzled," I say, watching him over the lip of my teacup as I finish. "He's not happy to be here. He doesn't trust you or Soren."

"He doesn't side with Blackstone, does he?" Michel says in alarm.

"No," I say and shake my head. "He doesn't trust anyone. The poor man has spent most of the last decade in such terrible conditions..."

Of course, then I remember that it was because of Michel that he was in that state, and my back stiffens a bit in response. It will make it hard for me to want to try to seduce him. I realize he did it to save my father from being killed, but still... he lived like an animal.

"I'm truly sorry about that," Michel says, his voice soft, with a hint of remorse. "I honestly thought it was the only way to keep him from getting himself killed and maybe you in the process."

I say nothing, resistant to accepting his story. Still, my father's alive and with me now, even if he is slightly crazy.

Michel pours himself some tea and drops some sugar into it, before tasting it. He looks like he wants to speak with me about something, but is hesitating.

"Eve," he says and puts his cup down. "Things will happen that appear to be a betrayal at first, but they aren't. Just remember that."

"I wish you didn't have to be so cryptic."

"You know why I have to."

I do know why. I inhale deeply and close my eyes, leaning against the back of my chair in an attempt to relax and let it go. I have to remember that this is all because Soren can read me and through me, know everything. I have to be in the dark. I understand now that to be the case.

Then I think that perhaps that's why Soren's trying to push us together. He wants to read Michel through me and discover whether Michel is plotting against him. Soren knows that the only time I can read him is when I'm connected to him when we make love. It will be different if we do. He's no longer a vampire or ascended so it will all be on me to connect with him.

Then of course, I think maybe he'll turn me down.

He's serious about his vows, but he did kiss me back and gladly lay on top of me when I kissed him…

There's nothing I can do so I try to shut off my mind and let what is going to happen, just happen.

He either will or he won't.

WE RETURN to our rooms and spend the rest of the day together, reading old newspapers, talking about the plague and Soren's cure for vampirism. We talk about nothing important. It's small talk, but it relaxes us both and I wonder what will happen if and when I'll have the chance to make my move.

Finally, Michel stands up and stretches. "It's almost time for dinner," he says and looks at me from under a frown. "How are you feeling? Are you recovered?"

I nod. "Yes."

"Good. If you need anything, let me know. I'll make sure you get it. I had better go and freshen up."

"Okay," I say and stand up. We stand there together, looking at each other, and then he smiles softly.

"I'll see you in the dining room."

"Okay."

I feel bad that I've missed my chance, and then he turns back to me.

"Eve," he says and steps closer.

I decide that now is as good a time as ever and I step closer to him as well. I place my hand behind his head and pull him down to me, our lips meeting like it was second nature to us and there hasn't been this divide between us all these past weeks. He kisses me back with abandon, his arms going around my waist, pulling me against him and the fact he's wearing a set of vestments doesn't seem to stop him, or slow him down, in any measurable way.

I pull back, breaking our kiss, my heart pounding, my breathing fast. "Michel," I say, wanting to say the words so I have cemented my bargain with Soren, but Michel doesn't give me a chance.

"Shh," he says. "You don't have to say anything." He pulls me against him once more and tries to kiss me but I stop him.

"Michel," I gasp when he kisses my throat. "Your vows…"

He pauses, his mouth lingering over my throat. "I want you, Eve. I don't care anymore about my vows."

He licks up my neck to my jaw and then kisses my ear and in spite of myself, a jolt of desire flows through my body right to my core. It would be so easy to let this happen, and not fight it. But I have to say the words.

"Michel, will you make love to me?"

Michel pulls away, frowning. "Why would you even have to ask?" he says, his voice hoarse with desire.

"But you said you were celibate."

I look in his eyes, trying to see what I can read in them. I don't want him to hate me because of this. He's frowning.

"Did Soren force you to offer yourself?" he says, his body suddenly stiff.

I don't know whether I can say yes or no without breaking the terms of my agreement with Soren.

So I don't answer. Instead, I kiss him again, hoping that he'll be the one to push me away.

"Stop, Eve," he says and holds me at arm's length. "Did Soren force you to try to seduce me?"

"Why would you ask?" I say, my arms crossed.

"Because," he says and runs his hands through his hair. "He told me that you'd eventually come to me and offer yourself to me. That you still loved me and wanted me. That I was your first love and you would never get over me. He told me that I had to accept your offer if I wanted him to keep you alive."

"Fuck," I say, surprising even myself. I glance away, my anger so strong at that moment, I want to punch something. "I'm sorry. He made me do it in return for proof that he would stop the plague."

Michel sits on the wing chair, running his hands through his hair. "He's playing us both. He's using my love of you to make me break my vows. He's using your sense of morality to make you try to tempt me."

I sigh and sit beside him on the other wing chair. "I should have known. I didn't think you'd willingly break your vows. I thought you'd resist. He really does want to torture us both."

He runs a hand through his hair. "I'm so sorry," he says and looks deeply in my eyes. "I never intended any of this to happen."

"The road to hell and all that..." I say, a sick feeling in my gut. "I fulfilled my side of the bargain," I say out loud to Soren. "I tried to seduce him. I kissed him."

"But you hesitated," Michel says from under a furrowed brow. "When you did, I felt a hesitancy in you. I didn't really believe Soren when he told me those things, although I wanted to."

"You wanted to believe it?"

"Of course. I love you, Eve. We just can't be together now. I've accepted that. I have other things to do than be your lover, as have you."

He looks resigned to it, his mouth pressed thin, his shoulders slumping.

Still, it warms my heart to think he wishes we could be together. As much as I love Julien, there is still a part of my heart that belongs only to Michel and I suspect it always will. There's a part of my heart that can never completely belong to Julien. But I'm afraid that I can't see Michel and me together again in any way. I know I have to choose, and when everything is considered, Julien is the man for me.

He loves me in a way that I need someone to love me. Completely. Totally.

Are you so sure?

I fist my hands, digging my nails into my palm. Damn him! I hate it when Soren peeks into my mind and torments me.

"Michel, do you think Julien truly loves me, or do you think Soren's compelled him to love me, just to spite you?"

Michel shrugs. "Would it make a difference? You love him more than you love me, so it would be over for us anyway."

"Why?" I say, frowning.

"You chose Julien over me. I'd always know that you'd be wishing you were with him instead of me."

"I'd rather be with someone who loves me completely and totally. If I thought that Julien didn't actually love me, I'd end it right away."

"There's no way to know. You just have to choose."

I sit in silence for a moment, mulling the situation over. I hate that Soren has forever ruined the innocent way I loved Julien and thought that he loved me. Even though Procel told me that Julien truly loved me, how can I believe him? How can I know that Procel isn't playing along with Soren, trying to screw with my mind? I can't believe Procel any more than I can believe Soren.

Soren may have done nothing to make Julien love me. Or maybe he sent Julien to me that day in the café when I first met him.

Michel is right. There's no way to ever know. I'm not sure anything could reverse the compulsion.

"Is it possible to stop compulsion? I mean, if the vampire who did the compulsion died, for example?"

Michel shrugs. "I've seen it happen before but that's when a vampire dies. His influence over the mortals and other vampires who are under his compulsion no longer has any force. But for Soren to actually truly die?" Michel shakes his head and blinks. "I don't know how to do that. If Blackstone's drug didn't work, I have no idea what could kill Soren except God Himself."

Of course, I don't believe in God Himself, so that means whatever kills Soren will have to be specific to whatever kind of being he is. If I could only understand what he is and where he comes from, then perhaps there would be a way to destroy him... If he died, I'd know that Julien would be free from his compulsion. I'd know whether Julien actually loved me.

I exhale heavily and get up from my chair. "I'm going to get changed. Soren will probably be mad that we didn't have sex. Time to face the music, I guess."

"He'll be happy that we're both filled with angst," Michel says and catches my eye. "That'll fuel his fire for a while. A being as old as he is has to keep amused or go mad, I expect."

I nod and leave Michel in the sitting room. I don't feel like eating dinner. I don't feel like sitting at a table filled with Soren and his Twelve, smirking at me over the whole business. I want to roll up into a ball of self-pity and sleep until Julien comes back home to me.

Instead, I get dressed in something that is more appropriate and when I come out of the bathroom, Michel is gone, no doubt to clean up before dinner.

While I'm brushing my hair, a knock comes at the door. Michel enters.

"Are you ready?" he asks in a soft voice. "I thought we could at least enter together. It will give Soren some satisfaction."

He gives me that de Cernay crooked grin and it's the first time I've seen him smile for a while.

"I guess," I say and then get into the mood. "Since he did stop the plague, it's the least I can do. I'll even take your arm and kiss your cheek when we enter the room. How does that sound?"

Michel holds out his arm and I take it, threading my arm through his. We smile at each other and walk down the hallway to where our guard waits.

When we enter the dining room, everyone is already there and standing around in groups, talking, the sound of their conversation like the ebb and flow of the ocean. They all turn when the two of us walk in, arm and arm, like I said. And like I said, I turn to Michel and stand on my tiptoes to kiss his cheek. He smiles softly when I do and he takes my hand in his and leads me to my place at the table, pulling out my chair like a medieval knight helping his lady.

I imagine it gives all the Twelve and Soren something to think about. It no doubt pleases them to see us together.

They must be dreadfully bored if our drama is so interesting to them.

We are, believe me. Your drama is what we exist for. The more, the better...

The servants bring in trays of food and so Soren and the Twelve put down their glasses of wine or blood and take their places at the table. The meal proceeds as it usually does, with the talk about the war, about what is happening at Blackstone's compound, and about the plague's halt. I listen with interest, hoping to hear how Julien is doing.

"Don't worry your little head, Eve," Soren says out loud. "Julien is as gallant a knight as ever and strong enough to fight off most of those he encounters. When I resurrected him, I made sure to restore him to his initial state as an ascended vampire. He'll be back with your dear sweet brother pretty soon. And, with the cure in a form that can be easily disseminated."

I smile in response, and lift my glass of wine up to toast him silently.

"Thank you," I mouth. He takes a sip of his glass of blood.

Once dinner is over, Michel walks me back to our rooms and we sit by the fire and talk about what we've heard.

"I'm glad Julien is okay," Michel says, and leans back, his hands on the armrests. He looks very tired and stressed.

"Me, too," I say, and it feels redundant for of course Michel knows how concerned I am. "I'm also glad that Dylan will be back with the cure."

Michel says nothing for a moment.

"Do you still see the future?" I ask him as he watches the fire.

He glances up, his eyes distant. "Not really," he says. "Not like before. When I was ascended, it was difficult for me sometimes to concentrate on the present. I kept getting streams of possible futures. I had to work hard to keep reality and my visions separate, so I knew what was really happening. I'm glad it's gone. Now, all I have are brief glimpses of the future, but nothing really clear enough or long enough to give me any kind of hope of influencing it."

"Now, you're just a mortal."

"I'm just a priest. Just a human. It's a relief."

He smiles but it's forced, and then he takes a sip of some tea the servant brought to us, as he does every night.

I finish my tea and then stand. "Well, it's time for me to go to sleep. I'm tired."

He stands, and we part. At one time, I would have wanted to take his hand and lead him with me to the bed, but now, I feel only regret. I think of Julien and wonder where he is and if he is all right. I don't trust Soren to tell me the truth about anything.

That's really too bad, because I'm the only one who has ever told you the truth, right from the start...

You didn't tell me the truth about Julien being compelled to love me, I think in my head, not wanting Michel to hear me talking to Soren.

I never told you a lie. I merely made a proposition – what if Julien didn't love you at all, but had been compelled to think he loved you? It was a suggestion to see how you responded and if you could handle doubt. You're all about science, Eve, and evidence. You need cold hard facts, but the truth is, even the cold hard facts you humans have are all fraught with risk, once you learn better science. Many of those facts get thrown by the wayside and you have new cold hard facts to absorb.

That's the way it is, I think in response. *A scientist always holds everything in suspended disbelief just in case.*

Well, think of Julien that way. Think of Michel that way, for that matter. What if neither of them truly loved you and were merely my servants?

I don't respond to him this time. I close the door and sit on the side of the tub, holding my head in my hands.

I don't believe you, I think. *Because Michel came to me despite his plans to let me go. He didn't want to come to me, and meet me, because...*

And with that, Soren throws my certainty that Michel loves me into suspicion. Did Soren force Michel to find me and to love me? Soren can't compel Michel, but he can manipulate him.

Do *neither* of the brothers truly love me?

I can handle that, I think to myself rather than Soren. It would mean I could forget all the drama and focus on doing the right thing – stopping the plague.

Which you have already done...

And getting the cure for vampirism, I think in response.

Which I've got in the works, thanks to your lovely brother and his half-sister...

Please leave me alone to my thoughts.

Actually, Soren says to me via our connection, *I think I want you to come down and have a little heart to heart. I'll send my guard to pick you up.*

I'm tired, I think, not wanting to go to speak with him at this point, only to have him torment me more.

I have some nice fresh blood that will give you a real boost. It's special. It's angel blood and will keep you up and ready all night.

I don't know if I want to be up all night," I think. But I know that if Soren wants me in his quarters, that's where I'm going. I leave the bathroom and Michel stands when I enter the sitting room.

"What's the matter?" he asks, dropping the newspaper onto the coffee table.

"Soren has summoned me," I say, making a face.

"When?" Michel says and he's confused for a moment. Then, he catches himself. "Of course. Your connection."

I nod and I hear a knock at the door. A guard pops his head inside the room. "Milady, my Lord Soren has requested your presence in his study. I'm to escort you there."

I go to the door and glance back at Michel, shrugging. I have no idea what to expect from Soren, and brace myself for anything. What would he possibly want to speak with me about, especially at this moment?

CHAPTER 19

I ENTER his quarters when the guard opens the doors. Procel is looking over Soren's shoulder at a map laid out on the top of Soren's desk. They're speaking in soft voices. Soren glances up when the guard clears his throat.

"My Lord Soren—"

"Leave us," Soren interrupts, dismissing the guard with a wave of his hand. The guard leaves and I remain where I'm standing, a few feet from the table.

"Well, come closer," Soren says with a wave. "I'm not going to bite." He glances up from the map. "Unless you want me to, that is." He grins and it's quite the evil grin.

I step closer and examine the map. It's a familiar one of the world with wide swaths of land covered in red. Now, there are parts of the map that are back to normal color.

I take it he wanted me back so he could brag about how far the antidote to the plague has spread in such a short time.

"No, actually," Soren says, glancing up at me from the map. "I brought you back so I could give you something."

He hands me a small vial. It has some blood in it. I take it that this is the "angel blood" he was speaking of.

"Take this," he says. "It will pep you up. I'm taking you to a late-night ceremony and I want you to be full of vim and vigor."

"Ceremony?" I ask. "Is Michel coming?"

He shakes his head. "No," he says. "It's just for the Twelve and me. And you, of course."

"Why do I need this?" I ask, taking off the small cork stopper and sniffing. It smells like ordinary blood.

"You said yourself that you're tired. This will get you through the night."

I take in a deep breath and then down the small vial of blood. Immediately, I feel its effects, as warmth spreads through me and then it hits me like a truck – a wave of euphoria stronger than anything I've ever felt before. I can't manage the intensity and stagger over to a sofa, where I sit and close my eyes as the sensations envelop my body.

"What is this?" I manage to whisper, unable to open my eyes, the pleasure and bliss is so intense.

"It's a little bit of manna from heaven."

I crack my eyes open, for even in that moment, I can't help but resist the implications of this being heavenly in any way. "It's heroin."

"Oh, ye of little faith," Soren says and shakes his head. "No matter what I do, you'll never believe, will you? What will it take, Eve, to make you a believer?"

"Why does it matter, if I do your bidding?"

"It matters," he says and stands up, coming over to where I am slumped, my head lolling back, my eyes almost rolling back into my head. He bends down and looks at me, his face only a few inches from mine. "I want you to believe."

"I do believe," I say, enjoying the feeling in my body. "I believe this is some amazing shit."

I crack my eyelids open and see his frown. "That's my blood," he says.

"It has some endorphins in it. Probably mimics morphine."

"Such a little scientist," he says and shakes his head. "Why can't you believe I'm an angel?"

"Because angels are just mutated humans with powers we don't understand or can't measure. Maybe aliens," I say and laugh at myself.

"Nothing is alien in this universe," he says but I can't understand what he's saying and I don't even want to try.

"So what did you want to talk to me about?" I ask, my eyes still closed.

He says nothing for a moment and so I open my eyes and lift my head with great difficulty. The bliss is starting to wear off, but I still feel energized and peaceful at the same time.

Soren sits across from me, watching me over his steepled hands, which are pressed against his lips. He looks contemplative, his eyes on me but distant, as if he's somewhere else.

Then he enters my mind, but in the way we do when we share blood as a group, and I feel his mind, and it scares me. I feel like I've fallen into an endless chasm, with no bottom in sight. I'm free falling in his mind and all around me are images coming into and out of focus, like I'm taking a tour of his memories.

He's somewhere in a desert and it's hot and dry, the ground is rough and red. Overhead, the sun is relentless. I glance around the vista that appears to go on forever. I know what it is. It's a desert in the Middle East, but it's mountainous and barren. There's no real life here except for that which lives underground. I'm walking on the hot dry earth, which cracks and breaks up under my sandaled feet, the crunch loud in my ears. Overhead, a hawk flies, crying out. In the distance, several vultures circle over a fire and I wonder if someone is burning a corpse.

Then the vision changes and I'm on a high cliff overlooking an azure sea. The sky is so blue. I think that I've never seen it so blue before. A few white clouds in the distance break up the vastness. The water below is calm, lapping softly against a sandy and rocky beach. Behind me is a circle of stones, megaliths, in a circular formation. In the center is a slab of stone over a base. I see blood on the stone. It's a makeshift altar and someone's sacrificed an animal – or human – there.

Where am I? I glance around, and it looks like the Mediterranean

Sea. I'm somewhere near Greece or perhaps farther around the coast toward Italy.

The scene changes again and now I'm in the far north, for the sky is a white blue and the air is cold, the ground is covered in snow. I stand on a cliff and see down its banks is an inlet, a fjord, so I take it I'm in some northern land like Norway or Sweden or Denmark. This is where Marguerite came from. Below me is a dead antelope of some species. I don't know it's proper name but I see antlers. It's fallen off the cliff, hitting the rocks below, the snow bloody beneath its head.

Why is he showing me this?

More scenes flash by and I'm in a hilly country that reminds me of images of Provence that I've seen in travelogues. A few dozen feet away is a small building made of stone. It's a temple of some sort. Inside, another altar, with trays and baskets of food, chalices of wine, and a dead goat spread out on the stone, its blood dripping out into a bowl. In another bowl lie its entrails. Someone was reading portents in its entrails, so I suspect I'm back in the days of Rome and this is a temple to a Roman god. I glance around and there is a statue of a god with wings on his feet. Apollo.

Is he giving me clues to what and who he is?

Is that why I'm seeing all this?

The images are flying by almost too fast for me to catch them all, but they are from everywhere, different landscapes, different climates.

Now I'm in a cave, deep in the back, and there's a torch throwing a yellow light against the wall, the soot lifting up and blackening the cave's roof. There are paintings on the wall – a deft image of an antelope, then another of a bird. There are hands on the wall, painted by blowing ochre over the artist's hand. This is old, and I get the sense we're far back in time, perhaps to the Stone Age, during the most recent ice age.

Now, I'm in the middle of a vast plain, at night, the sounds of the night all around me, lying on my back and staring up at the stars. A few feet away is a campfire, but it's burnt down to embers, and my eyes adjust so I can see the vast expanse of the Milky Way above me.

It's so huge and so distant that I have this deep sense of sadness despite how beautiful it is.

I feel so incredibly lonely in what seems like an endless night, and endless universe.

"Yes," Soren says. "It is lonely. It's terribly lonely. It was that way for me for thousands of years until I found others of my kind."

"Your kind?" I say and sit up, the night sky still above. I thought maybe it was just an image in my mind, but now I find I'm really here, in some far distant plain surrounded by hills, which are dark against the night sky. Or at least, I feel as if I'm really here, now. The dirt grits in my hand. I smell smoke from the burnt embers in the fire pit.

"I can't tell you what my kind are," he says, wrapping his arms around his bent knees as he sits beside me. "When I woke up, I had no idea who or what I was. All I knew was that I was here, naked, staring up at the sky very much like this and that I was missing something. I was missing the others. Once we were joined together and were one. When I woke up, here, I was alone. Ever since that day, I've been searching for others of my kind to join together again. You allow us to be together the way we once were."

"How long ago was that? It seems that a lot of time passed in the images you showed me."

"Forty thousand years," he says with a tired voice. Then he turns and meets my gaze, a smile on his lips. "If you wonder why I'm always surrounded by drama, that's why. I need it to keep me from going insane."

"Forty thousand years?" I say with a gasp. I turn away from his too-deep expression, which seems almost pained, and look back up at the night sky. I can see the Milky Way clearly, because there's no light pollution – no light except for a low moon that is almost sinking behind the far horizon. "Are we in Africa?"

He shakes his head. "No. Norway."

"But it should be winter…"

"We're in the past."

"How…"

He smiles again. "Don't expect to understand how. Just accept that it is.

"Are we back forty thousand years?"

"No," he says. "That would take too much energy. We're back in the summer. If you look in the distance, can you see a long black strip?"

I look in the direction he's pointing. "Yes," I say. "I see it."

"That's a road. This is one of the most remote places I could find. I come here now and then to escape everything and remember all the years I've been alive."

"How did you get here?" I ask, still in awe. "How come you're alive forty thousand years later? You're immortal, obviously but…"

"I'm immortal. The Twelve are immortal."

"From where? Who put you here?"

"I have no real idea. God? That's one explanation. Were we in some kind of Heaven before this? I don't know for sure. The Twelve and I are all that's left of about two hundred of our kind who came here, forty thousand years ago. I have no solid memories of who we were before. All I know is that we were united. Our minds were one – the way we are when we join through blood. Then, we were sent here, separated, each of us put in a different land, with different people."

"But why? Who sent you?"

He shrugs. "We have no idea. We think we were sent here to be your guardians. We became your gods. That can be the only reason. We were put here with no memories, but with powers that few humans possess and that has meant we've been your rulers, worshiped as gods ever since."

I shake my head in wonder. "You're obviously an alien."

"You believe that?" he says and turns to me, an expression of surprise on his face. "You'll happily believe I'm an alien with no evidence but you won't accept that I'm some kind of angel?"

"Angels are a way for humans to explain what you are. An alien is a more logical explanation for what you are. You're probably an alien race that sent emissaries to Earth to try to guide us, or uplift us or something," I say and exhale, satisfied that it accounts for what Soren and the Twelve are far better than the whole religious angle.

He doesn't say anything. "Who sent us, though?"

I laugh out loud at that. "Not God," I say with derision. "The God that everyone believes in – the God of the Bible as in the All-Knowing and All-Powerful? That god just doesn't exist. It's a fairy tale told to placate humans because we fear death. No," I say, satisfied. "You're probably aliens who thought we needed guidance and so you were sent here to prevent us from killing each other off by instilling in us morals so we wouldn't eat our brothers. *That* I could believe."

Soren grins and shakes his head. "Such a little skeptic."

"So which one were you?" I ask, stretching my legs out and leaning back on my hands. "What god did you impersonate?"

"Impersonate?" he says with disgust. "I was a god, Eve. I had worshipers. They gave me powers that allowed me to perform feats of wonder and keep them in line."

"Which one?"

He shakes his head. "Too many to list. I had all of what is now Western Europe. So, I was Cernunos, and I was Belinos and I was Teutates. I was all of their gods at one time or other. Whichever god was necessary at the time."

I nod and consider what he's said. "We're not really here."

"You mean, in the past summer in Norway?"

"Yes," I say. "You and I have joined minds and you're showing me a memory and you're able to manipulate my mind so that I see and feel and sense what you want me to sense."

"My little scientist."

"I can't help it. That's the way my mind works." We sit in silence for a while and I enjoy the quiet, the sounds of a light breeze through the grasses surrounding the camp, the chirp of insects. It's so real, I could believe we were really there.

"Why are you showing me this?"

He sighs heavily. "Because I know you want to destroy me. You fear me. You fear what I might become if I get too much power. I want you to understand what I am. What we are. You need us, Eve," he says and turns to me, frowning. "You still need us. Look around you, at the state of this world. Look at what it was like before the plague. Wars.

Massacres on a regular basis. Terrorism. Greed. Poverty. Murder, rape, pillage. It has always been like this, since you stepped out of the savannah and became self-aware. Once you did, you fought each other over territory. Killed each other from neighboring tribes. Ate the heart of your enemy for strength. Raped women, murdered children. Exposed newborns to the wolves."

"We need something," I say, unwilling to concede his point. "We don't need gods. We do need morals. We do need meaning. We do need to have a different view of ourselves and our planet."

"You needed gods, Eve."

I sigh. Is he right? Do we need gods to keep us from self-destructing? I fight against the notion. I think we can be moral without gods.

"Science isn't enough," he says. "It's a start, but it's not nearly enough."

"Religion hasn't been very good either."

Soren stands and wipes off his jeans. "Without religion to instill morals, you would have eaten each other. The weak would have served as food for the strong."

"What about vampires? Where are they from?"

He shakes his head. "A mistake. An experiment gone wrong." He extends a hand to help me up, but I stand without taking it.

"But vampirism lets you join with others and so you let it stand."

"Something like that, but it's a poor substitute for what we once had. Until you came along. You've given that back to us. You allow us to join all together instead of one at a time. You're the conduit, Eve. I've been waiting for decades and decades to create you. Despite all my powers, I had to wait for science to be able to create you. I finally have. You're not going to escape. Michel and your mother hid you for a decade, but now I have you. I won't let you go."

"What about what I want?" I say. "Maybe I don't want to be your conduit."

"It's that or die. Now that I can, I'll make another you."

I turn towards him, disgusted. "I thought you were here to instil morals in us barbaric humans."

"We are, but we also have needs. We need to be united. You're the way. Now, no more fighting me. I want you to understand who and what we are and why we're here so you'll stop fighting me. So you'll give up this ridiculous quest to destroy me and the Twelve. You *can't*. The most you could do was keep us in stasis for a while, but even then, we found a way. We've been around for far longer than you can imagine, Eve. We're not going anywhere and your technology can't destroy us."

"What about the other one hundred and eighty-seven of your kind? Where are they?"

"Gone. In stasis somewhere. Hidden. Hiding. Don't ask me where. I have no idea. We thirteen are all that's left acting in this world. The others are gone and no matter how far I look, I can't find them."

"Are they dead?"

He shakes his head. "We can't die, Eve. Hide us away in some cave or under the ocean or on the Moon. That's it. We'll come back – if we want to. Maybe the rest of my brethren simply got tired of it all and have gone to sleep permanently." He turns to me and he looks so sad. Almost defeated. "No matter what you do, you can't kill us. All you can do is steal our powers temporarily."

Maybe that has to be enough, I think. Of course Soren can hear my thoughts. Then, I blink and find myself back in Soren's room, slumped back in the sofa, Soren sitting beside me, his chin resting on his hand, his face a few inches from mine.

I sit up, and he remains close to me.

"Now, do you understand?"

I shrug. "If you think this changes things," I say, but don't finish. I was going to say, it doesn't. *I still want you stopped*, I think, but I don't say it.

"You can try to destroy me. Destroy us, Eve. We're far ahead of you. We have forty thousand years on you and Michel and your mother. Think of that before you do anything rash. And don't tell Michel or anyone what I've shown you."

"Why not?"

He shakes his head. "I want there to be some mystery about us. Humans need the mysterious. If everything is laid out for them, they get discouraged. They need to believe, Eve, even if you don't. Don't take that away from them. If you did destroy us, in some way, you'd be alone. That would frighten most of your kind immensely."

"Michel will ask. Julien will know unless I block him when we…"

"He won't hear anything you tell him, so you'll be talking to yourself. Remember that I know everything, Eve. Everything you do and think and say."

I sigh, frustrated that he has access to me at all times.

"Can I go?" I ask, wanting to leave. I feel incredibly burnt out from the mental journey Soren has taken me on and upset that I can't talk to anyone about it.

"Feel free," he says. "But let me warn you. Don't think you can stop us. This is pre-ordained. We were sent here for a reason and that reason is to be your guardians. To keep you from destroying yourselves. We take that seriously."

"And yet, you almost destroyed us."

"Not me," he says. "Blackstone. I never wanted this. I planned to stop it."

"You created vampires. You created him, in the end. You're responsible."

I leave without saying another word. I don't like what he's told me. I'm not sure I believe it. It's impossible to know if what he showed me was a story or the truth.

"Oh, ye of little faith," he calls out from the sofa before I can leave. "It must be incredibly lonely to not believe in anything."

"I believe in the truth. In evidence."

Then I leave him and close the door behind me.

CHAPTER 20

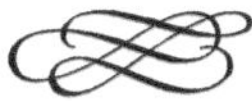

I WALK BACK down the hallway and up the stairs to my wing and my room. The guard trails behind me, making sure I arrive back without detour and I go inside. Michel's seated by the fire, reading. He glances up when I enter the door.

"What happened? You look tired."

I sit on the chair beside him, exhausted. "That was harrowing."

"Have some tea," Michel says. "It's fresh."

I nod and let him fix me a cup, glad for something to drink.

"What happened?" he says and hands me the cup.

I take it gladly. "Soren supposedly showed me what he is and what the Twelve are."

Michel puts his own cup down and frowns. "What did he say? How did he show you?"

I shake my head. "I'm not supposed to kiss and tell," I say.

He smiles ruefully. "I figured as much. Would I like what he told you?"

I purse my lips and consider. "Maybe. I don't know what to think of what he told me. It's like that old saying – turtles all the way down."

He sits back, eyeing me. "He didn't tell you everything, in other words."

"No. There's lots he doesn't know, if that's what you mean," I say, remembering what Soren said. "He did show me how he and the Twelve started, but it doesn't really answer any questions that I have."

"Consider yourself lucky," he says and sips his tea. "That's more than he's done for the rest of us."

"Michel, he showed me something, but I have no way of knowing if he was telling me the truth. So, really, it comes down to a question of faith versus evidence. You know where I stand on that issue."

"Only too well," he says with a sad smile. "Amazing that one of his creations would be such a skeptic."

I laugh. "I bet it really pisses him off that I'm not ready to fall down at his knees and worship him the way he thinks I should."

Michel shakes his head. "I think he enjoys your skepticism as long as it doesn't interfere too much with his plans."

I examine Michel, wondering how much he'll say – what he can say. "What do *you* think he is? I mean, really."

Michel puts down his cup and clasps his hands. He says nothing for a while, pursing his lips in thought. "I've always assumed he was a fallen angel. The Bible and other religions talk about the guardians who were sent to watch over us. They sinned, had sex with humans, created monsters – the Nephilim – and were cast into a pit on earth. All of that language is very poetic and mythical, and told as a story. What I've always believed is that they did in fact come here to watch over us. Guide us. They fell. They were punished by God. Condemned to an earthly existence instead of in heaven. That made them resentful and capricious. They use us. They manipulate us. They tempt us."

"So, to you, Soren and the Twelve are fallen angels."

He takes another sip of his tea like this conversation disturbs him. "The Twelve are probably Nephilim. The products of angels and humans. It explains the vampirism. The Nephilim and their offspring need to drink human blood to survive. Soren is something else."

"What?"

He shrugs as if helpless. "A fallen angel. Which one, I have no idea. Maybe Lucifer himself."

I say nothing, remembering that Soren said vampirism was an

experiment gone wrong. Did they, the original two hundred, try to mate with humans and accidentally created vampirism?

We sit in silence for a moment and then I decide that I've had enough drama and revelations for one night.

I stand. "I'm going to sleep."

Michel stands. "Go ahead. I'm going to do some reading before I go to bed."

I leave him behind and go to the bathroom to wash my face and brush my teeth. Then I crawl under the covers in my bed and close my eyes, sleep taking me before I can even think of what Soren revealed to me – whether it is a story or the truth.

I WAKE in the middle of the night to the sound of a commotion outside the door to our rooms. I sit up in bed to see Michel standing at the door, peering out. Then, Julien walks in and I see that he's covered in blood, his camo clothing ripped, cut and generally looking like he's been in a battle. Blood spatters his face and I see a bloody cut along his cheek that has already healed.

"Julien!" I run to the door, aware of my tiny nightgown with nothing underneath, but I'm relieved that he's here and alive. I wrap my arms around his neck and pull him down to me. We kiss, his arms around my waist, pulling me against him.

"Careful," he says and pulls away. "I'm a blood-covered warrior and you'll get dirty."

"Like I care." I pull him against me once more and we kiss again. Then, he ends the kiss and steps away. I see him eye Michel out of the corner of his eye. I know he feels uncomfortable showing affection in front of Michel and I do as well, but I was afraid I'd never see Julien again.

I take his hand and pull him over to the bathroom. "Let's wash you up. You look like you've been in a battle."

"I was," Julien says with a grin. "Blackstone and his crew didn't take too kindly to us releasing the antidote to the plague for some reason."

"Were you successful? Did you capture Blackstone?"

"Do you doubt it?"

I shake my head and start to wipe off his face with a wet cloth, but stop. "You really need a bath," I say and scrunch my nose up when I smell him. Mud, blood and sweat. Not a good mixture. "I'll get the servant to prepare one for you."

He grins. "Want to join me?" he asks, his voice conspiratorial. He grabs my hips and pulls me against him. "Battle – and you – always make me hard."

"I don't think so," I say, seeing Michel is still in the main room and the bathroom door is open. "Not when Michel's around. Besides, I know he'll want to hear what happened as much as I do."

"Okay," Julien says, frowning playfully. "But I expect to spend some quality time with you when we're finally alone."

I nod and leave him in the room, yawning when I close the door. I get my robe and go to the door to speak with the servant, who leaves to get hot water from the boiler room. I'm awake now, so I join Michel by the fire. I sit beside him.

"I'm glad he's all right," I say. "I was worried that he might not make it back."

"Me as well," Michel says, and smiles. "I understand he captured Blackstone and his son."

I nod, glad Julien is alive. I believe that Michel's glad as well. I know he loves Julien, despite their rivalry over me.

Soren was right. Michel does love me and if I did push things, I know he'd break his vows. He showed me that the other night – even before Soren sent me on my little errand to try to seduce Michel to make a point.

But I don't want to force the issue. I want Michel to be happy, and if that means he is a priest again and celibate, that's the way it has to be. I was happy for a short while – a very short while – when we thought Soren and the Twelve were in stasis and the brothers took turns being with me in the cottage by the ocean. How I wish I could go back to those days...

You can and you will... Cooperate with me and it will be so.

I don't respond to Soren's intrusion. Instead I wait for Julien to finish his bath so we can hear his story.

The servants lug in several large buckets of hot water for Julien's bath. When Julien's finished, he comes out into the living room with a towel wrapped around his waist and one around his head. He seems unconcerned that he's practically naked but of course, both Michel and I have seen him naked so I suppose it would be false modesty to be concerned now.

He stands beside my chair and towel dries his hair, throwing the towel onto a table and running his fingers through his hair to smooth it.

"Well," he says and puts his hands on his hips. "That's all she wrote for Blackstone's compound. We didn't think things would happen as fast as they did, but I'm glad it's over."

"He's captured?"

"In the brig as we speak, and spitting mad," Julien says. "It was a beautiful thing. Procel could have killed him, since he's older than every other vampire. In the end, he almost did. He went up to a wounded Blackstone, grabbed him by the throat and lifted him up off the ground. I thought he was going to break the man's neck and rip his head off right before our eyes," Julien says, a grin on his face.

I shake my head, but can't help but smile in response. He's so comfortable with the violence in war.

"He knew better," I say. "If anyone's going to kill Blackstone, it's Soren."

"Blackstone has many generals who will take up the cause if Soren kills him," Michel says thoughtfully. "They'll continue the fight for Dominion."

"What *will* stop them?" I ask.

Michel shrugs. "The cure. *That's* what will stop them. Dominion won't be necessary when humans are no longer a source of sustenance."

I nod, but I feel uncomfortable about the prospect of so many immortals running around, even if they don't need to drink blood.

"Won't the cure leave us in the same situation? I mean, there won't be any vampires, but there'll be thousands of immortals with centuries of experience and knowledge. They'll be hard to fight, if they decide they want to be our rulers," I say, uneasy with this truth. "What's the difference?"

"They won't have to enslave humans for blood. That will change the whole dynamic." Michel says.

"Will they all be cured?" I ask but just then, there is a light tap on the door. Dylan walks into the room and closes the door behind him. He's carrying a duffle bag and a large object that's wrapped in black cloth.

"Sorry to interrupt your debate," he says after laying the package down carefully by the door. Then he comes over to us. "I just this moment got in and haven't had a chance to go to my rooms yet." He turns to Julien, extending a hand. "Congratulations on your successful mission. I understand Blackstone's in Soren's offices right now, undergoing some well-deserved harsh interrogation techniques."

Julien shakes his hand and Dylan looks really pleased. "As to what you asked?" Dylan says and turns to me. "No, the cure won't kill all vampires. No, Soren won't be choosing who lives. Everyone will survive, but no longer be vampire. They'll be immortal. We'll *all* be immortal. There's no changing that."

"So immortals will become the new rulers. Hundreds of thousands of them," I say, dismayed at the prospect.

"I imagine there'll be some kind of war over who rules," Julien says, "but eventually, yes. No doubt that immortals will be the new rulers. It's inevitable, given their power and knowledge."

"Get rid of one despot only to have a new one take its place?" I say, sadness filling me. "Is that our only choice?"

"Unless we get rid of immortality itself, or make every human immortal, but that's far too much of a change," Dylan says. "I don't think humans are ready for it."

I exhale, and shake my head. "I think immortality is our destiny."

"Maybe," Dylan says. "Regardless, right now, Blackstone's in custody. Soon, he'll be dead. Probably most of his followers will be soon, too. At least, I hope so. The lot of them are committed to some kind of Dominion. I doubt they'll want to give it up."

Michel glances at the grandfather clock and stands. "I have to do a late mass, so I'll be gone for the rest of the evening." He turns to Julien and they hug briefly. "I'm glad you're back in one piece." He smiles at Julien and a nice moment passes between the two brothers. It makes my heart warm to see them be so loving, given everything that's happened.

We watch as Michel leaves and then Dylan yawns. "I guess I should leave as well. You look like you're ready for bed." He turns to me. "I'd like to speak with you alone, if you don't mind."

Julien points to the bathroom. "I'm going to go and get ready for bed. Brush my teeth, pajamas…"

He winks at me, because I know for damn sure he doesn't wear pajamas of any sort. He sleeps naked and the thought makes me warm. I hope that Dylan doesn't take too long so I can finally spend some time with Julien. I missed him while he was gone. I can't wait for us to finally be alone so I can touch him and reassure myself that he's all right.

I turn to Dylan once Julien leaves the room. "So tell me about it. What happened?"

Dylan holds his fingers up to his lips and goes to the door, where he picks up the black wrapped object. "This," he says and comes to my side, unwrapping the object which turns out to be a beautiful sword. He runs his fingers over the blade once he removes it. "This is key. Here," he says and hands it to me. "Hold it. Feel it. Tell me what you feel."

"What do you mean?" I say, although I have a sense of what he means. "You want me to feel its history?"

"Yes," he says. "Use that skill you were born with."

"Created with," I say. I take the blade and examine it. The metal is amazing – so smooth it looks unreal. It's sharp on both edges. There are some kind of hieroglyphs on the hilt that look very old. Sumerian. Akkadian. Some old and extinct language.

I get nothing from it, despite waiting. I glance up at Dylan. "I don't sense anything."

"That's strange," Dylan says and takes it back. "I thought you'd be able to feel the violence in this blade."

"What is it?" Then I glance up. "No," I say and shake my head quickly. "Don't tell me." I make a slicing sound across my throat, because I realize that Soren can pop in at any time and listen in. If Dylan knows something important, I don't want him giving it away to Soren by accident. "I don't want to know. In fact, it's better if I *don't* know."

"Why?" he says and frowns, taking the blade back and slipping it into the scabbard. "It's an amazing metal that comes from—."

I push my fingers against his mouth to stop him from speaking. "Shhh," I say, and shake my head vigorously. I point to my ears and then point in the direction of Soren's quarters, hoping that Dylan gets the message but he doesn't.

"I wanted to show you this because it's key. We thought the prophecy was about twins, you and me, and that we were key to destroying Soren, but it's really about this—."

I hold out my hand, palm out to stop him. "*Don't,*" I say forcefully. "Just don't, okay? Trust me."

He shrugs. "I went all the way to Scotland for this. You can ask Julien about it. He was up on all that Knights Templar history. He was probably one of them."

I make a face, scrunching my eyes closed, plugging my ears. Won't he stop talking? Doesn't he understand? I run my fingers over my mouth in a "zip your lip" gesture and he finally goes *ahh*, and points down the hallway towards Soren's chambers.

"Sorry," he says finally, and nods knowingly. "I was a bit exuberant. Need to know and all that, right?"

I nod, glad that he finally understands.

"Well, I better go," he says and stands, bending down to kiss my cheek. "I'll come back tomorrow. I'm going to spend some time with Sarah. She'll be eager to see me again."

"How is she?" I ask, curious about how she's doing now that she's been resurrected and cured.

"She's wonderful," he says with a huge smile. "We'll get together once this is all over. Everything's right on schedule. Antidote is released. Cure is ready to go. Other things," he says and pats his sword, which he wraps up once more in the black cloth, "are all in place. We're as ready as we'll ever be."

I nod. I know he's talking about the endgame. I don't know what it will be, but he knows, as does Michel and my mother. The three of them are the only ones who can plot against Soren without his direct knowledge. He was hoping to use me to find out what their plans are. I have to make sure he doesn't succeed.

Whatever the case, I know it has something to do with the sword Dylan showed me, and something about Scotland and the Knights Templar. I'll have to shut that out of my mind and let them plot and plan without my knowledge. It irks me, but at least now I understand why.

CHAPTER 21

As Dylan leaves the room, I remember the documents I read when I was going through my mother's files about the Sword of Megiddo and the prophecy of St. Therese of the Reeds. She foretold of the Sword of Megiddo being used to kill the dragon. At that moment, I want to slip back to Michel's home in Cambridge and find the box of my mother's research so I can find the document and read it over again. At the time I read it, I thought it was a bunch of drivel, the ramblings of some medieval zealot who was high or had lost touch with reality.

Now, I want to look more closely at it. Then, I realize that whatever it is, I shouldn't think too closely about it. That might be giving Soren too many clues about what the rebels are planning. I don't want to be the one to ruin their plans.

So I put it entirely out of my mind and smile when Julien walks into the room, dressed in a silk robe that's obviously not his usual attire. In fact, Julien usually walks out of the bathroom naked without any hint of modesty. He has a beautiful warrior's body, strong, well-built and honed, his muscles clearly defined.

He's beautiful and desirable. And all man.

"You like?" he says and turns in a circle.

"I'd like it better if it was hanging up in the wardrobe," I say and remove my robe as I go to him, wrapping my arms around his neck. His arms slip around my waist to pull me against his body. He glances around the room.

"I'm glad our uninvited guest is gone, as much as I enjoy his company. I was wondering if he'd go or blab on all evening. I *want* you."

I smile at him and stand on my tiptoes for a kiss. "He's gone."

"What did he want to talk about?" Julien asks, his voice light.

"Nothing."

"Come on," Julien says. "He must have said something. He's busy working on the cure, I take it."

"Yes," I say, determined not to say anything about the dagger or Scotland or the Knights Templar. Or my thoughts about St. Therese's prophecy. Instead, I pull him down for another kiss and press myself against him. "Enough talk," I say, my voice smoky with desire. "More action. We don't have much time."

"You mean before my brother finishes saying mass?" Julien says, pulling my robe off, then taking my hips and pulling them against his body. "He'll be gone for at least an hour so we have time."

"We do."

He pulls me over to the bed and lies on top of me.

"I need you," he says. "It's been too long since we've indulged. I want to taste you."

My heart does a serious flip at that, because he's right. It's been too long since we were alone and had time to do things right. His mouth moves over my body, as if he's trying to decide where to bite me. I know that wherever he chooses, it will be both painful and erotic at the same time. Even now, it arouses me – the thought he'll feed on me and we'll connect so deeply that we feel everything the other feels, our emotions and senses joining.

"Bite me," I say, for he needs to drink my blood so he'll get the intense high off an ascended vampire's blood. He does finally, his teeth piercing the skin on my inner thigh, the pain sharp and short. His tongue soothes the hurt and soon, I feel no pain. Soon, the endorphins in my blood take away any pain and euphoria fills me. When it hits Julien, I feel our connection, our senses joining, and I lose myself in him. Then, I can no longer sense the boundaries between us, and we're just one big mass of lust and flesh and pleasure.

He forgets everything except my mouth on him, his mouth devouring me, bringing us both to ecstasy.

~

WE HAVE ONLY a few moments to catch our breath and compose ourselves before Michel returns, earlier than Julien expected. He enters the sitting room just as I come out of the bathroom in my robe and nightgown. Julien's fully dressed and sitting by the fire, reading the latest newspaper. I hope it looks perfectly innocent.

Michel takes a seat by Julien and the two talk about the battle.

"I'm going to sleep," I say and smile at the two of them.

"Good night," Michel says and smiles back. When his head is turned, Julien mouths *I love you*, to me and it warms my heart.

As much as I would like him to join me in bed, I know he can't. We have to appear to not be together. I wonder if Michel suspects that we were together while he was away…

I fall asleep listening to their soft voices in the corner, the crackle of the fire the only other sound.

~

I WAKE in the morning to the sound of my servant stoking the fire in my room, to take the chill out of the air.

"You're awake, miss?" she asks, standing at the foot of my bed.

"I am now," I say and stretch.

She goes to pull open the heavy drapes at the window and the dim gray light of a winter storm fills the room. Outside, it's a blizzard. A cold wind blows the trees that surround the house, their barren limbs scratching at my window. I can't help but think the weather is appropriate for the dark deeds that will be done today. No doubt, Soren will want to kill Blackstone and make us watch.

"Will you bring me a tray with my breakfast?"

The servant shakes her head. "Lord Soren wants you to attend the dining room for breakfast."

I sigh, eager to eat. I had hoped to do so alone so I wouldn't have to face Michel and Julien at the same time.

The servant has prepared my bath and I soak in it, enjoying the heat. Once I'm finished and dressed, I follow the guard to the dining hall and see that the rest of Soren's entourage is already there, seated around the great table with Soren at the head.

"There you are," Soren says when he sees me. "Take your place. We have some delicious food on the menu as well as stimulating entertainment." He winks at me and I turn my head away, not wanting to see his gloating expression. I find my place and of course, it's sandwiched between the brothers. They both stand and pull out my chair together, and I sit, trying not to respond and give Soren any pleasure.

Your discomfort always gives me pleasure, Eve. You are so beautiful when you're being petulant.

I smile at him and hold up my glass of blood, wiping away whatever petulant expression I had on my face. I don't want to give him the satisfaction.

We're served a nice meal of an English breakfast with all the fixings, eggs, sausages, bacon, hash browned potatoes. There's even fruit on the table.

Soren holds up a pineapple. "We had visitors from afar. Now that the plague has been stopped, a few supply trains have gotten through now that the blockades have been removed." He raises his eyebrows and people clap in response. Then, he takes a sharp knife and cuts the pineapple in front of us, slurping down the juice and passing pieces around for the others.

When the servants clear off our plates and bring refills of the tea and coffee, Soren stands.

"And now for the main event. A little payback I've been waiting a long, *long* time to deliver. Please, everyone get on your coats and boots and assemble in the front entry. We're taking a little trip."

"Where are we going?" I say despite my intention not to resist.

"Oh, you'll like this, Eve," Soren says and motions to the door. "Some great theatre for all those who lived in fear of the vampire all this time. I hope you enjoy it."

He winks at me and a sense of dread fills me. What Soren *thinks* I'll enjoy and what I *will* enjoy are two different things, I suspect.

We do as he commands and get our coats and boots, and wait by the front doors. Outside, there are several large vehicles waiting, their engines running and I think it's strange. I haven't heard a combustion engine for a long time. Compared to the electric engines we've been using since the plague, it's so loud and I can smell the scent of fuel burning in the vehicle exhaust.

We really are back in the fossil fuel age once more and I wonder whether that was a good decision. Regardless, it's the new reality and so I stand beside Julien and Michel and wait for further instructions.

Soren arrives, wearing a long white leather trench coat, a white scarf and gloves. He looks like a male model in a photo shoot for a spy movie and once again, and in spite of my dislike of him in general, I have to admit that he is strikingly beautiful for a man. His fair skin, his platinum hair, chiseled features and piercing blue-grey eyes make him almost too beautiful.

He catches my eye as he walks by and the smallest smile graces his lips.

If you want it, you can have it. You just have to ask...

I grit my teeth. *Bastard.* Of course I have absolutely no interest in him sexually, but he loves to tease me.

Not a tease. An offer. It's Michel's greatest fear. Wouldn't that just make his little heart break? You and me together? It would be almost too good to bear...

Never gonna happen, I think to myself.

Never say never...

Then he laughs and turns away, waving the group of us through the doors and to the waiting vehicles.

"Come on people," he says, his voice ebullient. "Let's get this show on the road. Time for some payback."

We enter the five vehicles and I end up with Michel and Julien plus

Soren and Kael. Soren sits in the front passenger seat, his arm on the back of the seat, his neck craned so he can watch us. He's smiling, excited for whatever event he's taking us to.

Is this going to be one of his feats of wonder? A miracle?

"No mere miracle, Eve," Soren says out loud, his eyes narrowed as he examines me from the front seat. "Just amazing biotechnology, thanks to your wonderful brother. Did I ever tell you the story of your brother's birth?"

"I already know," I say. "He told me. He was conceived via my mother's frozen eggs and whatever genetic trickery your scientists worked up to create a warrior for your use. You put him inside his crack-addicted surrogate mother in England and left him to rot so that his skills as an adept would develop."

"Actually, no," he says. "But it's a nice story. He's your twin. Same mother, different egg. One boy. One girl. A perfect pair. We made three of each of you, but sadly, both of your triplet siblings died, leaving only you two."

As we drive through the snowy streets of Boston, I frown as I try to take in this new bit of information. "We were never twins. He was raised by one mother, and I by another."

"Yes, but you started out life together. The truth is that you were separated at birth. Natalia and your father donated their egg and sperm, but I was the architect. After you were born, we split you up to keep you safe. Didn't want to expose either of you to too much risk."

Soren turns around and says nothing more and I sit frowning, wondering why he told me this.

"Did you know about this?" I say softly to Michel.

He shakes his head, his brow furrowed. "No," he says. "As far as I knew, Natalia gave birth to a singleton. There was no mention of twins in her records."

"Of course not," Soren said. "I had to hide that reality. But today, I can reveal it because the threat I've been hiding it from is now going to end."

"What do you mean?" I ask, completely confused.

He turns and looks at me, his eyes dark. "The only one who knows what you two are and could use you two against me. Luckily, I've won this battle. Now, for the dénouement. The final blow that ends the war between us."

I think about Dylan and wonder where he is. Like me, his early abuse made him sensitive, brought out his powers of prescience. Like me, he had an abiding interest in science. Like me, he became a vampire and ascended. Like me, he's working for Soren. Helping Soren set himself up for his own form of religious Dominion. Were we really fraternal twins? If so, no one ever said anything about it. Not my mother. Not Dylan's parents. We shared my mother's womb right up until birth and then were separated?

Who would Soren want to keep us from and who could use us against Soren? What does that mean?

I'm so tired of all the cryptic messages, I give up trying to understand and instead, I watch out the window. We're approaching the park where Soren raised Kael from the tank and Kael killed all those civilians. I can see that crowds have gathered in the central clearing of the park, actually walking on the graves of those who came before them. They stand around in clusters, their breath visible in the cold air. Some stomp their feet and rub their hands together. The day is gray and chill, the skies filled with thick clouds.

The cars stop and we get out, joining Soren as he walks into the center of the park along a path that has been cleared by the guards. Soren extends his wings, great grey-white monsters that stretch out eight feet on each side of his body. I can see and feel the awe in the crowd. When the Twelve follow suit, it's a fearsome sight.

A phalanx of soldiers stands together in a tight circle just off to the left of the clearing. Soren motions to the soldiers and they part. As we watch, several soldiers drag forward a bloodied Lord Blackstone and his son. Both are in shackles and are badly beaten, faces swollen almost beyond recognition. Both need help to stand. The son wavers on his feet and has to be propped up, his head bowed, pink-tinged drool hanging from bleeding lips.

"Michel," Soren says, and Michel goes to his side. "Did you bring it?"

Michel removes a chalice from a shoulder bag I hadn't noticed when we first arrived. Then, we go through the blood sharing ceremony. Michel uses a small sharp dagger, and slices my wrist, blood dripping into the chalice. Michel repeats this with Soren and the Twelve, going to each of them one after the other, so that their blood mingles in the cup. Finally, he takes the chalice around to them all and when I drink, as before, I'm assaulted by the force of their minds, the strength of it almost making me fall to my knees.

I feel it immediately – the emotions of the congregation gathered to watch this ceremony – or execution – whatever it is. They feel fear and hope, dread and awe.

Soren strides to where the guards stand with the two men and he lifts Lord Blackstone's chin so that he looks at Soren through the one eye that is not swollen shut.

"So, old friend, ancient nemesis," Soren says, his voice soft. "The vampire who would be king, we meet on the final battlefield. Surprised it's a park in my territory instead of a field outside your compound like you planned? Remember what Sun Tzu wrote – *the wise general wins the war before going to battle.*"

Lord Blackstone says nothing, but spits on the ground a few inches from Soren's feet.

"Nothing to say, hmm?" Soren shakes his head and moves to the son and does the same, lifting his chin and staring into his face. He looks unconscious, his eyes rolling back in his head.

"I have something for you," Soren says and snaps his fingers. Immediately, a guard comes forward and hands Soren a vial. I realize that it must be the cure.

Soren takes the vial, breaks the top off and then pours the liquid down the younger Blackstone's throat while the guard holds his mouth open. He swallows the liquid and within moments, while we watch, he starts to cough, then his body is wracked with convulsions and the soldiers drop him to the snow-covered ground where he shakes and wheezes, gasping, blood foaming out of his mouth, staining the snow beneath him. He gurgles as his last breath escapes his red lips.

Finally, he lies still and I see Lord Blackstone finally raise his head and stare directly at Soren.

"I've been waiting for this for a long time," Soren says. "You served your purpose, and now, here's some payback for all my brethren you killed."

Blackstone struggles, and I wonder what he means – Blackstone killed Soren's brethren? Some of those two hundred of his kind who went missing over the forty thousand years since they arrived?

How?

If this is true, no wonder Soren has hated Blackstone so much.

"Aren't you going to resurrect him?" Blackstone demands.

"Oh, I don't think so," Soren says lightly.

"You son of a bitch," Blackstone rasps, his mouth still bleeding. "You said you had a cure."

"Actually, not a son of anyone," Soren says and winks at me.

I turn to Michel. "I didn't know Blackstone killed some Ancients," I whisper. "Soren never said anything about that."

"No, he didn't," Michel says, keeping his voice low. "Probably didn't want anyone to know that he has vulnerabilities. Not something you want to get around, especially if you tend to the tyrannical side."

So Soren *can* die...

I told you we don't die, Eve, so don't get your hopes up. I don't plan on dying – not anytime soon.

As I watch the guards drag the dead body of Blackstone's son in front of the crowd, I realize that I don't want Soren dead. However, I don't necessarily want him to rule the world as a god.

I always have. It's what I was meant to do until Blackstone and his kind came along and reduced our numbers and our powers... I've been waiting all these years, planning and plotting, putting things in place so that we could get back what we lost. You're key, Eve. You've already done so much. You have one more task and then you'll be free to live your precious eternal life with your beloved brothers...

I try to blank my mind so he doesn't know my true feelings, but I'm happy to have him reveal more of his plans. I wonder what task I have left – probably helping him perform feats of magic, miracles, and other wondrous events to channel more worship his way, and towards the Twelve, so they can be even more powerful and take over the Church...

Precisely. As soon as you do, you and every other vampire will be cured and immortal. You and your lovely brothers can go off and live by the ocean if you want, for all I care. Do your part, and I guarantee you'll get your reward. Not in heaven, but here on earth. Think of it – the brothers, yours for all eternity...

I force myself not to react to that suggestion. Instead, I do my best to keep my mind blank. The three of us are silent. Witnessing the death of your fellow man, or vampire, whatever the case may be, is unsettling. I know that Soren could do the same to me if I displease him.

And Michel and Julien, too...

I make fists and dig my nails into my palms.

"When will he release the cure more widely?"

Julien shrugs. "He doesn't tell me his plans."

Michel nods in response. "Me, either. I imagine when it suits him. All we can do is wait. I do know that he's planning some feat of wonder to prove that he has godly powers, so be prepared."

"I imagine he'll need us to share blood and channel worshipers to do that," I say, dreading being part of another one of his charades.

"He will."

I sigh heavily. I'm tired of all this. I want to go to St. David's and sit on the beach, listen to the roar of the ocean and watch the stars come out one by one when the sun sets...

You will, Eve. You will. Soon enough, I promise.

I squeeze my eyes shut, wishing I could find something that would block him.

No, you don't, Eve. If you did, I'd have to kill you. Now, grow up. I'm the only hope for humanity. Accept it.

I open my eyes and try to relax. It's no use trying to fight Soren. I have to just live with this constant intrusion into my mind.

Then, Kael shouts to a group of soldiers and they part, exposing shackled vampires dressed in black, hidden behind a high fence. They begin to walk down the pathway towards Soren and the Twelve, each one chained to the person in front of them. Their pale skin marks them as vampires and the fact they can exist in the sunlight means they're ascended.

They're all Blackstone's soldiers, each bearing his family crest on their jackets.

I count them as they pass and stop once I reach seventy-five. More and more file past and it's then I realize Soren's going to do a mass cure in front of the crowd to prove he can do what he promised – cure vampirism.

Bingo.

Soren snaps his fingers once more and a guard hands him another vial. He motions to his own soldiers and they hold Blackstone firm, one soldier opening Blackstone's mouth while Soren breaks off the top of the glass vial.

"The world will be better off without the two of you or any of your followers. While I gave your son a cure tailored specifically for him, this cure is for your entire line. You should know that once I give you this cure, all of your line will die within minutes of your death. Thanks for developing it, by the way," Soren says, a smug expression on his face. "I know you intended it for me and the Twelve, but that attempt failed terribly. I imagine you didn't expect to have it used against you and your line. I was going to tweak it so that it merely removed your need for blood, but I decided to hell with it. I want you and yours gone for good."

Soren shoves the vial into Blackstone's mouth, which is held open by the soldier behind him, and soon, he falls to the ground, quivering and shuddering, gasping and coughing out blood and foam as he is cured of vampirism and of life itself.

Soren watches, silent, his face expressionless. When Blackstone is lying deathly still on the ground at his feet, Soren looks up and meets my eyes. In them, I see such darkness that I feel actual fear and revulsion...

"*Don't* look at me like that," Soren says, his voice low. "He destroyed the Twelve originally and kept me from them for a thousand years. If he died a million painful deaths, it wouldn't be enough."

Now, the rest of Blackstone's men start to show the same symptoms. They cough, and wheeze, holding their throats. Some fall to their knees, knowing their fate, blood dripping from their mouths. There must be over two hundred shackled soldiers and other vampires standing in rough rows behind the main stage where Soren and his men stand with Blackstone and his son dead at their feet. Soon, the air is filled with the horrific sound of two hundred vampires gasping for breath, gagging, their bodies now writhing on the blood-stained ground.

I turn and watch the crowd for their response. They're horrified, fascinated, ecstatic, confused and their emotions flood into me and through me, into Soren and the Twelve who have joined minds through the blood ceremony.

Some in the crowd move closer to watch the carnage, others shrink back, covering their eyes, their ears against the horrific sound the dying vampires make.

"You're going to kill them all?" I manage, shocked that he's not going to resurrect them as immortals like he said he would.

"They're my enemies, Eve," Soren says, his voice hard to match his eyes. "This is war. In war, we kill our enemies or else we face them on the battlefield again and again. I made that mistake long ago, when I exercised mercy for Blackstone and his son instead of administering justice."

"But all of them?"

"Every single one."

CHAPTER 22

IT TAKES five minutes before the last vampire is finally silent, the coughing stopped, the thrashing finished. On the ground lie over two hundred dead, the white snow stained with their own blood, coughed up during their death throes.

Soren turns to the crowd, and lifts up his arms, bright white light streaming off him, almost blinding it's so white.

"This is what I promised you," he says in a deep voice. "This is my pledge to you. Accept me as your Lord and I'll rid the world of these monsters, one bloodline after the other until there are none left to threaten you ever again."

He looks out over the crowd and then closes his eyes.

"On your knees," he commands, and one by one, the mortals do exactly that, falling to their knees, their heads bowed, fear and reverence mixing in a wave of emotion that takes my breath away. It empowers Soren and the Twelve, who stand on either side of him, their wings outspread. Together, the thirteen create an awesome sight. I can understand why the people cower and fall to the ground in fear.

Soren *is* fearsome. He's ruthless. He thinks nothing of killing over two hundred vampires at once in the most horrific manner. Yes, those two hundred vampires have been responsible for thousands and tens of thousands of deaths during their existence, but still... to see them writhing on the ground, blood pouring out of their mouths...

I'm standing behind Soren and the Twelve, in their shadows, as they soak up the adoration of the crowd, and they seem oblivious to everything but this moment when they gather more power for themselves.

Then, Dylan appears at my side from behind some trees that separate the main clearing from the rest of the forest. He glances down to meet my eyes and his expression is grim, his eyes dark. He's dressed in a long cloak over a black uniform with the symbol of the Council of Clairveaux on his jacket. When he pulls aside his cloak, I see he has brought his sword, his hand on the hilt as if he's ready to draw it.

"Don't you agree that he has to be stopped, sister?" Dylan whispers, his hand on my shoulder. I look at Soren's back, and in the gap between him and Procel, I see the mass of humans on their knees before him on one side of the field, and the mass of dead vampires on the bloody ground on the other side.

"Yes," I reply, barely able to speak.

"Then do it," he whispers and withdraws his sword. He takes my hand and places it on the hilt. "Let's do it together, the way we were meant to."

The Twelve and Soren are too busy soaking up the crowd's awe, fear and worship to notice the two of us, directly behind them. Before they can react, Dylan whispers to me.

"*Now*, sister, my twin," and together, we shove the blade into Soren's back, below where his wings protrude, the extremely thin, light and sharp blade easily slicing through Soren's leather jacket and piercing his flesh. It slips into him like a hot knife into butter, ripping his clothes, scraping against bone making a wet sound as it emerges through his body to protrude through the other side.

The blade has gone completely through Soren's chest up to the hilt. I hear rather than see Soren's response. He gasps, a long indrawn breath and his wings disappear, folding up into nothing before our eyes. From where I stand, I can just see that he reaches to the blade protruding from the front of his chest, right where his heart would be. He grips it and tries to pull at it, cutting his hands in the process. When he realizes he can't pull it through, he tries to push it back, but it slides through his palms, and he screams out loud, wrestling his hands from the blade, each palm pierced and bloody.

"It's made of a metal that is their only weakness," Dylan says, his voice louder. "It was put here for us to use against them," he says and meets my eyes. "They've tried to keep it hidden from us, but we found it, and kept it hidden from them."

Then Soren tries to pull off the blade but Dylan reaches out and grabs Soren by the shoulder to stop him. I keep the pressure on so that the blade stays in his body.

"Now, take his power," Dylan says, his hands grasped around mine. "This blade was meant to help destroy his kind. Keep it in as long as you can and then take his power."

"How?" I ask, struggling to keep hold of the sword's hilt even as Soren tries to twist around and dislodge the two of us.

"Take his power!" Dylan yells but I don't know what he means. "You can give him power. *Take* it instead," Dylan says, his teeth gritted as he fights to keep his hand on mine and the blade firmly in Soren's chest.

Then Julien sees us and rushes over, holding Soren still so that we can keep the blade in him.

"Take it all back," Dylan says. "The sword temporarily keeps him from using his power so an adept like you can take all of it. That's how the others were destroyed."

Julien holds Soren firmly, his expression dark.

Dylan speaks through gritted teeth. "He'll be nothing but an empty shell when he has none left."

I have no idea what to do, but I close my eyes, and try to imagine sucking up Soren's power rather than channeling it to him. I feel the awe of the humans on their knees as they see what they believe are angels in front of them – avenging angels come to rescue them from the threat of vampire rule. I usually feel the power of their awe flow through me and into Soren. Now, I try to reverse it, letting it fill me instead, keeping it to myself. I'm aware of Soren and the Twelve – I feel their minds joining with mine. I feel their power, only now, I'm taking it instead of giving it.

They feel it, too, and it's only then that they start to realize something's wrong.

Procel turns to look at us, and finally sees the blade protruding out of Soren's chest, sees his bloody hands, sees his face contorted in anger and fear and pain.

"*No...*" Procel says, reaching out, but it's like he's frozen in place. His wings disappear, and so do those of the others. Soon they're all screaming in my mind, for me to stop. That I'll destroy them all... That I have no idea what I'm doing and what will happen if they no longer have any power...

They fall to the ground as if none have enough physical energy to even stand.

Michel rushes to Soren who manages to grab Michel and pull him roughly against his body so that the sword pierces Michel's chest, right into his heart. I feel it through Soren, feel Soren sapping Michel of life in an effort to save his own.

"Stop or I'll kill him," Soren manages to say, his voice barely audible. "I'll take his life if you disable me. I'll save him if you let me keep my powers."

Now Julien fights with Soren to pull Michel out of Soren's grasp. I see Michel's face contorted in pain, his teeth gritted.

"You don't deserve to be a god," Michel says and grabs hold of Soren's shoulders, pulling himself onto the sword even harder. Although Julien tries, he can't dislodge Michel. Both men are holding onto the other with all their remaining strength.

"Eve," Soren whispers, gritting his teeth from pain. I can tell he's weakening because he can barely speak. "You'll get everything you want. *Everything...*"

I hesitate, my eyes completely blocked by tears. Michel's face is deathly pale, and I know he'll die in moments if I don't stop.

"No," Michel says and meets my eyes. I see the pleading in them despite his pain. "Don't save me. Let me die." He closes his eyes and I can see it's taking all his strength to even speak. "Someone has to die. It's the only way to stop him."

"You said you wouldn't die," I cry, tears blurring my vision. "You *promised* me..."

At that moment, I don't know what to do. I want to stop Soren but I don't want Michel to die. Michel struggles to keep his mouth next to Soren, his whole body shaking from the effort. I hear him whisper in Soren's ear.

"Take me with you."

Then both Soren and Michel go limp, the blade sliding out and they crumple to the ground, Soren on top of Michel.

"Is he dead?" Dylan kneels beside them, the bloody blade in his grip. I cover my mouth with my hands, for Michel is still, his eyes closed beneath a bloody Soren. I kneel down, pushing Soren off him and taking him into my arms.

"Michel," I cry, my fingers on his neck, feeling for a pulse, but there is none. "Michel!"

He's dead.

Julien kneels down beside me. "Save him," he says, his voice urgent, taking my hands and placing them on Michel's chest. "Make his heart beat. Keep him alive. You have Soren's power now. Do it!"

I frown, but do as he says, my hands on Michel's chest. I close my eyes tightly and have no idea what I'm doing. I focus on where I think Michel's heart is located and will it to beat again. Warmth flows down my arms and into Michel, a bright light glowing from where my hand meets his chest.

I hold my hands against Michel's chest, my eyes filled with tears. I feel Michel's heart beat finally. He's alive but he's bleeding heavily, and I sob, a hand covering my mouth. "Michel," I say, taking Michel's hand and squeezing it, but there's no response. He's unconscious, his blood seeping out of him and spreading onto my hands.

"I'm going to save him," Julien says, his eyes filled with tears. "I've got to save him, Eve." With that, Julien bites his own wrist and holds it over Michel's mouth, his blood dripping into it. He closes Michel's mouth in an attempt to get him to swallow. Only a few drops are needed to save his life. Julien looks up into my eyes, his own wet, tears streaming down his cheeks. "I had to do it. I can't let him die."

I say nothing for what can I say? Julien knows that the very last thing Michel would want is to become a vampire again. When the time comes, I know Michel won't drink blood to finish the transition. He'd rather die, no matter what Julien does to convince him otherwise.

The deed done, Julien pulls Michel out of my arms and cradles him in his own.

Dylan bends down and rolls Soren over. He places two fingers on Soren's neck to check for a pulse then glances up at me.

"He's still alive, but I think you stole all his power. Look," he says and points to the wound. "He can't even heal himself."

I bend down and sure enough, the wound is still there, blood oozing out. If he keeps bleeding like that, he'll die. "I tried to take all his power, but I had no idea what I was doing," I say, glad that I was successful.

Lying on the ground a few feet away are the Twelve. They look as lifeless as Michel, their faces pale. Soren lies on his back, his arms spread out, his blue-grey eyes open, staring blankly up at the sky. I see his bloody chest rising slowly, very slowly.

"What have you done?" he whispers. He blinks rapidly and I wonder if he's dying.

I survey the carnage surrounding us. Then I go to each of the Twelve and check their pulses, but they're all silent, cold. Are they dead? Or are they in some kind of limbo? Did Soren's power keep them alive?

"They look dead," I say. With that, I hear a sob from the crowd, who look on at the scene before them with horror. What must they be thinking? Their angel overlords dead, the most powerful angel stabbed and lying bloody on the ground.

"Go," I say to them and point to the exit from the park. "Go away. This place isn't safe any longer."

A few linger, but most in the crowd seem happy to leave as quickly as possible. I turn back and now one of Soren's guards comes up to me, ready to take me into custody but Dylan stands in front of me, his sword drawn.

"Stay away from my sister," he says in a low menacing voice. "She just saved the world from the worst tyrant it has ever seen. Stand down. Your master's no longer able to lead you. Go home."

A few of Soren's soldiers hesitate, muttering amongst themselves, not certain what to do.

Dylan turns to me, re-sheathing the sword after he wipes it on his cloak to clean the blade. "What are we going to do about Soren? He's still alive, but I suspect he'll die soon if he doesn't heal. The Twelve are dead – or something like it."

I kneel down beside Soren while Julien picks Michel up.

"What should we do with you?" I say as much to myself as to Soren. "All your Twelve are dead."

"Not dead," Soren says. His eyes are open, and he's barely able to speak, hardly any sound comes out.

I see one of Michel's priests standing at the side of the makeshift stage and I point to him.

"We should take Soren with us. I don't want him to somehow gain enough strength to go and hide somewhere. We'll have to take him with us."

Dylan surveys the bloody field covered with Blackstone's dead soldiers. "We'll have to burn the bodies or else we'll have a public health problem in the spring." He turns to a few of the guards who don't seem to know what to do with themselves. "Gather the bodies up and burn them. Take the Twelve with us. Who knows what to do with them?"

Dylan appoints one of the men as foreman and we leave them to their ghastly job.

While Julien carries Michel to the vehicle waiting on the road bordering the park, two of Soren's guards carry him. Instead of going back to Soren's, we drive to Michel's home in Cambridge – his old mansion.

The last time I was there with Michel, I thought I'd never see it again. When we drive up the lane to the entry, I remember reading my journal about the first time I saw this place, when Michel and I were first together and I was so much in love with him.

Now, I wonder when the time comes for him to drink blood and transition to vampire, whether he'll choose to die.

CHAPTER 23

WHILE MICHEL SLEEPS in his room, I read the documents Dylan hands me. Julien is with me and the three of us stand outside Soren's cell-like room in the basement. Close by stands a guard, his hand on a sword at his hip. Soren is totally silent, motionless. I can barely even detect his heart beat.

"Is he dead?"

Julien shakes his head. "He's done this before," he says and I hear resignation in his voice. He peers into the room through a small window. "It is only a matter of time before he gets his powers back. It seems like a natural process that happens over time. Like he absorbs power from the earth itself. Hopefully, it will take a few centuries before he's a threat and maybe by then, we'll find the way to destroy him for good."

"How is it you can say all this now?"

Julien shrugs. "Now that he has no power, his compulsion is gone. I'm free."

He smiles and my heart does a little flip. Will he still love me even though he's not under Soren's compulsion?

I don't say anything. Instead, I continue to read the documents that Dylan provided. They describe the Sword of Megiddo, which is made of a metal alloy that is of unknown origin, and which the analysts think was what they used against each other in a battle over power. The design of the blade is from the fourth century, but the alloy is not even made now. In fact, it can't be made. The document, a study by experts in metallurgy, claim it is not of terrestrial origin.

"Alien?" I say and turn to Dylan.

He raises his eyebrows and smiles. "Not of this earth, whatever it is."

"But it was forged into a sword in the fourth century?"

He takes the blade out of its sheath. "Before that, it was a dagger. See the lettering here?" he says and points to a line of symbols on the blade. "This is a very rare sword, made of Damascus steel. It's made of a type of steel produced from special iron ore from India, called Wootz steel. It was forged in the Middle East – close to the fields of Megiddo. This is a blade that was made in the early fourth century BC and used to destroy Ancients."

"Where did you find it?"

"I did some sleuthing after talking to Julien about his time in the Knights Templar. They left the Middle East and went to Scotland after the death of their leader during the Crusades. They were sworn to protect a secret – one that they were willing to die for. It was this sword – which is the only tool known to disable the Ancients so they can be destroyed, an Adept taking their power. I believe Blackstone had it when he was first created and used it against Soren's kind. But it was lost in the intervening years, and only recently was it recovered at a site in Wales."

"Did you know about this?" I ask Julien, who was examining the blade.

"Yes," he says. "So did Michel. But Soren compelled me not to speak of it. Michel knew but he couldn't tell you or Soren would know we had it. Your mother knew, but she couldn't tell you, either. When Dylan came to me to speak about it, I could only shrug and say I didn't know."

"That made me suspicious," Dylan says. "I knew Julien was in the Templars, and had fled to Scotland in the 14th Century, so I thought if the legend was true, he'd know about it since he was alive then."

"How do you know all this?" I ask.

"The manuscript. It details the location of the sword, where it was hidden, its history. That's why Michel was so intent on keeping the manuscript from you."

I turn to look at Julien. "And I thought it was because of how it made Michel look."

Julien shrugs. "No," he says. "The manuscript contained secrets that you couldn't know."

I look through the window in the room where Soren lies flat on a cot. His clothes are bloody. His eyes are closed. He seems lifeless.

"That's why Michel couldn't tell you anything," Julien says, continuing his story. "Soren threatened him with your death and my death. Soren compelled me so I couldn't say anything either, but we both knew what you really were. You were the only one who could use this to destroy Soren, steal his power."

I lean in and take another look at Soren, wondering what the alloy was and who made it. "You said the alloy wasn't from Earth, but how did the smiths make it

"They had Wootz steel and mixed the alloy in," Dylan says. "Gives it a special deadliness for Soren and all the Ancients."

I nod, and then I remember what Soren said to Blackstone when he died.

"He said that Blackstone destroyed his brethren. Did Blackstone use this sword?"

"Yes," Dylan says.

"How did you learn all this?

"I've been busy, sister," Dylan says. "My time with Blackstone, him taking me under his wing, so to speak, was very profitable. I heard all his old stories, including the one about how he was responsible for the destruction of a dozen Ancients using this sword. Soren's Twelve. But he had no idea where it was. He knew the Knights protected it but what happened to it after De Molay was burned to death by the Church was unknown."

"How did you find it?"

"I went looking for it and found it in Wales. The secret was kept by a group of monks known as the Pure. When the Templars were disbanded, some of them fled to Scotland and then Wales, where they kept the sword in a small Catholic Church on the Pembrokeshire coast. St. David's Cathedral."

"St. David's?" I said in shock. "That's where we use to spend summers..."

"I know," Dylan said and smiled. "Your mother knew. Michel knew. They didn't want you to have to use it. They were afraid it would kill you and tried to find a way that saved your life. We tried to develop a biotech weapon to destroy Soren, but it didn't work. So in the end, we knew we had to use the sword. Michel saw what happened in his mind. He knew that Soren would try to force you to save him. Michel chose to sacrifice himself so you could live."

I cover my mouth, overwhelmed with emotion. *Michel...*

Finally, at the very end, I learn the truth.

Michel thought I would die if I used the sword and did what I was destined to do – destroy Soren, prevent him from becoming a tyrant. They didn't want me to die and weren't going to use it. It was in St. David's Cathedral for seven hundred years. Waiting to be used...

But Dylan found it and wanted to use it. He was brave enough to try...

THE NEXT DAY, after waiting outside Michel's room hoping to hear some news about his choice, I turn to Julien and struggle with what I want to say to him. It's the elephant in the room and I have to just get it out.

"Julien," I start, not meeting his eyes just in case. "When Soren was still powerful, he compelled you to, well, to not speak about many things. He suggested—."

"Shh," he says and shakes his head, reaching out and pulling me off my chair and onto his lap. "I know what he suggested. It wasn't true. He didn't compel me to love you."

I exhale and meet his eyes, mine filling with tears because that's been bothering me ever since Soren said it.

"That's good to know," I say, my voice breaking.

"I fell in love with you all by myself," he says and smiles, and I smile back, despite my tears because it feels as if a huge hole in my chest has just been filled.

"Me, too," I say and wrap my arms around him.

"No, you didn't," he says and pulls back. "I had to work hard to win you. Damn hard. You resisted me every step of the way, if I recall correctly."

I laugh, tears running down my cheeks. I wipe them with the back of my hand. "I did resist you, but that's because I felt terribly guilty. You were everything I wanted in a man," I say, remembering my journal entries from that time of my life. "You wanted me as your equal, even if I was only a mortal. You were so easy and fun and..."

I think to myself – not uptight. Michel was always uptight about his emotions for me.

"Not a controlling bastard?" Julien says with a grin.

"Not into the whole chain of command thing."

Julien's serious for a moment. "Michel only did what he felt was necessary to keep you safe. You were so damn stubborn and unwilling to follow rules. He felt he had to get you in the right head space to function in Soren's world and that of Blackstone." Julien plays with a lock of my hair for a moment and I know he wants to say something, but is holding back.

Finally, he meets my eyes. "He does love you, Eve. I can't deny that. He loves you almost as much as his damn Church."

"Almost," I say. "It isn't good enough."

"I know," he says and pulls me down for a kiss. "I don't feel as if you and I have had nearly enough quality time together since Soren was resurrected. I expect to spend at least two weeks in bed once we're free of all this."

"He compelled you to either avoid me or try to seduce me,

depending on what pleased him at the time," I say. "I'm glad losing his powers cancelled the compulsion."

"Me, too. I miss you, Eve."

I run my hands over his hair, which is getting longer and starting to fall into his eyes. With his hair longer, he almost looks identical to Michel now. In truth, if you put a cassock on him, he'd be indistinguishable from Michel. Except for that characteristic Julien gleam in his eye.

"Will he drink the blood and transition?"

Julien sighs heavily and leans back. "I don't know. I'll do my best to convince him. I don't know if it will be good enough. He hated being a vampire."

He glances over at the grandfather clock. "I have to go and meet with the guards, but I won't be too long. When I get back," he says and kisses my neck. "I intend to make you scream out my name in delirious pleasure."

I smile and kiss him. "I'll hold you to that."

He leaves and I sit alone in the room for a while, trying to decide what to do now. With nothing else to do, I go to Soren's makeshift cell, which was quickly constructed using metal bars taken from the local jail. He lies on a cot in the center of the room, his eyes closed. Apparently, he doesn't have enough strength to even open them. The guard tells me that he was responsive to pain but hasn't uttered a word since he was brought to the cell. His hands and feet are shackled to the cot, so he's going nowhere and is supposedly no longer a threat to me.

I stand by the cot and stare down at him.

"So," I say as much to myself as to him. "I hear you're pretty much an empty shell." I try hard not to gloat too much.

For now. Give me time. You can't destroy me completely. Only disarm me for a while. I'm eternal, Eve. Never forget it.

I frown in shock that he can still speak to me in my mind.

Will I *never* be rid of him?

"What about the Twelve?" I ask. "They're not even conscious.

Their bodies are technically dead, but they don't seem to be rotting. The doctor is amazed."

Adamantine, Soren says. Undying. Without me, though, they have no power. I gave it to them using you. When it was taken away from me, you took it away from them as well. When I'm restored, I'll find them, even if it takes me a thousand years. A thousand years is nothing to me.

I sigh, because what he says is true. "They're going to put you down an abandoned mine and keep you there, locked in a sealed room and guarded by two miles of earth. There'll be no one there for you to steal power from and get back your strength. I don't see how you'll regain your former glory."

I will, he says. You'll just have to wait and see.

"You'll go mad before that happens."

No, I won't. My memories will sustain me. I can live in my memories for a thousand years, if that's what it takes. My memories are so real, even you felt that they were reality. You can't get rid of me, Eve. Not that easily.

"Will I never be free of you?"

There's a pause. *Never. We're connected, Eve, and have been ever since we first shared blood. Nothing will sever that connection, so give up trying.*

"I'll find a way to block you. I blocked Michel."

You can't block an omniscient god.

"You're *not* all knowing," I say dismissively, although it bothers me that he can still read my mind. "And you're not a god. Obviously or you wouldn't be here."

Through you, I am. That's why I'll never let you go. Get used to it. I'll always be there in the background, listening in. When you fuck Julien. When you fuck Michel.

"I won't be fucking Michel," I say. "He's not going to drink blood so he'll die."

Not going to happen. Julien will convince him to become vampire again and then take the cure when it's available. You'll see. I told you that you'd get everything you want, Eve. I'll be here to help you.

I turn and leave him in the cell. There's no reason for me to be there any longer since he can dip into my mind any time he wants.

Anytime I want. Don't forget.

"My own personal hell," I say out loud as I close the door. When I emerge into the anteroom outside the cell, Julien's waiting.

"You were talking to yourself," he says, frowning. "It sounded like you were talking to Soren."

"I was," I say and wrap my arms around him, needing a hug. "He's still able to go into my mind, even the way he is." I pull back and look in his blue eyes. "I'll never be free of him. He'll *always* know what we're doing. What the Council's doing."

"So what?" Julien says and pulls me closer. "He'll be three miles down in a mine shaft, in a cell with three feet of steel and cement and then rock and earth between him and us. He'll be no threat."

"He claims he'll regain power. It will take a while, but he says he'll never be destroyed. Only temporarily powerless."

"Crap." Julien looks in my eyes. "And he'll always be able to access your mind?"

I nod. "Unless I can find a way to block him."

He pulls me closer and rocks me in his arms. "So, he'll be like the devil sitting on your left shoulder, whispering in your ear. You'll have to find a way to shut him out."

I shake my head. "He says it's permanent. Once we connected via blood, we're joined forever.

"Great," Julien says, his hands on my shoulders. He bends down and looks in my eyes. "You have to learn to ignore him. Don't think about him any more than you have to. Otherwise, you'll go crazy. We're supposed to start our new life without him and the Twelve and without Blackstone and his army. We're supposed to start recovering, restoring the world, getting back to normal."

I nod, but I have my doubts. How can we go back to normal after what's happened? So much of the world has fallen. The economy is in ruins. So many people have died from the secondary effects of the plague, starvation when the methods we relied on to transport food around the world failed. Not to mention being rounded up and used as blood bags...

"I want to go to Wales and live by the ocean," I say, exhaling in mental and physical exhaustion. "I've had enough of the wars and plague and everything."

"I know," Julien says and pulls me closer. "If anyone deserves peace and quiet for a while, it's you. I'll look into getting us passage on the transatlantic crossing."

I look up in his eyes. "Michel?"

He shakes his head softly. "Stubborn bastard," he says. "Still refusing."

"Let me talk to him," I say, squeezing his arms.

"No can do," Julien replies. "You're the last person he wants to see, Eve. He knows that you could tempt him."

"I'll go and see him even if he doesn't want me."

"Give me some time," Julien says as we walk arm in arm back to the main floor. "I'm trying to guilt him into living. You know, *I can't live without you. We've been together for eight centuries...*"

We arrive in the living room, where a fire is blazing in the huge hearth. My family is there, my mother and father, my foster parents, Dylan, his foster parents, and Sarah. Everyone's been able to come out of hiding and make their way to Michel's house at Dylan's invitation. It's the first time I've seen my mother since we saw each other in secret. I'm overwhelmed with emotion, now that I know why she had to leave me.

"Eve," she says and holds open her arms.

I go to her, and let her embrace me, even though it can't make up for all the lost years. Still, it feels good. My father watches from his chair by the fire. He and my mother are still on the outs, and they've been separated for so many years that there's no hope for any reconciliation. The most I can hope is that they can be friends and allies as we try to figure out this new world we've inherited.

I see my foster parents on the couch and go over to give them each a hug, glad to know that they are, in fact, safe.

"Sister," Dylan says and comes over to give me a hug as well. He kisses the top of my head and holds on for a long moment. When he pulls back, he smiles at me. "You did it. I knew you would."

I smile back. "I'm glad it's over."

He leads me over to the sofa. Sarah and I hug before I sit beside him, across from his parents and mine. Julien sits on the arm of the sofa beside me, his arm on my shoulder, stroking the bare skin on my neck.

We talk for a while, catching up on everyone's experiences over the past few weeks.

Once the focus is on the tea and sandwiches a servant brings in, I turn to Dylan.

"What are your plans for the long term?"

Dylan pours some tea for me and himself. "I'm staying at the university and will keep up the research. We're close to a cure that doesn't kill the host. Soren wanted to rush a cure that killed the host line so he could get rid of the entire Blackstone bloodline all at once, so we haven't perfected it yet. When we do, all of us will get it."

"No more bloodlust," I say with a sigh.

I glance around. The only person missing is Michel.

AFTER WE SAY OUR GOODBYES, Julien pulls me aside.

"I'm going to Michel now," he says and strokes my cheek. "I'll try to convince him. I have to convince him."

"You have to, but I don't believe he'll accept."

He bends down to kiss me. "Either way, I'll come to you when it's done."

I let him go and return to my rooms. Finally exhausted after everything that's happened, I go to bed.

Later that night, I wake and find the bed is still empty. Julien hasn't returned from Michel's room. He's no doubt trying to convince Michel to remain alive. I pull on my gown and make my way through the dim hallways of the mansion, past the main foyer to the other wing where Michel's staying. There's a guard outside the door and when he sees me, he steps forward.

"I'm sorry, Miss, but you're not allowed inside."

I touch him and look in his eyes, using whatever power I have left in me, that I took from Soren, to compel him.

"It's okay," I say, making eye and skin-on-skin contact with him. "You can let me through now. Do you understand?"

"I can let you through."

He steps back and I'm able to open the door and step inside the darkened anteroom. I glance around the corner of the open door into Michel's bedroom. He lies on the bed, looking as pale as the sheets beneath his head. Kneeling on the floor beside the bed is Julien, holding Michel's hand. I can hear his sobs from where I stand.

"Please," Julien whispers. "Don't leave me alone for all eternity…"

"You're not alone," Michel says.

"Don't make me do it without you." Julien presses Michel's hand against his forehead.

It reminds me of the first time Michel was turned. Snatches of the manuscript come back to my mind…

In the end, it's his love for me that convinces Michel to relent. He was prepared to die, to endure the pain but I kneel at his bedside for days on end, my hands clasped around his, weeping like a boy for him not to leave me.

"Forgive me," I say, choking with emotion. "I tried to stop her. She has such power over me. I tried, Michel. I really tried but God has forsaken us both."

Michel finally reaches out a hand to me, stroking my head as if in a blessing.

"I won't forsake you," he whispers.

By then, he's too weak to take a mortal himself, and so I drain one of the girls and capture her blood in a chalice – one from the altar at the Basilica.

Just one more sacrilege to accompany the rest.

He drinks and becomes immortal.

WILL Michel drink the glass of blood that sits on the bedside table?

I step closer. "Michel, please drink," I say, emotion making my throat choke up. "Don't choose death."

Michel closes his eyes when he hears me. "Keep her away from me," he whispers. "I don't want to see her ever again."

I step back farther into the shadows, but he can't see me. Then I understand what he means. He's going to drink the blood. He's going to transition but he wants Julien to keep me from him. He doesn't want to see me again.

"I will," Julien says.

"Make me forget her," Michel adds. "Use the drug to make me forget."

"I will. I promise."

Then Julien helps Michel sit up and hands him the glass of blood.

CHAPTER 24

OVER THE NEXT WEEK, I spend my time in my rooms, uncertain of how I feel about what's happened. My family come for visits, but most of the time I'm alone. Julien's off getting things ready for Soren, overseeing the construction of the cell in which Soren will be imprisoned.

The containment room is in an abandoned mineshaft in New Jersey. Construction is almost finished on the vault in which he'll be kept. His body doesn't decay. It remains intact, but he has no ability to do anything but stay alive. He can't even open his eyes, and so there will be only a weekly check on him to ensure he's still captive.

I stand in the hallway and watch as they wheel him out of the cell where he's been kept and into the vehicle to be transported to the mine. I hope it's the last I'll see of him, but if he truly is immortal, and if he will regain power one day, I have no doubt he'll come looking for me for revenge.

Count on it.

I try not to respond to Soren's intrusions into my mind, but it's difficult. He'll probably do his best to interfere as much as he can in my life. There has to be something I can do to block him, and I'm going to do whatever it takes to find out how.

Michel has so far remained secluded in his own rooms. I know he didn't want to be a vampire again, but there was no way Julien would let him die for good. I don't think Julien could stand to live without Michel. As I watch the vehicle drive off, Julien returns to our suite and closes the door, a heavy sigh escaping his lips. He comes over to where I stand by the window and wraps his arms around me. It feels so good, so comforting, to have him with me.

"How's Michel?" I ask, my arms around his as he stands behind me and kisses the top of my head.

"Grumpy, but he'll get over it. As soon as we get the cure, the real cure, he'll be happier. For now, he's angry to have to feel bloodlust again."

"It's only temporary," I say, frustrated with Michel that he wanted to die.

"I know, but he hated being a vampire, Eve. It defined his life. Being free of blood lust even for a short while made him happy. Being a priest again made him happy."

I shake my head, unable to understand Michel's love for the Church, given everything that's happened.

"Now what?" I ask, turning around in Julien's arms so that we face each other. "What's the first thing on our new post-Soren post-Blackstone post-Plague agenda?"

"What's next?" Julien says and squeezes me tightly. "First on my agenda is spending a week in bed with you, that's what."

I smile. "You said two weeks."

"Two weeks." He kisses me, his strong arms around me, his mouth hungry on mine, one hand slipping down to squeeze one of my buttocks. "I feel completely deprived and in serious need of TLC."

"Mmm," I say when he pulls my hips against his. "I think a week in bed is the least we can do. More like a month."

He pulls me over to the bed and for the next hour, we try to make up lost time, rolling naked together under the covers.

Later, a servant enters with a tray of tea and sandwiches for our lunch. We're both dressed but lying on the bed, reading the daily paper together, discussing the reconstruction efforts underway to get the city back up and running again now that the plague has passed.

Life is still precarious and fraught with danger, but there is a semblance of order now that Blackstone is no longer in power.

We spend the day like that, staying in bed, eating our meals alone rather than in the main dining room, and Julien only leaves me briefly to speak with Michel or the other officers who remained loyal to him or who joined him once Soren was destroyed.

Each time I ask Julien about Michel and what he plans to do, Julien's noncommittal, as if he doesn't want to speak to me about Michel. Finally, a few weeks later, when I still haven't seen or heard from Michel, I push as hard as I can for some news.

"Tell me how Michel is or I'll go looking for him myself. Did he take the drug to make him forget?"

Julien puts down the paper and lies on his side, facing me.

"Yes, he took the drug. He's forgotten about you. He doesn't know anything about your relationship. All he knows is that he was almost killed when Soren was disabled."

"What does he remember?"

"About you? Nothing. About Soren? He remembers our past history. I told him that he had a brain injury when he was almost killed by Soren and has some memory loss. Eve, he can't remember anything starting from just before he met your mother until now. He knows the basic story of Soren's rise and his fall, but not your relationship. He knows you and I are together and have been since the start."

I nod, and there's a part of me that's sad. I wish we could have just come to terms with what happened and go our separate ways, but apparently it was too painful for Michel. He didn't want to live knowing that we were once lovers and that I chose Julien instead of him.

Still, I can't deny that it hurts me that he wants to forget it all. I hated not knowing what happened to me. When I first found my online journal and read all my entries, I felt as if there was this huge hole in my life and more than anything, I wanted to fill it with knowledge of who Michel was to me and why everything happened.

Maybe Michel will feel differently about the hole in his past. I don't know what he'll feel but I cried a few nights when Julien told me about the drug and how far back the memory loss went in Michel's past.

"He doesn't remember my mother? My father?"

Julien shakes his head. "Nothing from the time he met your mother when she was a child. He doesn't even know the story of you. You're just a name in a list of other names of people who were involved in stopping Soren."

"What's he going to do?"

Julien heaves a deep sigh. "He wants to go to England and stay there, find a small parish, and be a parish priest. Nothing big. Just a small town with a small congregation. He left instructions for me before he took the drug."

"Where's he going?"

Julien shakes his head. "That's going to remain secret," he says softy. "He didn't want you to know at first, just in case you had second thoughts." He looks at me guiltily. "Sorry."

I frown. That makes it feel even worse. I have no interest in being with Michel any longer. Although I no longer feel anger towards him for lying all those years and for keeping me in the dark, I still have chosen Julien, and that's the way I want it. I have no interest in getting back with Michel or restarting what the three of us had before.

There's a knock at the door and Michel enters, dressed in a black cassock with a large wooden cross. His hair is longer, and a bit wild. I see that the shoulders of his cassock are wet from snow. He's been out walking in the courtyard, probably saying goodbye to his property.

His eyes meet mine and I see no recognition in them. I'm glossed over quickly and his gaze comes to rest on Julien, who is sitting beside me.

"Sorry," Michel says and smiles. "I didn't want to bother you, but my car is here so I'm going."

Julien gets up and crosses the floor to Michel. "So soon?"

"Yes," Michel says. "No sense in delaying." Michel puts his arms around Julien, his eyes closing as they briefly embrace.

"I'll miss you brother," Julien says and I hear the emotion in his voice, which is almost breaking. "Don't be a stranger."

Michel pulls back and smiles, squeezing Julien's shoulder. "We could never be strangers. You'll come to stay now and then."

"I will."

They embrace once more and then Michel turns to leave, without even a glance back.

He really has forgotten me. I thought that he might be surprised to see how much I look like Danielle, but he said nothing and didn't respond at all to seeing me. I get up from the bed and stand at the window, staring outside at the falling snow.

When Julien comes to stand beside me, I can't help it. "I thought he'd be surprised at how much I resemble Danielle," I say, a little hurt.

"I told him you were almost a dead ringer for her, but I guess he's so glad to be getting a parish, and that he'll have a flock, that he's not all that focused on women and how much they remind him of his first lover."

Julien pulls me into his arms and hugs me tightly. He pulls back and bends down to look in my eyes. "Does it hurt that he doesn't even recognize you?"

I nod without speaking, not sure I can say anything without my voice breaking with emotion.

Julien hugs me again. "Maybe someday, he'll remember. Who knows how long the effects of the drug will last?"

I sigh and lean into his arms, and his warmth and his love washes away all the pain and sadness of the past months. Although there is a part of me who will always love Michel, Julien is more my type. He's passionate but has a great sense of humor. He's strong, but can let down his guard and be vulnerable. We're a team, and now, we'll start our new life together as founding members of the new Council of Clairveaux. We, and the others who join us, will work to ensure that the rules are followed so that vampires and humans can at least live in peace while we perfect the cure and end vampirism.

"I'm glad we ended up together," I say, and kiss him softly.

He pulls back and strokes my cheek. "When I saw you in the diner that first day we met again, I was so jealous that Michel found you first. When I saw your dimples, and your hazel eyes, you were so much like Danielle that it took my breath away. As angry as I was that Michel got to you first, I couldn't blame him, but I knew then that I'd do everything I could to weasel my way into your life because you were meant for me."

"I was," I say and lean up on my tiptoes to kiss him once more. "I'm yours."

"You are," he says and lifts me off my feet, kissing me hungrily while the soft light of the early spring morning fills the room.

EPILOGUE

Twenty Years Later...

SEEKING to forget makes exile all the longer; the secret of redemption lies in remembrance.

Richard von Weizsaecker

OUR COTTAGE IS IN ST. Brides, about thirty kilometers south of St. David's, on the southern coast of Wales. It's a good walk from the three-bedroom house to the Lockley Lodge information center, in Martin's Haven and the cliffs nearby. I often go there and sit with my binoculars so I can watch the birds flying back and forth to the cliff faces of Skomer Island where they'll nest and lay their eggs. I take the boats to the island on occasion and spend time walking around, watching the birds and breathing in the salt air.

Sometimes, Julien joins me, but most of the time, he stays at home, reading or working on some project. Dylan and Sarah were down for a visit and left yesterday, and I feel a bit lonely with them gone. They live in Manchester with their parents. Both took the cure, like Julien and I did. Now, we no longer feel the need for blood, but now we face a new reality.

Eternity.

It stretches out in front of us all and means that unless we can find a way to harness the Adamantine nature of vampirism and transmit it to humans, we'll all have to say goodbye to the mortals we've all grown to know and love. So far, we've had no luck. The only route to immortality at this point is via vampirism, and no one wants to start that scourge again, even with the cure. Work continues on trying to find the secrets to the Adamantine genes, with Dylan and his team at the forefront.

Until that happens, we all face the prospect of losing the humans in our lives as they age and eventually die. That means my foster parents, Dylan and Sarah's parents and everyone we know who was never vampire. I remember what Soren said to me about watching humans be born and live out their lives and then die. It's not something I want to have happen to me.

Tonight, I'm going out to watch the meteor shower.

"Are you coming?' I ask Julien. He comes to me where I'm busy lacing up my boots. While it's warm during the day, the nights get cool.

"Not tonight." He pulls me into his arms when I stand up. "You go alone. I have some things I want to do. Some reading to catch up on."

"You've been awfully mysterious lately," I say and kiss him. "Off gallivanting around by yourself in the town. Do you have some kind of secret life I know nothing about?"

He laughs and pulls me closer. "No secret life," he says with a grin. "Just some Council business that needed my attention."

I frown, thinking he's being deceptive, but I say nothing more. He'll tell me when I need to know.

After I gather my things, I leave the cottage and walk along the path that follows the cliffs. In the summer, when the weather's warm, I stay out all night and watch the stars. When I do, I remember a time years ago when I watched the night sky, taking time lapse photographs of the Milky Way as it rises above the earth.

It's mid-August and that means it's time for the annual Perseid meteor shower and I intend to stay out all night and watch. It's an annual event for me, and I always stay alone for the peak, remembering another time when I watched the meteor shower. It seems so long ago that I can barely remember how I felt, but I know that I fell in love on a beach in Massachusetts with a man who also loved the stars. Most of the time, I block Michel out of my mind, but during the annual meteor shower, it's impossible and while I wish Julien were with me, part of me is glad. I need to spend the time alone, to soothe that small still-broken part of my heart.

I walk to the cliffs along the coast. I've brought with me a sleeping bag and my camera equipment for I want to capture the meteors as they streak across the heavens. The Perseids are remnants of the Swift-Tuttle comet, which makes a pass every 133 years. The biggest known threat to Earth, if the comet hit, it would be far worse than the one that killed off the dinosaurs. That likely won't happen for several thousand years if at all, and it feels strange to think that I will likely be around that far in the future.

The sun doesn't set until late this time of year and so I have a sandwich and some tea in a thermos to keep me from getting too hungry. As I walk along the cliff face, looking for the perfect place to set up my camera tripod, I see a figure walking along the cliff towards me. He's too far off to see who it is, and so I focus on the task at hand. I unpack my bag and check the horizon for clouds but it's clear. The best time for viewing will be right after midnight, and since there's a new moon and the skies are cloudless, it's a perfect night for viewing and capturing the shower on camera.

While I'm pulling out the tripod from its carrying case, I realize that the man has stopped and is standing a few feet away. I frown, because it's not really proper for him to intrude. When I turn to see who it is, a shock runs through me for it's Michel, dressed not in his vestments, which he wears for mass on Sundays at the cathedral in St. David's, but in a black sweater and jeans, with a light jacket.

He stares at me and I wonder if he recognizes me or whether this is the biggest coincidence ever. We haven't spoken since the night he transitioned, although I've spent many a Sunday in the past few years sitting in the back of the cathedral while he said Mass. He never appeared to recognize me and I never tried to speak to him, so it comes as a shock that he's out here tonight, walking along the cliffs when I'm here.

The coincidence is too much to accept.

He meets my eyes and I'm at a total loss for words, my cheeks heating, a choke in my throat as my emotions roil. I've only seen him from a distance in the past twenty years since it all happened, but even so, despite my love for Julien, there's still a part of me that misses Michel. A part that still loves him.

"I remember everything," he says, his voice soft.

For a moment, I can't speak. Michel glances out at the water.

Finally, I clear my throat. "I thought the drug…"

He shakes his head. "The drug wore off. It'll wear off for you too, eventually, but you had it used on you twice, so it's had a longer effect."

"When did it wear off?"

"A decade ago."

I'm silent, trying to understand the implications. It means he *did* recognize me each time I went to his church and sat during Mass in the summers when Julien and I returned. It means he's chosen to stay away these last ten years, despite remembering everything.

"Why are you here?" I say stupidly.

"Julien told me you were walking along the cliffs looking for a good place to take some time lapse photographs."

"You spoke to him about me?"

Michel nods but says nothing else.

"Why?" I ask, totally flummoxed by his presence and the fact he sought me out deliberately. "I thought—"

"I thought I never wanted to see you again," he says, reaching out to place a finger over my lips to stop me. "I thought it would be better for us all if I forgot who you were. That I'd be happy as a priest, but that was when I was mortal. Staring down the face of eternity? No. I miss you."

"I don't understand…"

He shakes his head, his expression sad, his large blue eyes wet. "I still love you. Back then, I wanted Soren to die," he says, his voice almost a whisper. "I wanted to kill Soren, so that you wouldn't have to. I failed," he says and holds out his hands, pleadingly. "It's because of me that he's still alive."

"No," I say and shake my head. "It's my fault. I hesitated because I didn't," I say and stop, my throat closing up. I have to bite back a sob and tears spring to my eyes, remembering that day. "I didn't want you to die."

We stand like that, me biting back tears, him with his hands now in his pockets, glancing away as if he's embarrassed to see me cry. I wipe my eyes, overcome with emotions.

"*Don't*," he says and steps closer, wiping my cheek with his thumb. He slips it into his mouth and closes his eyes and I remember…

Then I'm in his arms, and his face is buried in the crook of my neck. I'm crying and I don't care anymore because he's here, and he remembers me.

He remembers us.

I remember how much I loved him once upon a time, before all this happened, and we were together.

Before the world fell apart.

He holds me and rocks me slowly back and forth in his arms and he's warm and solid and smells like sandalwood.

We stand like that for a long while, not speaking, enjoying each other's embrace. No words are spoken because none are needed. All this time, he didn't want me to know that to destroy Soren meant he had to die. He was afraid it would be me and he couldn't let me die.

In the end, neither of us wanted the other to die.

He's wrong, of course. Soren's still alive because he can't be killed. Only neutralized for a time.

That's right. I'm eternal. My power comes from life itself. Keep me down in the mine, keep me on top of a high mountain. It doesn't matter. I'll be back.

I was put here for a reason, I have powers for a reason and I don't die for a reason.

Think about that.

I exhale and pull away, smiling up at Michel.

"I should get the camera set up and running." I glance around at the darkening sky. "The Milky Way should rise pretty soon. I want to catch it."

Michel lets go of me with clear reluctance, but then he helps me finish setting up the camera. We get it set on the tripod and the timer programmed to take a long-exposure image every twenty seconds, then I roll out the sleeping bag and we sit side by side, the way we did what feels like ages ago.

"What happens now?" I ask. If I'm not mistaken, Michel has come in search of me for a reason. I think he wants to be with me again. If so, he has to know that means sharing me with Julien.

I don't know how I feel about that.

Hell. I *do* know.

I want him, despite everything. Maybe because of everything. It was never because he thought I couldn't handle the truth that he never told it to me. It was because he knew Soren had direct access to me. It was because he thought that I wouldn't do what was necessary in order to destroy Soren. I wouldn't pay the price and let Michel die.

He was right. I couldn't let Michel die. I didn't have to but I never got the chance to tell him that Soren can't be killed. He wanted to forget me, and live as a priest the way he always wanted back before he first became a vampire. Now, he's had two decades to do just that.

"I want you back," he says softly. "I want the three of us to be together again."

I say nothing for a moment, feeling incredibly guilty that I'm even considering it. How will Julien feel if I admit I want Michel again?

"What does Julien think about this?"

Michel smiles and leans his head on his knee, looking in my eyes. "He said it's up to you."

"It's up to both of you as well," I say, still not sure what I think. I want them both. I want them both to be okay about it.

"He told me that he knew that one day, we'd all be together again."

"He never said that to me."

Michel says nothing. "He said you weren't ready to hear it yet."

"And I am now?"

Michel reaches out and takes my hand, stroking my palm with his thumb. It sends a shiver through me and my body still remembers his touch.

It brings tears to my eyes and I have to cover my mouth with my other hand. Then Michel pulls me onto his lap and holds me in his arms.

Finally, he kisses me and I let him. Despite the intervening twenty years, I still feel the same thrill at his touch. We kiss and it's tender, sweet. It feels like relief.

Like my heart and mind are saying *finally…*

The kiss ends and I turn my head and settle back in his arms.

Soren's words echo in my mind.

You'll get everything you want. Everything.

He was right.

I blocked that idea from my mind. A selfish part of me wanted both brothers but the better angels of my nature said I had to choose.

I was wrong, because as much as I thought I loved only Julien, and wanted only Julien, there was a part of me that wanted them both

Now, I have them.

In the distance, a bright falling star burns across the sky, a long white streak ending a bright flash of light fading into darkness.

THE END

ALSO BY S. E. LUND

PARANORMAL ROMANCE / URBAN FANTASY ROMANCE

THE DOMINION SERIES

Dominion: Book 1 in the Dominion Series

Ascension: Book 2 in the Dominion Series

Retribution: Book 3 in the Dominion Series

Resurrection: Book 4 in the Dominion Series

Redemption: Book 5 in the Dominion Series

Eternity: Book 6 in the Dominion Series

~

Contemporary Erotic Romance

THE UNRESTRAINED SERIES

The Agreement: Book 1

The Commitment: Book 2

Unrestrained: Book 3

Unbreakable: Book 4

Forever After: Book 5

Everlasting: Book 6

Drake Forever: Book 7

Endless: Book 8

Limitless: Book 9

THE DRAKE SERIES (The Unrestrained Series from Drake's Point of View)

Drake Restrained

Drake Unwound

Drake Unbound

THE MR. BIG SERIES

Mr. Big Shot: Book 1

Mr. Big Love: Book 2

Mr. Big Daddy: Book 3

Mr. Big Deal: Book 4

THE MCINTYRE BROTHERS SERIES

Tempt Me: Book 1

Tease Me: Book 2

Tame Me: Book 3

Military Romance / Romantic Suspense

THE BAD BOY SERIES

Bad Boy Saint: Book 1

Bad Boy Sinner: Book 2

Bad Boy Soldier: Book 3

Bad Boy Savior: Book 4

THE BOYFRIEND SERIES

Boy Toy: Book 1

Man Bun: Book 2

STANDALONE BOOKS:

Matched

If You Fall

ABOUT THE AUTHOR

S. E. Lund lives on the side of a mountain in the shadow of an active volcano with her family of humans and pets. Besides writing paranormal romance, urban fantasy and contemporary romance, she dreams of living in a warm climate where snow is just a word in a dictionary.

Sign up for her newsletter and get information on new releases, sales and news. She hates spam and will never share your email!

https://www.subscribepage.com/x8t1t7

www.selundauthor.com

selund2012@gmail.com